Books By Rick Bentsen

The Blademaster Chronicles
The Blademaster
Willowdale
The Age of Darkness

The Chronicles of Xarin
The Crucible

Gamma Strike
+* Dawn of a New Age
The Dawning of a New Age

** The Chocolate Sheriff

+ Out of print
* Released through iUniverse
** Forthcoming

The Age of Darkness

By Rick Bentsen

Steel Drake Press
Taunton

The Age of Darkness
Book 3: The Blademaster Chronicles

First Print Edition

Cover image: © Sundraw | Dreamstime.com

For information, contact the author at
rickbentsen@gmail.com

www.facebook.com/RickBentsenAuthor

ISBN: 0692676864
ISBN-13: 978-0692676868

Praise for The Blademaster

"Up until I'd read "The Blademaster" by Rick Bentsen, the closest thing I'd come to reading or seeing a story in this genre was "The Lord Of The Rings" that I saw at the theater several years ago because my husband wanted to see it.

I wanted to read "The Blademaster" because Rick and I have been cyber friends since around 2000 and I wanted to support him and his new book.

So, kind of to my own surprise, when I started reading the saga of Alana Steeldrake (First Blademaster to be named in over 300 years) and Colwyn Starseeker (Protector to Alana Steeldrake and heir to the title of First Lord of the Valendale Territory) I found myself really enjoying it!

The story flows with just enough descriptions that keep the story moving and on course.

All the characters, even the secondary ones, are really well developed. I felt like I knew all the characters in the book, even the bad guys, by the time I'd finished it.

I'm impressed with Rick's writing ability. I'm amazed at his imagination. I'm intrigued with the names of places, characters, and phrases he came up with and how they perfectly fit the tone of the story. And I appreciated the underlying moral code of love and honor that he threaded throughout the story.

And I can totally see this story becoming a movie!"

--Pat Ballard, author (Abigail's Revenge, Wanted One Groom, and others... The Queen of Rubenesque Romances...)

The Age of Darkness

Foreward

July 9, 2016

I, sadly, owe all of my readers an apology with this one. This book was due out three months ago, and it is just coming out now.

It has been an adventure, and not a fun one at that.

It started innocently enough. The book surprised me a couple times as I was writing the opening couple of chapters, spiraling off in directions I wasn't expecting and giving me Laws of the Blades and characters I wasn't really planning on introducing just yet. Which is fine. I like surprises to a degree.

And then came the third section, which was supposed to introduce a Blademaster by the name of Tunera Ironmoon. You'll notice if you flip forward to the contents page that the third section is now titled "Talby Swiftfoot".

I had an entire section of book completely derailed by a character that did not want to be a part of the story. At least not yet. I'm still hoping to introduce Tunera in book 4 as there are some key events coming up that she's a rather large part of.

And so, I had a large part of the plot of this book derailed. Which is fine. I like to think on my feet, as it were. The problem was, I did not have a plan B and had to learn a whole new batch of characters.

And so, here we are. The book is three months late, but it is done and should be in all of your hands shortly.

I am truly sorry that the book is late, though. I know how frustrating it can be to wait for a book and have it delayed. (I'm looking at you, George R. R. Martin!) It frustrates me to no end that I have had such a delay happen with one of these books. I can't promise that it will not happen again, but I will do my best to keep it from happening again.

As we rush towards the Great War of Souls in these Blademaster Chronicles, I would like to thank you all again for your love of these stories. I love writing these books, and it touches my heart to know that they are enjoyed.

The Age of Darkness

The War of Souls starts in earnest three books hence. I know it feels like a good deal of a wait before we get there, but I am sure that the ride will be very satisfying. And there are some loose ends that need at least a little bit of tying before the War starts.

Coming soon, I will be releasing the first book in a companion series to The Blademaster Chronickes. The Legacy of the Blademasters will be a series of five story arcs over 10 books. Each of the story arcs will focus on a different Blademaster of old. I really am excited to bring these stories to you, and I really think that they will enhance the world of Calthea. And what better place to start than with the story of the very first Blademaster?

So be on the lookout for more information about The First Blademaster, which will be coming soon enough. If you enjoy my Blademaster Chronicles, than the Legacy of the Blademasters will definitely be a must read series.

Please enjoy this book, and once again, I am sorry this one was late!

Dia duit,
Rick Bentsen

Rick Bentsen

Acknowledgements

I can hear it now. "Oh, goodness me, the author is about to blather on and on about who did what to help him... Do we really have to read this?" First of all, I love the word blather and I now firmly promise to use the word far more often.

Second, no, you don't have to read this. But I would be remiss if I did not include my thanks. So, yes. Feel free to skip this section, but I shall now blather (told you I would use the word more often) on about Team Rick Bentsen and all they've done.

First of all, thanks to God for the gifts that make the writing possible. A little bit of imagination goes a long way, it would seem.

To my parents, who have been arranging many in person appearances for me to sign and sell my books. It has been a very interesting journey over the past several months, but I have enjoyed every bit of it.

To my brother without whom I would likely never have been introduced to Dungeons and Dragons. Without which.... No Blademaster.

To my continuity expert and editor, Joanna, for everything she does. As I said in *The Blademaster*, Joanna knows the characters as well, if not better, than I do. It makes it easier to hand these books off to her when I know she will take good care of them.

To my readers, because without you, there would be no point to doing this. I love each and every one of you.

Finally to Alana and Colwyn. You came into my life like a whirlwind and have made the past several years very interesting. You two are very special to me. Thank you for letting me tell your story to the world.

The Age of Darkness

.

Rick Bentsen

For the woman who, as I have really come to
Understand this year, keeps me
fully in balance as I work.

The Age of Darkness

Rick Bentsen

The Age of Darkness

The third book in The Blademaster Chronicles

The Age of Darkness

Chapters

The Prophecy of the Coming of the Age of Darkness
As prophecied by Bahalla Maranal, the Dream Weaver
31 Years after the Great Purge

In the waning days of the Age of Light, one who wears the white shall fall to the rites of the Dark One. Only the true power of the Child of Light can save her soul.

When the One born of the Light goes to the twice dead city, she shall fall to the darkness, as one of her own shall betray her. Only the slim blade of the Second Law of the Blades can save her.

When the twice dead city falls empty a third time, the storm clouds will gather, and sabres will rattle in their scabbards. The blight of war shall be upon the land, and only the One born of the Light can lead the charge against the darkness.

On the wings of war comes the Age of Darkness.

What came before...

In *The Blademaster...*

In the town of Ravendale in the Southern Dales of Calthea, a warrior woman, Alana Steeldrake, who knows nothing of her parentage awoke one morning. The man she loved, Colwyn Starseeker came to find her that morning to bring her to see the High Priest of Taelin.

When they got to the Temple of Taelin, they were sent on a quest to discover what happened to a priestess in Tornith, a city in the northern part of the continent of Calthea. Tornith is a dark city dedicated to the Dark God, Thraal.

On their way to Tornith, Alana, Colwyn, and their companions, William Stonehands (a mage), Meryn Swiftfoot (a halfling), and Balaam Otakis (the High Priest of Taelin) journeyed to the city of Valendale to consult the sage, Isaiah Talon.

They found the city completely deserted, save for some warriors of Thraal who were there to try to catch them. After defeating the warriors, Alana consulted the sage who directed her to the Elven Woods, where she would finally learn her destiny.

In the Elven Woods, the companions were given directions to a hidden temple at the heart of the forest. In the Temple of the Blades, Alana learned that she is the first Blademaster in 300 years. After hearing all that is entailed with her new position and that she must marry someone she truly loves, Alana and Colwyn agreed to get married. Colwyn underwent the Test of the Blades and succeeded, thereby earning the right to marry Alana.

After the wedding, the companions started north towards Tornith. Along the way, they found a new companion, a dragon named Cobalthaxillius.

Once they crossed the border from the Southern Dales into Dracomyr, the companions came to the Stonegate Mountains where they were taken prisoner by goblins. The goblins began to take the companions to Tornith in cages. Partway there, the companions escaped and made their way the rest of the way to Tornith.

In Tornith, Alana tried to infiltrate the ziggurat of Thraal, but was captured. She was told she would be sacrificed to Thraal.

When the time came for the sacrifice, she was bound to the altar on the top of the ziggurat. Before she could be sacrificed, Balaam threw himself over her body, forcing the ceremonial dagger to kill him instead of her.

Alana got free and killed the High Priest of Thraal.

Balaam was sent to Limbo, where he freed the people that had been sent there by the High Priest of Thraal when he sacrificed them. Also freed was the Dark God himself.

The companions buried Balaam's body at sea and then returned to Ravendale, knowing that their next adventure would come soon...

In *Willowdale*...

Not long after the companions defeated the High Priest of Thraal and leave the ziggurat of Thraal, the Dark God appeared to his new High Priest, Adouon Darkholme. Thraal gave his High Priest instructions on how to create a fighter to counter the Blademaster called the Nightstalker. Kera Rayden was turned into the first Nightstalker and sent to Willowdale to wait for the Blademaster and her companions.

In Ravendale, Alana and her companions spent a month recovering from their trip to Tornith before their next adventure comes along. One day, the proprietor of the White Horse Inn in Valendale, Marcus Whelan, appeared at the Lucky Minotaur in bad shape. Alana made sure he was taken care of.

Marcus told Alana and Colwyn about how the people of Valendale were captured and taken to Willowdale. The Blademaster agreed to go help the people of Valendale.

After hearing prophecies from the sage Isaiah Talon, the companions left for Willowdale.

Just outside the city limits, the companions were stopped by a woman named Silvestra Knightwing. Silvestra, as it turned out, was an old friend of William. She gave them a tour of Willowdale, but the companions were captured on their way back out of the city.

The companions escaped from the dungeons in the palace, but only Colwyn was able to get away.

Colwyn flew to the Elven Woods so that he could go to the Temple of the Blades and consult with the Legacy of the Blademasters about the situation in Willowdale. While in the Elven Woods, Colwyn was tempted to stray from his marriage by the Queen of the Forestwalker Elves. After turning aside the Queen's advances, Colwyn went to the Temple of the Blades and got what information he could about the situation in Willowdale and the Nightstalker.

When he returned to Willowdale, Colwyn freed the rest of his companions. They went to a cavern overlooking the city so they could plan their attack.

The companions scouted the city so that the Blademaster would have all the information she could when she planned the attack. After listening to all of the reports, Alana planned out the attack on the Zeraphim forces that were holding the city.

During his watch during the night before the attack, William talked to Silvestra about their past. They realized that they still loved each other and were supposed to be together. Meryn overheard their conversation and went to the Nightstalker in Tornith in a fit of jealous anger and gave away the plan for the attack.

The next morning when Meryn was discovered missing, William and Silvestra went to rescue her while Alana and Colwyn roused the leaders of the Resistance in Willowdale to fight for themselves. Lord Taelin himself spoke to the leaders of the Resistance to get them to help themselves.

Alana issued the challenge to the Nightstalker and Colwyn led the citizens of Valendale into battle against the Zeraphim.

During the course of battle, the Nightsalker's undead dragon attacked. Cobalt fought the dragon, but ended up losing the battle and dying. Silvestra Knightwing assumed her dragon form and fought the undead dragon, ultimately destroying it.

Alana and the Nightstalker fought one on one in the ramparts of the palace. When her undead dragon was defeated, the Nightstalker escaped through a portal to Tornith.

With the Zeraphim and the Nightstalker defeated, Alana and her companions brought the people of Valendale back to their homes before returning to Ravendale themselves.

And so begins the next part of The Blademaster Chronicles....

The Age of Darkness

Prologue
The Dream Weaver

Lthough it had been many years since anyone had called him anything other than the Dream Weaver, he remembered his name. He doubted there was anyone else still living that remembered it. He was called only by his title. The Dream Weaver.

No one truly understood what it meant to be a Dream Weaver. Having been the Dream Weaver for almost three hundred years, he knew better than anyone that no one could understand what a Dream Weaver was unless they had spent any time searching the weavings for their meanings. Not even the Mages of the Inner Circle knew exactly what the Dream Weaver did. In the end, the Mages of the Inner Circle did not need to know what the Dream Weaver did. All they needed to know was how to perform the ritual when the Dream Weaver passed on the mantle of power to his replacement.

Unlike any of the other types of magic users, there was only ever one Dream Weaver at a time. Currently, Roald Vilas held the title of Dream Weaver as he had for close to three hundred years. He knew, though, that his time as the Dream Weaver was coming to an end.

He had seen it in his most recent weaving.

It had been something that he had known would be coming for a while. That did not make it any easier to see. But he was almost three hundred years old, and he knew that he was finally nearing the end of his life. He knew that it was time to pass on the mantle to the next Dream Weaver as Bahala Maranal had, once upon a time, placed the mantle firmly around Roald's neck.

While it was not easy to see that the end was coming, it did come as something of a relief. He was tired. He was especially tired of people coming to him for prophecy. People did not understand that his form of prophecy was limited. He could only see what the future held while he was dreaming. That was the core of a Dream Weaver. But people simply assumed that he could do some form of magic in order to tell them their future.

No matter how many times he told them that it was not the case, they still believed what they wanted to believe.

He looked forward to no longer having to deal with all the little problems people brought him on a regular basis. Soon, he would be off on his last journey before his walk with the gods of magic. He was content in the knowledge that he had earned his walk. He knew that this last journey would finally bring him full circle and the mantle would be passed to another, younger man.

But he had one last task left to do before he passed on the mantle.

The dream he had woken up from this morning had left him disturbed. It was true that he did not always understand the dreams he wove as part of his duties as the Dream Weaver. This one was clearer than almost all of the other dreams he'd woven in his close to three hundred years.

And it terrified him.

In his dream, he had seen the army of Thraal stretched out before him. Whole companies of undead, grouped into different types, slowly gathered together in the land surrounding the city of Tornith. He saw wraiths and spectres, zombies and skeletons and even a few ghouls.

But by far the scariest was the vampire lord in command of the army. The most disconcerting part was that Roald had felt that the vampire lord was staring right at him in his dreams. The vampire lord's eyes had been a deep dark red. Roald knew that he would see those eyes every night that he went to sleep for the rest of his life.

There had been, as there always was, words to go with the weaving. As soon as he woke, he had written those words down with a shaking hand. He tried hard not to focus on what he was writing for fear of seeing those terrible eyes once more.

When he finished writing down the prophecy, he began to pack. For the first time in many years, Torval, the god of magic that Roald served, came to him after a weaving. The god had told him that he needed to share this weaving with the Blademaster, Alana Steeldrake. The god had also said that during this final journey as the Dream Weaver, he would meet the man who would replace him.

Roald remembered the Blademaster. He had sent her off on her journey to Ravendale long before she had known who and what she was. He had known though. And he had given her what aid he could.

And now he would aid the Blademaster one last time.

It did not take him long to pack for his journey. He did not need much, just some clothes and his bedroll. It was not so long a journey to Ravendale and he would travel by the main roads. He would stay at inns when he could at night, but it would take over a week to arrive in the capitol city of the Southern Dales. It did not matter. He knew the Blademaster would be there when he arrived, no matter how long it took.

He simply hoped he arrived in time to help her before the owner of those terrible red eyes arrived to start the war that was coming.

The Age of Darkness

Part 1
The Calm Before
the Storm

Chapter 1
The Council of Dragons

ad he wished it, the old man could have simply willed them to their destination. That would have taken the fun out of the journey for him, however.

It had been a great many years since the old man felt the wind through his hair. It was a feeling that he missed. He loved to fly on the back of a dragon. There was a great deal of joy to be had in the experience.

Perhaps that is why he had decided that his Blademasters should have a dragon with them. Their duty was a serious one. In all things, there needed to be balance, so he felt that perhaps the joy of flying on the back of a dragon would be the balance to the seriousness of their duty.

The journey did not last as long as he would have liked it to. Silvestra was still a fairly young adult dragon, and she was a very strong and fast flier. And he knew that she was anxious to get back to her husband and her Blademaster.

And he was anxious to get her back to the Blademaster and her companions. While he knew that the journey that she was about to take to search for new Blademasters would not be all that dangerous, he knew that there was a great darkness on the horizon. Alana Steeldrake would need every possible defense when that darkness came.

Soon enough, though, they landed. He slid off of Silvestra's back and stood on the sandy beach of the island. As soon as he had slid off her back, she began to transform into her human form. Looking around, he sighed softly to himself, knowing that this was not going to be an enjoyable visit.

The Isle of Dragons had not changed from the last time he had visited. It was odd to be on an island that had never changed. The rest of Calthea had changed over the years. The rise of the different races in different parts of the world had caused those areas of the world to change greatly over the years. Vast cities had formed.

But during it all, the island that had been set aside for the dragons remained constant.

In a way, Taelin found it a comfort that the dragons had maintained their island the way they had. Because all of the dragons lived on the Isle of Dragons. Good dragons, neutral dragons, and evil dragons all lived in the same location with very little conflict. Oh, sure. Occasionally, dragons would fight each other, but for the most part, the Isle of Dragons was a place of peace.

It gave the god some measure of hope for the rest of the world.

"Well, Silvestra," Taelin said into the quiet of the approaching dawn. "I guess we should get this done. I know that neither you nor I are looking forward to this confrontation, but we must."

"Eliazar is not going to be happy with what you have done, my lord," Silvestra reminded him. "He fought to keep William and I apart. He will not be happy that you have put us back together."

"No, I imagine he will not be," Taelin shrugged as he grabbed his staff and set the end of it firmly against the ground. "Nor do I care. You two were meant to be together. I could not let him keep you apart."

"He may use that against you when you demand he appoint some nathair an aeir a chosnaíonns," Silvestra warned her god. "Eliazar can be a very stubborn old dragon."

"Eliazar and I have clashed before," Taelin's voice was soft. "Your predecessor, Cobalthaxillius, was one of those clashes."

"I know, my lord," Silvestra nodded, lowering her eyes away from Taelin. "I just want you to be prepared for what could happen with the Council."

"The Council will argue with me as they always do," the god barked a deep laugh. "I would expect nothing less. In the end, though, I expect that there will be dragons that will volunteer to guard our new Blademasters."

"I hope you are right, my lord," Silvestra nodded. She looked off in the direction of where the Council of Dragons met. "I cannot be the only nathair an aeir a chosnaíonn in service to the Blademasters. I can only do so much."

Taelin put his hand on Silvestra's shoulder in comfort. Warmth spread from his touch bringing calm to the young woman. As her god had intended, she took great comfort in that calming touch.

"Come," he smiled at her. "We have much to do."

They started across the beach to where it met the forest. By the time they had crossed half the beach, an older silver haired woman had come out of a path leading deeper into the forest. The woman started to shuffle slowly across the beach towards them.

When Silvestra saw who the woman was, she smiled a broad smile and raced across the beach to greet the older woman. Unable to control herself when she got there, she wrapped her arms around the woman and drew her close in a ferocious hug.

The older woman smiled and gently patted Silvestra on the back.

"It is good to see you on the Isle of Dragons once more, Silvestra Knightwing," the older woman's soft voice said into

Silvestra's ear. "It has been too long since you have come home."

"I have missed you, Talonwing," Silvestra said through tears. "I have not forgotten your words the last time we met. And I thank you for them."

"I see that you still wear the heartstone that I returned to you, child," Talonwing smiled as she held her at arm's length to look at her. "Good. True love should not be dismissed out of hand."

"A great deal has happened since I saw you last," Silvestra said. "That is why we are here."

"We?" the older dragon raised an eyebrow. She looked past Silvestra and saw Taelin standing there for the first time. "My Lord Taelin, I apologize. I did not see you there at first."

"No apology necessary," Taelin smiled. "I know that you have taken a special interest in Silvestra. It is only natural that you would only have eyes for her when we arrived."

"Indeed," Talonwing nodded. She shuffled over to Taelin and bowed slightly to him. "I can only think that since you have accompanied Silvestra to the Isle of Dragons that you wish to address the Council of Dragons."

"Indeed," Taelin nodded. "It is imperative that we speak to the Council right away. We will need to be off again as soon as possible. As Silvestra said, a great many things have happened and the dragons will once again be called on to do their duty."

"You have brought the Blademasters back then," Talonwing raised an eyebrow. "Are things that bleak that we need them?"

"Thraal has returned to Calthea," Taelin said quietly. His voice was very quiet, but there was no questioning the trouble that that statement would cause.

"I see," the older dragon turned away. "We will, of course, convene the Council as soon as possible, then."

"Thank you, Talonwing," Taelin smiled at the dragon. "I only hope Eliazar is in a mood to listen today."

"He is as ornery as usual," Talonwing sighed. "I daresay he is not going to be pleased to see either of you.

Nor will he be pleased to see that you once again wear the heartstone, Silvestra."

"He will be even less pleased once he learns that William and I have married," Silvestra whispered.

The light in Talonwing's eyes brightened, and a slow smile spread across her face.

"You did heed my words, child," the older dragon embraced Silvestra again. "I am glad for you. And what is your part in that, Lord Taelin?"

"Who do you think blessed their union?" the god laughed a hearty laugh. "I could not see them apart any more than you could."

"Eliazar will definitely not like that," Talonwing nodded. "But then you already knew that."

"Of course," Taelin nodded. "It is not the first thing we have clashed on. I daresay it will not be the last."

"Indeed not. Eliazar is a stubborn old dragon," Talonwing nodded. She motioned for Silvestra and Taelin to follow her. "Come, I will take you to the Council chambers."

As they entered the Great Hall of the Temple of Dragons, Taelin glanced around. It was not the first time that he had ever been in the presence of the entire Draconic Council. But it never ceased to amaze him. It was an imposing sight to be sure. There were five great tables arranged in an arc around the seating area. Three dragons perched at each of the tables save one, and none of the dragons were in their human forms. In order to accommodate the council, the room had to be huge. It was also open to the sky, and the early morning sunlight lit the room with an orange tint. The wall at the end of the room across from the center table was open. It was through this entrance that petitioners to the Council entered.

Each of the five tables hosted one of each of the three alignments of dragons: one good, one evil, and one neutral. The Council was arranged in such a way so as to prevent undue alignment influence. It was a practical solution, one that the dragons had come up with on their own.

The center table was where the leaders of the three respective alignments of dragons: the great gold wyrm Eliazar, the ancient red dragon, Shakaaris, and the oldest diamond dragon that Taelin had ever seen, Mintakis. It was these three dragons that would preside over the Draconic Council, and it was these dragons that would make the final decisions about assigning dragons to serve as nathair an aeir a chosnaíonn to new Blademasters. Taelin knew that it would be a difficult thing to convince them, but he also knew that it was important that he succeed in the attempt.

As they entered, Talonwing started towards her table. When she got to it, she transformed into her dragon form and took her place.

Taelin and Silvestra strode to the center of the room, and the god stared directly at Eliazar. Their eyes locked, and both knew that the battle had begun.

"You have been absent from the Isle of Dragons for many years, Lord Taelin," Eliazar rumbled. "I assume that since you are here now, you want something of the dragons."

"Why must you assume I am here because I want something?" Taelin raised an eyebrow. "It's possible I just missed your acerbic tone."

"You always want something when you appear before the Council, Lord Taelin," Eliazar rumbled, his tone hostile. "Do not trifle with us. Speak your peace and have done."

"Have some care, Eliazar," Taelin's voice came out with a note of warning. "I am patient, but my patience with you will someday come to an end."

"Very well," Eliazar heaved a deep sigh. "But what is it you wish of us?"

"A great deal has happened, Eliazar," Taelin said quietly. "As I told Talonwing when she greeted us, the time has come once more for the dragons to do their duty. Silvestra, here, has already bonded herself in duty to a Blademaster. I would have you listen to her."

"Silvestra Knightwing, you will take your dragon form before you may address the Council," Eliazar turned his gaze to the young silver haired woman.

Silvestra nodded and began the transformation. There was no way to hide the heartstone from view when she transformed, nor did she care to. She knew that Eliazar would have something to say about it, but she did not care. What was done was done and it was too late for him to change things now. The worst he could do would be to banish her from the Isle of Dragons altogether.

"Very well, Eliazar," she said quietly once she finished the transformation. "I will address the Council now."

"What is that you are wearing?" Eliazar roared. "I took that from you years ago."

"And I returned it to her," Talonwing's calm voice interrupted the tirade. "You were wrong then, and you are wrong to be upset about it now."

"She was forbidden to see the human mage again," Eliazar thundered.

"Forbidden by you, but not by me," Taelin's quiet voice cut through the room, silencing the gold dragon.

"What have you done, old man?" Eliazar's eyes narrowed as he looked at Taelin.

The Lightbringer took a step forward and crossed his arms, unimpressed with the show of aggression from the gold wyrm. He raised one eyebrow. It was enough to back Eliazar down just slightly.

"I have been cleaning up your messes, Eliazar," Taelin said. "I have seen to Cobalt's redemption. And I have married Silvestra Knightwing to her true love, William Stonehands. Both of which are acts that you cannot undo."

"You dare!" Eliazar reared back his head and glared at the god. Taelin wondered if he was going to be foolish enough to unleash his breath weapon. "You dare meddle in the affairs of the dragons?"

Taelin raised an eyebrow at the ancient gold dragon. Shakaaris and Mintakis shuffled to the side, giving Taelin a great deal of room to deal with Eliazar.

"Are you challenging me, Eliazar?" Taelin's voice was barely more than a whisper. "After all that I have done for the dragons, do you now challenge my word of law?"

"I am saying that you do not have the right to undo edicts of this Council," Eliazar roared.

"The Council's edicts?" Taelin inquired. "Or yours?"

The great gold dragon reared back his head in anger.

"They are one and the same!" he roared.

"Silvestra, my dear," he said as he turned to face his companion. "Do me a favor and go stand by Talonwing. I suspect this is about to get a little messy." He waited for her to get over by the table where Talonwing was curled up before turning back to face Eliazar. "You forget yourself, Eliazar. I am still the Lord of the Dragons."

"Perhaps we no longer need you, Lord Taelin," Eliazar rumbled. "Perhaps it is best if you leave."

"Does the rest of the Council agree with Eliazar that I should leave?" Taelin asked. He looked at each of the dragons in turn. Not one of them indicated that they agreed with Eliazar. "No one stands with you, Eliazar. Perhaps, I am not the one whose time to leave has come."

"An appointment to the Council of Dragons is a lifetime one," the dragon roared. "You cannot remove me."

"Must you continue to challenge me?" the god sighed. "I would prefer to retire you from the Council while you yet live. Whether you live on or not is beside the point. Your service to this Council is over."

Eliazar roared in anger and released a torrent of flame at Taelin. The flame grew into a great ball of flame as it rolled towards the god.

Taelin simply stood there. When the fire was just about to him, he held his staff out in front of him. When the fire reached his staff, it split into two and went around him. The god sighed and pointed at the ancient gold dragon.

The gold dragon sputtered as his flow of air was cut off. His eyes opened wide as he realized he could no longer breathe. The dragon thrashed about as he tried to draw air in. It only took a few moments for the thrashing to stop. The great dragon's head crashed down onto the ground and his eyes glazed over.

Taelin walked over to the dragon and laid his hand on the great wyrm's snout.

"I am sorry, old friend," he whispered. "You left me no choice once you attacked me. I truly wish this could have ended differently."

"We all bear witness to the fact that he forced you into this, Lord Taelin," Shakaaris intoned, his deep voice softer than normal. "I take no pleasure in my old opponent dying this way. I will miss him greatly."

"We will all miss him," Mintakis croaked. "But this may be for the better."

"The gold dragons will need a new representative to the Council before we continue," Taelin said, a tear rolling down his cheek. "Take Eliazar's body to where you bury your honored dead. The Council will reconvene when Eliazar's replacement is named. Silvestra and I will wait here."

Taelin was sitting on the ground with his back against one of the legs to the center table in the Hall of Dragons two hours later. Silvestra was lying on the ground nearby in her dragon form. She had fallen asleep fifteen minutes earlier, and her rumbling snores carried in the late morning sun.

He did not know how long it would take for the gold dragons to choose a new representative to the Council, but they could ill afford for it to take a long time. They needed to hear what he had to say and agree to send dragons to serve as nathair an aeir a chosnaíonn to the new Blademasters.

The god closed his eyes and leaned his head back against the leg of the table. He figured he would take a little nap while he waited. Even though he was a god and did not need sleep, there was no reason for him to stay awake when there was nothing he could do but wait.

He did not hear the dragon walk into the Hall of Dragons in its human form. Nor did he see the dragon walk across the floor of the Hall of Dragons towards the center table. Had he, he would not have been surprised to see who it was.

"I see that you are still causing trouble, old friend," the new arrival's soft voice came from right next to him.

Taelin was startled awake and he stood to face the dragon that had arrived. Both eyebrows raised in surprise, going so far up his forehead that they threatened to join his hair.

"Well, this is a surprise," Taelin laughed. Although he was surprised, he could not be happier to see who it was. "I take it you are the new representative for the gold dragons to the Council?"

"Yes," the dragon man nodded. "My people saw Eliazar's need for a replacement coming and had decided that I would be the next gold dragon to serve on the Council some time ago. You are not the first to say that his time to leave the Council had passed. I am sorry it took his death to make it come to pass. I am even sorrier that his death had to come at your hands."

"He left me no choice, old friend," Taelin fought tears as he continued. "It was not what I would have chosen."

"No one on the Isle of Dragons blames you, Lord Taelin," he laid his hand on the god's shoulder in comfort. "You need to know that."

"It does help to know this, yes," Taelin nodded. He turned to Silvestra and tossed a rock gently against her snout. "Wake up, Silvestra. We have company."

The silver dragon opened one eye and looked at Taelin. She opened her other eye when she saw who was with him.

"Is that...?" she trailed off.

"Aurientallus," the dragon man nodded. "Yes. I was the first nathair an aeir a chosnaíonn."

"As the nathair an aeir a chosnaíonn to a Blademaster now, it is an honor to meet you," she dipped her head towards him in respect.

"What now?" Aurientallus said. He turned to Taelin. "What does she mean that she is the nathair an aeir a chosnaíonn to a Blademaster? I thought all of the Blademasters had died in the Great Purge."

"A great deal has happened, old friend," Taelin said, his voice sad. "That is why we are here. The dragons are going to once again be called into service to the Blademasters. Silvestra is actually the second. The first, Cobalthaxillius, died protecting his Blademaster. Silvestra replaced him."

"If you have brought the Blademasters back, that can only mean one thing," the dragon man sighed.

"Yes," Taelin nodded. "Thraal has escaped his prison in Limbo and is once again trying to rule Calthea."

"I believe that you will find that, with Eliazar gone, the Council will be more ready to agree to assist this time," Aurientallus said. "I will help to convince them."

"Thank you, old friend," Taelin's face lit up in a broad smile. "It is good to see you again."

"It is good to see you as well, Lord Taelin," the dragon man returned the smile. "Please don't take so long to visit us next time."

The three of them waited for the rest of the Council to arrive once more.

Chapter II
The Nightstalker Returns

The portal had not taken her back to Tornith.

She had assumed when she'd stepped through the portal in Willowdale, that it would have taken her back to Tornith. And so, when she exited the portal and found herself somewhere in the middle of the Stonegate Mountains, she was surprised.

And angry.

It was a long walk to Tornith from the Stonegate Mountains. The time spent walking would only fuel her fury at being beaten by the Blademaster. She did not know how the Blademaster had bested her. It had, however, incensed her. She would not make the mistake of underestimating the Blademaster the next time that they met.

And there would be a next time. Of that, Kera Rayden was sure.

She could not be sure where exactly in the Stonegate Mountains the portal had dropped her. She knew that Tornith was generally north of the mountain range, though. By foot, it would take over a week to get to Tornith. If she could get her hands on a horse, though, she could easily cut that time in half.

There was a tribe of goblins that lived in the Stonegate Mountains, she knew. And she knew that the goblins would have horses. She would get a horse from them, she decided. The goblins were loyal to Thraal, after all, so they should be willing to help her. As a representative of the High Priest of Thraal, she would go and see their Legate and demand a horse. And if he did not want to give her one, she would just force him to.

Now decided on a course of action, she set about finding where the goblins lived. *It shouldn't be too hard to find such a large clan of goblins*, she mused to herself.

It took most of her first day in the Stonegate Mountains to find the cavern entrance that led to where the goblins lived. She was careful enough when she passed the sentries that she did not think that they saw her.

She skulked down the corridor of the cavern, quietly making her way towards where the clan lived. She kept to the shadows as much as she could, hoping that her black armor would allow her to easier blend into the shadows. While she wanted to make her demand of the Legate of the clan, she wanted to make the demand on her own terms and not appear before the Legate as a prisoner.

She knew how goblins handled their prisoners.

As she made her way down the corridor, she heard the sounds of goblin merriment coming through the walls. The various families that made up the clan were clearly having a good time. She knew that goblins tended to enjoy life, much like their cousins the dwarves did. She was not sure she wanted to know what constituted a goblin party, though.

All she wanted was to get a horse and get on her way to Tornith as quickly as she could.

She tried not to think about what the High Priest of Thraal would do to her for her failure in Willowdale. She hoped that she would survive the High Priest's rage. She could not get her revenge on the Blademaster if she were dead.

Up ahead of her, Kera caught sight of a goblin warrior heading up the corridor towards her. It was probably a sentry going out to relieve one of the ones she'd passed on the way in. She turned away and hunched her body up, hoping the darkness of the cavern and her black armor would hide her from the goblin. She waited for the goblin to pass by her. When he did, she launched herself at the warrior, wrapping her arm around his throat. The tip of her knife pressed into the goblin's throat.

"Make so much as a whimper and you die," the Nightstalker hissed into the goblin's ear.

The goblin nodded once in understanding, not wanting to test the veracity of the threat. When she pulled the knife away, he asked in a very soft voice, "What do you want of us, human?"

"Take me to your Legate," she hissed into his ear. "I will discuss my business with him. The sooner I talk to him, the sooner I am out of your caverns."

"I understand," the goblin nodded. He turned to start to lead her to where the Legate was, but he was caught up short by the Nightstalker's arm across his throat.

"Remember," she admonished. "Make one wrong move, or if you set off any kind of alarm, and you will die where you stand."

The goblin nodded his understanding, and Kera released his throat. The goblin led her through the tunnels of the goblins' home, carefully taking her around the more heavily populated parts of the colony. She took note of the route he was taking. She approved of the decision to avoid the majority of the colony, realizing that if they went through the heavily populated areas, his kinfolk would set upon her. She decided that the goblin knew that, were that to happen, he would be the first to die. He clearly wanted to avoid that.

It took what felt like several hours before the goblin led Kera to a nondescript door at the end of a side hallway. He looked back at her and pointed at the door.

"Legate Altas lives in these quarters," the goblin said in a soft voice. "You'll find him in there. I have done as you asked and so I will be on my way."

"Not so fast, little one," Kera yanked the goblin up short. "You are going in there with me. If it is not as you say, then you will die before any harm can come to me."

The goblin paled, but nodded. He pushed open the door and led the Nightstalker in to meet the Legate.

What greeted Kera Rayden was not anything like she expected.

She had expected to see that the Legate was living a life of luxury and excess. As he was the leader of a whole clan of goblins, it was a reasonable expectation. But Legate Altas lived in a relatively small and austere room. Certainly, it was likely a cut above most of the quarters where his goblins lived, but it was far from the extravagant quarters that she had been expecting. In the room they entered, there was a small writing desk along one wall and several comfortable chairs to sit in, although she expected that they would only be comfortable for someone who was goblin sized. She did not think she would find any comfort in any of those chairs. There was another plain door on the back wall that Kera assumed led to the Legate's bedroom.

The Legate himself was not as she expected either. He was as fat as she suspected, but he wore simple leathers instead of more elaborate clothing. His large goblin feet were bare. She had noticed that most of the goblins that she had seen in his clan tended to go barefoot. All in all, the Legate just did not fit the picture she had fixed in her mind.

"Legate Altas," the goblin that had led her to the Legate said into the silence of the room. "This human has business with you. Or at least she says she does."

"Leave ussss," the Legate said. "I will hear what thissss human hassss to ssssay to me."

The goblin bowed to the Legate and made his way out of the little room. Having gotten what she wanted, the Nightstalker let the goblin go without incident. She put her knife back on her belt and turned to face the goblin Legate with her arms crossed across her chest. The look on her face made it clear that she was in no mood for games.

"Do you know who I am?" she asked in a soft voice.

"You are a human female that will ssssoon die at the handssss of my goblinssss," the Legate hissed. "We do not take kindly to intruderssss here in the Sssstonegate Mountainssss."

"Oh, I'm not going to die today, Legate Altas," she flashed a wicked grin at the goblin leader. "I'm just here for a horse."

"A horssssse?" the Legate laughed. "And why do you think that I would give you a horssssse?"

"Which god do you serve, Legate?" the Nightstalker asked.

"The goblinssss honor Lord Thraal, of coursssse," the Legate hissed. "Which god do you honor?"

"I am the balance to the Blademaster," Kera announced in a whisper. "As she serves the light, so do I serve the darkness. I am Lord Thraal's chosen champion."

"The Nightsssstalker?" the Legate rose from his chair. "We have heard of you, of coursssse. But we thought you jusssst a myth."

"I am no more a myth than the accursed Blademasters are a myth," she spat out. "I will yet have my revenge on that cursed woman."

"We, too, wish for revenge on the Blademasssster and her companionssss," Altas hissed as he came towards the Nightstalker. "When we had her captive, she killed a great many of usssss. We would ssssee her dessssstroyed."

"I must return to Tornith to report to the High Priest of Thraal. But the portal I was to take back to Tornith brought me to the Stonegate Mountains instead," she explained. She uncrossed her arms and heaved a deep sigh. "I would like a horse so that I can return to Tornith quickly. Will you help me?"

"Assss you ssssserve the Dark God assss we do, we will provide you with a horssssse," the goblin Legate nodded. "There issss a condition, though."

"And what condition would that be, Legate Altas?" the Nightstalker raised an eyebrow at him.

"You musssst promisssse to kill the Blademasssster," the Legate hissed. "We will have our revenge on that woman through you."

"I promise that the Blademaster will die by my hand," the Nightstalker grinned wickedly. "I can also promise that she will suffer greatly before I permit her to die."

"That issss all that we assssk," the Legate returned her wicked grin. "We will show you to your horsssse. But know thissss, Nightsssstalker. We will be watching and waiting for you to fulfill your promisssse."

The horse that the goblins had provided her had been a good, fast one. She arrived in Tornith in four days after riding out from the Stonegate Mountains. She made good time, and it did not hurt that the Nightstalker did not care much for petty comforts. She rode hard and fast, only stopping when she needed to in order to rest the horse. Her stops at night were just long enough for her to get a little sleep. She stopped well after the sun went down and got started again long before the sun rose the following morning.

She was in a hurry to get back to Tornith. By moving fast, she was able to keep from thinking about what would happen when she arrived at the ziggurat of Thraal. She knew that the High Priest would not be happy that she had failed in her mission to rid the world of the Blademaster. While she did not know Adouon Darkholme as well as she had known the lich that had been the High Priest before him, she knew that failing the High Priest of Thraal was often fatal.

She did not want to die while the Blademaster was still alive.

When she got to Tornith, she made her way directly to the ziggurat of Thraal, not wanting to put off the confrontation with the High Priest of Thraal any longer than she needed to. When she got to the ziggurat, she stabled the horse. Carefully, she made her way directly to the High Priest's sanctuary. She went over in her head all the reasons that she could give for her failure. But she knew full well that the why of her failure did not matter nearly as much as the fact that she had failed did.

That she had failed was all that the High Priest was likely to consider when he decided her fate.

She did not hesitate when she got to the door of the sanctuary, but instead knocked twice. She knew better than to just barge into the High Priest's sanctuary without having been invited in.

"Enter, Kera," Adouon's soft voice came from inside the sanctuary.

She did not wonder how he knew it was her. She had long ago accepted the fact that the High Priest knew far more than everyone gave him credit for. As such, it came as no surprise to her that the High Priest would know when she'd arrive.

She took a deep breath and opened the door to the sanctuary. Once inside, she just stood there, just inside the door. She faced forward, her eyes riveted on the High Priest.

"You are earlier than I expected you," Adouon said without looking up from the paper he was writing on. "Clearly you did not walk all the way from the Stonegate Mountains or you would be several days out from Tornith yet."

"I made a deal with Legate Altas of the Stonegate goblins," Kera shrugged. "He gave me a horse. It took me far less time to get here on the back of a horse than if I had walked."

"I see," Adouon nodded. He continued to write on the paper in front of him as he had since she'd entered the sanctuary. "And what did you have to promise the good Legate in return for the horse?"

"I had to promise a bloody and violent death for the Blademaster," she shrugged a second time. "Of course, it is up to you whether or not I will be able to fulfill that promise."

"Yes, it is," Adouon said. He looked up from the paper and smiled at her. "Fear not, my dear," he continued. "I am not going to kill you for failing our Lord Thraal this time. It was foreseen that you would not succeed in killing the Blademaster at this time. I knew even before I sent you to Willowdale that you would fail."

"Then why send me?" she asked. "If you knew I was not going to kill her, then what was the point of sending me just to fail?"

"I wanted to see what you would do." It was Adouon's turn to shrug. "Besides. Prophecy is not, in and of itself, infallible. Just because it said you would fail to kill the Blademaster does not mean that there was no chance of your success. As long as there was the slightest chance of your killing the Blademaster, I had to send you to try."

"So I will not be punished for failure?"

"On the contrary, my dear," Adouon smiled wickedly. "I intend to give you every chance to fulfill your promise to the goblin Legate."

"What do you have in mind, my lord?" she asked.

"I am sending you to the edge of the Wilds, Kera," Adouon said. He turned back to the paper and signed it, folded it and sealed it with wax. "When you get there, you will give these orders to the commanding general of the army of undead. I am placing the entire army under your command. You will lead the attack on the Southern Dales."

"I understand," she nodded.

"Before the end of the war that is to come, you and the Blademaster will face off again."

"And when we do, she will die by my hand."

Adouon smiled at her and motioned towards the door.

"Head on down to the portal, and I will send you on your way to your army," he said. "I know you are eager to get going."

ChapTeR III
The Calm BeFoRe the SToRM

illiam Stonehands was deep inside the forest outside of Ravendale tracking a flock of thrynda birds.

The companions had been back in Ravendale for two weeks. Winter was fast approaching, but as far south in the Southern Dales as they were, they still had some time before the snows came. Winter was going to be a blessing, though, as it would give the companions time to prepare for the battle that prophecy said was coming.

For his part, William knew that preparation involved making sure he had all of the spell components he would need to do his part.

And so he found himself tracking a flock of thrynda birds so that he could harvest some of their tail feathers that he needed for certain attack spells.

He had been tracking them for most of the day, hoping that they would stop long enough at some point for him to sneak up on them and pull out a few tail feathers. The feathers had to be harvested directly from living birds in order for them to be useful. He had tried to use tail feathers that he had collected off the ground, but they just did not have the same potency as the freshly harvested feathers did.

His pouches were full of spell components. Once he harvested the thrynda bird tail feathers, he would have all of the spell components he figured he would need for their next journey. He knew that there was one more journey for them to take before winter hit.

He figured that he had just enough time to finishing harvesting spell components before they had to leave again.

It would be hard on him, though. They would have to leave before Silvestra got back from her journey to the Isle of Dragons with Taelin. He missed her greatly and wished she would hurry home.

It wasn't just that he wanted her near him, although that was certainly part of it. He knew that there was danger coming for the Bladeamster, and he knew that she would need her nathair an aeir a chosnaíonn to be there with them. He did not know what exactly the danger entailed, but he knew it was coming.

He knew they would all feel safer having Silvestra there with them.

He checked the progress of the thrynda birds and saw that they were still flying. He followed them as quietly as he could. The birds paid him no attention as he followed them.

It amazed him how the birds flowed through the forest, winding their way around the trees. Most birds preferred to fly in open sky, but the thrynda birds seemed to thrive best deep in a forest.

In a way, he and his companions were just like the thrynda birds, simply flowing through whatever life threw at them. He was just as amazed at the way that Alana and Colwyn were able to get through anything that came there way.

He envied them that ease, although he knew it was nowhere near as easy as they made it appear. In the end, what he really envied them was their sense of purpose. She was the Blademaster. He was her Protector and the heir to a noble seat in one of the Dales. Their destinies were set and all they had to do was follow their destinies through to the end.

William had no idea what he was to become.

He was a powerful mage, and he was content, for the moment, to be a companion to a Blademaster. He enjoyed his travels with Alana and the others. But he knew that there was more to his life than just slinging spells in support of the Blademaster. That he had found love with Silvestra was, in a way, proof of that.

If he were meant to be just a mere mage, then why would he have ended up with so unique a mate as a dragon woman?

When he had been at the Tower of the White, none of the Mages of the Inner Circle had been able to tell him what path his life was to take. They only knew that he was to protect the Blademaster.

Silvestra knew, though. He remembered that she had seen the path that his life was to take the last time they had seen each other at the Tower of the White. But she had not been able to tell him what she had seen.

He had a feeling that he was going to soon learn what path he was supposed to take. It was just a feeling, but it was a strong one. Someday soon, he would be given a choice, he felt. And when that day came, he would know the truth.

He would just have to wait.

As he tracked the flock of thrynda birds, he felt that he was being tracked as well. He cast his senses around him, but he could not feel anyone near him. That did not ease the feeling that he was being watched.

He thought that if he was being watched by magic, he might not be able to detect such conjuring.

That was an unsettling thought to him.

He kept his senses cast about him, trying very hard to sense whoever might be out there watching him as he continued to track the birds. It was the only thing he could think to do. He needed the feathers too much to abandon his quest.

It took another hour, but the flock of birds finally came to roost in the branches of a great oak tree. He slowly made his way over to the tree that they had settled in. He moved carefully and quietly so as to not scare the birds off.

When he got to where the birds were roosting, he slowly inched his hand towards two of them, carefully aiming for the tail feathers. He quickly pulled tail feathers from both birds at the same time. He was rewarded with four tail feathers, which went into a pouch.

The thrynda birds screamed in anger at him and the entire flock took off once more.

"What is it with you and those birds?" a voice called from below William.

The mage looked down and saw a man in white robes standing there watching him. The man had close cropped light brown hair that was greying at the temples. His blue eyes were deep and timeless. The man was smiling, but William was sure that he was capable of a world class scowl. The white robes were unadorned, but the man was holding an ornate staff topped with a red gem the size of William's head that was held onto the staff by what looked to be a silver dragon's clawed hand. William wasn't sure, but he thought it was an actual dragon hand, not one made out of metal.

"That explains why I couldn't sense you watching me," William said as he dropped down from the tree to stand in front of the other man.

"I know," the man chuckled. "I felt you trying to find who was watching you. I couldn't let you sense me. That would ruin the surprise."

"To what do I owe the honor of your visit, Lord Ferrin," the mage asked. He had, of course, recognized the man immediately. When one is visited by one's god, recognition tends to be immediate.

"Just thought we should talk," the god shrugged. "Walk with me, and we will discuss your future."

"Odd that you mention my future," William chuckled as he fell in step with Ferrin. They started walking towards Ravendale. There was no hurry in Ferrin's step, so William was in no hurry either. "I was just thinking that I was going to finally be facing my destiny soon."

"And what makes you say that?" the god asked him.

"It is just a feeling I've been having for a while," the mage shrugged. He shifted his staff from one hand to the other. "I keep feeling like there should be more to my life than this."

"Oh, there most certainly is," Ferrin laughed a hearty laugh. "And you are right. You will be given a choice very soon. I think you will find yourself at the Tower of the White by the spring thaw, in fact."

"Is there anything you can tell me about what is coming?" William looked over at the god. He did not expect that Ferrin would be forthcoming with an answer. He knew that things did not work that way when it came to destiny.

"You already know I won't answer that any more than your wife can," Ferrin said softly. "I can tell you that it will not be an easy road. You will definitely need Silvestra by your side. You are lucky that you have her. Lord Taelin did a very good thing by putting you two back together."

"We never should have been split apart," William sighed. "There was meddling."

"There is always meddling," Ferrin said. "It is what you mortals do when there is meddling that we gods find interesting. I have taken an interest in you and Silvestra. You have both served me well. And when the time comes, I will ask a great deal of both of you."

They walked in silence for a while. William thought about what the god had said to him. It reinforced things that he'd already thought about.

"Is the Blademaster, as I suspect, about to go on one last journey before the winter sets in?" the mage asked.

"You've already forseen it," Ferrin shrugged. "Why ask me? Trust your senses. Trust your instincts. They will serve you well. They always have. They always will."

"My instincts tell me that the prophecy of the Great War of Souls is being fulfilled," William said in almost a whisper after a few moments. "I am afraid that people I love are not going to make it through."

They walked in silence for a while. William wondered if Ferrin was going to respond or not. It was clear to the mage that the god was weighing what, if anything, he could say.

"I can tell you only this," the god eventually said. "The prophecy of the Great War of Souls has, indeed, been invoked. But you already knew that. This will be a difficult time for you and your companions. But you are the right people to be leading the side of light in this conflict. And if you are to have any chance in succeeding, then the Blademaster must find some of the other children of the light that are out there to be found."

"That's where we are headed soon, then," William nodded. "We're going to find some of these children of the light."

"As I said, your instincts serve you well, William Stonehands," Ferrin smiled. It was a warm smile that filled William with some comfort. "They will guide you down the right path if you listen to them."

"I have never told anyone this before, my Lord Ferrin, but I am scared of making a mistake," William said. "If we are, indeed, heading into this Great War of Souls, such a mistake could be fatal."

Ferrin stopped and put a hand on William's shoulder. William stopped and turned to face his god. Ferrin smiled a sad smile and squeezed William's shoulder in encouragement.

"We all make mistakes, my child," he said after a moment. "The true test of a person is his reaction to making a mistake. Only by accepting the mistake and doing one's best to make amends can a person keep on the correct path."

"That sounds like something that would be in the Law of the Blades," William frowned.

"The Nineteenth, actually," Ferrin shrugged. "You are no less bound by it than the Blademaster, though. What the High Priestess of the Blades has never quite understood is that, more than a rigid set of rules that a Blademaster must obey, the Laws of the Blades are a code that, if adhered to, will make any person the best person they can be."

"I never looked at it that way before," William stroked his chin thoughtfully. "But I suppose you're right."

"Your Blademaster already understands this." The god started back towards Ravendale. "Alana Steeldrake is a very special woman. I am glad that you and Silvestra are there to help protect her."

William hurried to catch up to his god. He still had questions to ask, although he doubted he would get answers.

"You arranged for me to end up as one of Alana's companions," William commented. It was a statement of fact rather than a question, because he already knew the truth of it. "You gave the message to the sage Isaiah who subsequently told the Mages of the Inner Circle to send a mage to Ravendale."

"Indeed," the god nodded. "And why do you think I might have done that?"

"Because you knew how important this Blademaster would be," the mage said. "You know. You know how bad the war is going to be. So you chose to make sure she had as much protection as you could."

"I can only do so much. The fact that she now has both you and Silvestra was not planned. It is welcome though."

"Is there anything else you can tell me that might help, my lord?" he asked in earnest.

The god kept walking, his staff digging a small hole with each step. "I can tell you only that you will leave Alana for a time very soon. When you return to her, you and Silvestra must never be too far from your charge. There are many dangers she will yet face. And that is before the War of Souls begins in earnest. Alana will receive a visitor very soon. You must not tell her anything about his coming. She must choose to heed his words of her own volition. And so, my child, must you."

The god turned away and started to walk swiftly away. William hurried to catch up to him.

"Lord Ferrin, I must know who the visitor is," he called after his god.

Ferrin turned to face him. "I have told you too much already, my child. Heed my words." With that, the god vanished in a flash of light.

William started back towards Ravendale, far more confused than when he had left his companions to go hunting for spell components.

Chapter IV
The High Priestess of the Blades

he Temple of the Blades had been very quiet since Colwyn Starseeker had left after getting the answers that he needed regarding the situation in Willowdale. Solara Moonfire, the High Priestess of the Blades, had not seen much of Colwyn during his visit. He had been very angry with her for arranging for the Elven Queen to seduce him.

She supposed she could not blame him.

She had heard about the Protector's visit though. She had also heard the rumors of the prophecy that Colwyn and his Blademaster had invoked with their actions in the city of Willowdale.

And she was not overly pleased.

She knew what it would mean for the Southern Dales if the War of Souls were to begin. And she knew what it would mean for those that lived in the Temple of the Blades.

She had asked the Legacy of the Blademasters to assemble whatever information they could on the War of Souls now that the prophecy had been invoked. All they were able to bring her, though, was the prophecy of the War of Souls itself. She had read the prophecy over several times, puzzling out exactly what it would mean for the Temple of the Blades, for the well being of the Temple and of the Legacy of the Blademasters was her primary concern.

She sat in her sanctuary and read over the text of the prophecy one more time, trying to puzzle out the intricate meanings that the Dream Weaver had hidden in the words he had set down.

"The prophecy of the Great War of Souls
After three hundred years of peace in the world comes the Age of Darkness. The Dark God will return to begin his conquest of the world once more.

In the early days of the Age of Darkness, after the Blademasters have returned to the world of Calthea, the army of the dead shall arise in service to the Dark God. The dead shall rise and wage war across the face of Calthea.

When the twice dead city falls empty for a third time, the storm clouds will gather and the sabres will rattle in their scabbards. The blight of war shall be upon the land and only the one born of the light can lead the charge against the darkness.

The army of the light must uncork the magic of the bean sidhe to turn back the darkness. The one born of the light must lead the legacy of the Blademasters onto the field of battle.

When the soul of the captured bean sidhe wails, the stones of the stronghold of the light will shatter and crumble upon one another. The spirits of the chosen of Taelin will once more take the field of battle in the war against the darkness.

The fire of the sun and the moon will dim and fade to darkness. The one born of the light must walk out from the shadow of the fire of the sun and the moon and lead the chosen of Taelin.

The Twenty Third Law of the Blades will be violated for some of the chosen of Taelin.

If the one born of the light does not lead the charge against the army of the dead, the world will fall into a darkness that will be without end. Only the power of the First Law of the Blades can guide the hand of the one born of the light.

In this battle as in all others the one born of the light will fight, there will be no guarantees. Only by following the wisdom of Taelin and by the luck of Laeyra will the one born of the light prevail.

Should the one born of the light be successful in leading the forces of the light, the world will live in relative peace for a time, but only for a time for the Dark God shall never give up his quest.

If the one born of the light wishes to undo the damage caused by the wailing soul of the captured bean sidhe, she must find the Light of Taelin and use its magic to once more build the stronghold of the light.

In the years after the end of the great war of souls, should the one born of the light in turning back the darkness for a time, she will extend the light three times. But with the third, she will take her place among the spirits of the chosen of Taelin.

So ends the words of the final prophecy of Bahala, the Dream Weaver. With the gifting of this prophecy, I turn the mantle of power of the Dream Weaver over to a new and much younger Dream Weaver. Heed these words, for all that is written here shall come to pass.

May these words one day find their way to the one born of the light. The one who protects her will be able to translate these words for her, although neither will know the meaning behind the words when they find them.

Written by my hand,
Bahala Maranal, the Dream Weaver
Thirty seven years past the Great Purge."

She had no more insight as to what the prophecy meant this time as she had any other time she'd read it. It was infuriating to have in her hands such a critical prophecy of events that were coming to pass and to have so little understanding as to what was going on. It was something she needed some guidance on.

"I hope that I can be of assistance," a soft female voice said, breaking the High Priestess out of her thoughts.

When Solara saw who it was that had spoken, she dropped to her knees in reverence. It was rare that Laeyra made an appearance in the Temple of the Blades. More often, it was Taelin that dealt with matters pertaining to the Blademasters.

"Lady Laeyra, you honor me with your presence."

"Get up, Solara," Laeyra smiled down at the High Priestess of the Blades. "You sought guidance on the prophecy of the Great War of Souls. I have come to guide you."

"Where is Lord Taelin?" Solara asked, frowning. "I mean no disrespect, my lady. It is just that he is usually the one to come discuss things with me here."

"No offense is taken," Laeyra laughed. Her laughter was filled with joyful music. "My husband is off playing with the dragons. He is doing his best to enlist their help for the Blademasters. And so it is left to me to guide you."

"I am so confused by this prophecy, my lady," Solara said. "I know that the prophecy has been invoked. Your Blademaster has seen to that. Nut I cannot tell just what it means for the Temple of the Blades."

"There is much to discuss," Laeyra said. "Much of it you will not like. There is little that we can do about that, however."'

"I do not like any of it," Solara thundered. "I have not liked any of what has gone on since Lord Taelin brought the Blademasters back. I felt it was a mistake then, and I still think it is a mistake. Had the Blademaster not gone to Tornith, the Dark God would still be in his prison in Limbo. Had the Blademaster not gone to Willowdale, we would not be on the precipice of the War of Souls. The woman is reckless. She acts without considering the consequences of her actions. No, I do not think that making Alana Steeldrake a Blademaster was a wise move on the part of Lord Taelin."

"Alana may be reckless, as you have named it, but everything she has done has been important," the goddess of luck said as she took a seat near to where Solara was still standing. "Everything she has done has been according to the Law of the Blades. And everything she has done has been something that Taelin and I have wanted her to do."

"You wanted the Dark God freed?" Solara gasped. "I cannot believe that."

"Do you know that the High Priest of Thraal had been sending the souls of those he sacrificed to that same prison?" Laeyra raised an eyebrow at Solara. "Did you know that there were hundreds of souls trapped in Limbo that could not go to walk with their gods? Did you know that there was at least one priestess of Taelin trapped there?"

"No," Solara sighed. She slumped in her chair. "I guess you and Taelin could not leave them there."

"No, we could not," Laeyra smiled sadly. "But to let them go, the Dark God had to also be freed. There are consequences to every action."

"And her actions in Willowdale?" Solara asked. "What purpose could driving the Zeraphim out of Willowdale serve?"

"Ask the people of Valendale," Laeyra shrugged.

"What do you mean?"

"The Zeraphim had captured the people of Valendale, enslaved them, and brought them to Willowdale," Laeyra explained. "Had the Blademaster and her companions not gone to Willowdale, those people would still be slaves to the Zeraphim."

"I had not known that," the High Priestess turned away. "I suppose I owe the Blademaster an apology. She truly was doing as she was supposed to."

"Never forget the Fourteenth Law of the Blades when looking at what Alana is doing," Laeyra admonished Solara softly. "There are many things in life that are but mere illusions. Things are not always as they appear. A Blademaster must depend on the wisdom of Taelin to understand what is real and what is an illusion. Confusion brought on by false realities can lead to a gruesome death. Always remember to let Lord Taelin be your guide in everything you do. Remembering this will cause you to see through any illusion that is in your path."

"She has been following her path," Solara nodded. "I have just been assuming she was being reckless."

"Don't be hard on yourself, Solara," the goddess smiled. "You were only reacting to what you could see."

Solara stood and walked over to her bookshelf. She scanned the titles of the books on the shelf for several long minutes before turning back to Laeyra.

"The Temple is not going to survive the War of Souls is it?" she asked softly.

"I cannot lie to you," Laeyra sighed deeply. "There are some that live in the Temple of the Blades that will die a second death. When they do, they will go to walk with Lord Taelin and I."

"But the Legacy of the Blademasters..."

"The Legacy will be broken," Laeyra shrugged. "There is little that can be done about that."

"But what will happen to the knowledge the Legacy protects?" Solara asked, aghast.

"Some will be lost. Some will be retained," Laeyra shrugged. "All things end. Nothing is forever."

"I never thought the Twenty Fifth Law of the Blades would apply to the Temple of the Blades or the Legacy of the Blademasters," Solara slumped back in her chair.

"All things end, not some things," the goddess said in a whisper. "One day, even the gods might go away."

"Well, that's a sobering thought," the High Priestess of the Blades grunted.

"Indeed it is," Laeyra nodded.

"What must we do to prepare for the War of Souls at the Temple of Blades?" Solara asked the next question she needed an answer to.

"The Legacy of the Blademasters must prepare to take the field again. As the prophecy says, the spirits of the chosen of Taelin will once more take the field of battle in the war against the darkness."

"I fear some of them have forgotten how to fight," Solara's sad voice said.

"Then you must remind them," the goddess ordered. "They must be ready to fight when they take the field."

"They will be," Solara nodded.

"One more thing," Laeyra added. "You must name Alana as the Master Blademaster as you once named Raven Windrider such."

"She's not ready!"

"Neither was Raven," Laeyra reminded her. "But she is needed. She is the only one that can lead the Blademasters into battle. The prophecy says that too. If the one born of the light does not lead the charge against the army of the dead, the world will fall into a darkness that will be without end. Only the power of the First Law of the Blades can guide the hand of the one born of the light."

"And Alana is the one born of the light mentioned in the prophecy," Solara sighed.

"She is."

"Then I guess I have no choice but to name her the Master Blademaster. May the consequences of this action not be dire."

Laeyra stood and moved to the center of the room. She looked back at the High Priestess of the Blades and smiled.

"Yes, you must," the goddess said softly. "I must leave you now, Solara. I have given you all the guidance that I can give you. It is up to you and the Blademaster now. There is nothing more that Taelin and I can do to prepare you."

With that, Laeyra vanished. Solara kept looking at where she had been standing for several long minutes before standing up herself.

"Raven!" she bellowed, knowing that the first Blademaster could hear her.

Sure enough, before too long, the spirit of Raven Windrider floated through the door of the sanctuary, her Protector by her side as he always was.

"You wanted to see me, Lady Solara?" Raven said.

"Yes. The Legacy of the Blademasters needs to be prepared to take the field in the very near future," Solara ordered.

"Some of them haven't practiced with their swords in years," Raven shrugged. "It won't be easy to get them into shape."

"Nonetheless, they must be ready," Solara said. "I do not know when we will be called upon to take the field, but everyone must be ready when that time comes."

"We will see to it," Richard Kale said softly. "Come, Raven. We have a great deal of work to do."

Solara watched Raven and Richard leave the sanctuary and slumped back in her chair. There was a great deal to do before Alana returned to the Temple of the Blades.

Chapter V
Two Visitors

The tap room of the Lucky Minotaur was relatively empty at that time of day. Alana, Colwyn and William were sitting at a table in the corner having lunch. It had been a good lunch. As always, Albert's food was excellent.

But it had also been a subdued lunch. Alana knew that there was war brewing and that prophecy said that she would be the one to lead the side of light. She wished that she knew just what they were going to be up against.

All she knew was that Lord Taelin had said that she would need help. He had suggested that there were other Blademasters for her to find. She just wished she had an idea of where to look for them.

They needed some help if they were going to find the new Blademasters. Searching all of the Southern Dales for the women that Taelin had chosen to bear the mantle of the Blademasters would take too long.

Alana did not see Albert come over to their table. But she noticed when he, without saying a word, left a large slice of chocolate pie in front of Alana. She knew that he had seen the way the three of them had eaten their lunch in subdued silence. The innkeeper was not stupid and knew that, when she and Colwyn, who were normally so cheerful, were so sullen, there was trouble afoot. There was little that Albert could offer, but he knew that his chocolate pies had often helped Alana through difficult times.

And they never failed to make her smile.

She smiled up at Albert, appreciating his gesture. He returned her smile and moved off over to the bar.

Alana took a bite of the chocolate pie, still warm from the oven, and sighed happily. The silky chocolate filling slid down her throat, warming her and comforting her.

The door to the tap room opened, and an old man shuffled in. Alana watched him make his way to the bar. As she looked long and hard at the old man, recognition set in and she dropped her fork.

"Well, this is going to be trouble," she muttered.

"What?" Colwyn asked. His eyes followed her gaze. He frowned when he saw the old man. "It's just an old man. I don't see how one old man can be trouble."

"I do," William's soft voice cut in. "That's not just any old man, Colwyn. He's called the Dream Weaver. He is a very powerful magic user. And a prophet."

"Oh," Colwyn groaned. "Yes, I can see where a prophet could be trouble."

"He lives just outside of Talondale," Alana added. "I talked to him just before I left for Ravendale." She turned to face Colwyn. "He was the one who told me that I would meet my true love in Ravendale." She turned back to look at the old man. "I wonder what he is doing here."

"Looks like we are about to find out," William shrugged. "He is, not surprisingly, coming over here."

Sure enough, the old man was shuffling his way across the tap room towards their table. None of them were overly surprised that he was coming to see them. Alana would have been much more surprised if he had been in Ravendale looking for anyone else.

She remembered the old man quite well. It had been an early spring morning when she had gone to see him before setting out for Ravendale...

The air was still chilly. The spring had only just arrived two weeks before and had not had a chance to fully thaw winter's chill. But Alana did not want to wait any longer to start on her journey. And she wanted to see the Dream Weaver before she left.

Something told her that he had vital information about her journey.

The young warrior woman made her way to the small cottage just ouside Talondale where the old man lived. She had never visited the Dream Weaver before, but, like everyone else who lived in Talondale, she knew where he lived.

When she got to the cottage, she reached up to knock on the door, but the door swung open before she could. She stood there gaping at the old man who had opened the door, her fist still in the air on its journey to knock on the door.

"Come in, Alana Steeldrake," the old man said, his wrinkled face crinkling in a wide smile. "I have been expecting you."

"You have?" she asked, lowering her hand. "How did you know I was going to come to see you?"

"I would not be much of a Dream Weaver if I did not see events surrounding people that are as important as you are," the old man shrugged. "Now come in. It is still quite chilly. Come in where it is warm."

She followed the old man into the cottage, still not believing that he knew she would be coming.

"I'm no one important," she protested after he closed the door. "I don't know what events you are talking about."

"You will," he said cryptically. "And before too much longer. Events are starting to happen. And whether you want to admit it or not, you are at the heart of many of them. I have seen it."

"What can you tell me about what you have seen?" she asked, curiosity getting the better of her.

"Only this. Not long after you arrive in Ravendale, there will be a young man that will come to your aid," the old man said. He sat down and looked at her. "I do not know who he is or what he will do to aid you. I only know that he will stand at your side and offer you his sword. He is the one you are meant to be with. Do not decline his aid."

"I was hoping for something more than romantic advice," she sighed as she slumped in a chair.

"It is far more than romantic advice," the old man raised an eyebrow. "This advice will save your life one day."

"Romantic relationships don't save lives," she frowned.

"Let love be your protection," the old man continued. "And remember. Dark and light. Good and evil. Black and white. These are two sides of the same coin. Both sides must exist or neither will."

"I don't understand," her frown deepened. "None of this makes any sense."

"It will make sense in time," the old man stood. "And now, my dear, I have told you all I can. I will see you once more before I die, I think."

"And will you confuse me as much then as you have now?" she asked as she stood.

"I am quite sure I will, yes," the Dream Weaver smiled. He put his arms around her and gave her a hug. She resisted his embrace, but he was insistent. "Just know that you are the right person for what is to come. You will be able to do what needs to be done. And you will be able to do what no one else can do."

Alana left the old man's house, feeling far more confused than she had when she arrived.

Three years later, she still felt confused as she watched the old man approaching their table. She sighed, knowing that the old man was going to say things that would mean just as little to her now as his words had meant to her back in Talondale.

"Alana Steeldrake," the old man said as he got to their table. "It is good to see you once more."

"And you, sir," she bowed slightly to him in respect. "As you can see, I did take your words to heart when last we spoke. This man is the man you told me of." She looked over at Colwyn, a bright smile crossing her face. "I could not wish for a better partner and Protector."

"You have done well, Alana," the Dream Weaver smiled. The smile was tinged with great sadness, however. "Your journey has only just begun, however."

"I know," Alana sighed. "War is coming to the Southern Dales."

"You have no idea as to what is coming," the old man shivered. "Reread Bahala Maranal's words. Even then, you will not know. That is why I am here. You must know what you are to face if you are to succeed in leading the forces of the Light."

The old man reached into the pouch on his belt and withdrew a small roll of parchment. The parchment had been sealed and Alana knew that it was meant for her eyes alone.

"You have had a weaving," William interjected.

"Yes," the old man nodded. His hand shook as he handed the parchment over to Alana. "I have never had a weaving that so scared me in my life."

"That sounds ominous," Alana frowned as she took the parchment from him.

She cracked the seal and opened the parchment. She read over the words written there and then read them a second time. Her frown deepened as she read. When she was done reading, she passed the parchment over to Colwyn who also frowned while reading what was written.

"When the twice dead city falls empty a third time, the age of darkness will spread across the land.

A wave of shadows shall block out the sun. The undead shall spread across the land in waves. Their number will be as close to endless. And they shall be led by the red eyed demon.

Only the one truly born of the light can lead the army of light against the army of darkness."

Alana turned to the old man and nodded once. The old man sighed softly knowing that the message had been received. Even though the prophecy had not been the clearest that she had ever read, the words still sent a shudder up her back. She did not know what the red eyed demon was, but the way the handwriting seemed to get more shaky at that point, she knew that whatever it was could not be good.

"Is there anything else that you can tell us, sir?" the Blademaster asked.

"Just that one that you seek for is in Barandale," he grunted. "I know not who just that there is one in Barandale."

"Barandale?" Colwyn raised an eyebrow.

"Barandale," the Dream Weaver confirmed.

"There's a halfling that is meant to be a Blademaster?" Colwyn gasped.

"So it would appear," the old man nodded.

"That's going to be no end of trouble," Colwyn groaned.

"Thank you for bringing me this, sir," Alana placed her hand on his arm. "It helps to know what we are up against. It makes it far more important that we find the other Blademasters now."

"Much depends on what you do now, Blademaster," the old man said. "But I believe that Calthea is in good hands."

The old man started to leave but stopped. An odd look crossed his face and he turned to face the young mage. William had kept quiet throughout the conversation between the Blademaster and the Dream Weaver save for the one revelation at the beginning. Alana wondered what the mage thought about the army of darkness that was coming. She knew that William would give her his thoughts in time.

But now, Alana was interested in the look that the Dream Weaver was giving William.

"I would speak to you before I leave, mage," the Dream Weaver said to William.

"I expected as much when I saw you," William shrugged. "Let us go over there where we can talk in private. What you would say to me, I suspect, is not for everyone to hear."

"Indeed not," the old man nodded. He shuffled towards where William had indicated. "What I must say to you is for you and you alone. In time, you may tell your Blademaster, but only as it affects your duties to her."

William shrugged at Alana and Colwyn before following the old man across the room. Alana watched the two mages walk across the room. She strained to hear what they said to each other, but she could not.

As he followed the Dream Weaver to an empty table, William thought back to the conversation he had had with Ferrin. When he had seen the Dream Weaver enter the tap room, William had no doubt that this was the visitor that the god of magic had been talking about.

And William had no doubt about what the Dream Weaver wished to discuss with William.

"Can I get you anything?" William asked the old man with concern. I imagine it has been a long ride from Talondale."

"It has been, yes," the Dream Weaver nodded. "Worry not for my comfort, young mage, though, and attend to my words."

"I know why you wish to talk to me," William shrugged and took a sip of his juice.

"You have already had a weaving then?" the old man raised an eyebrow.

"No," William put his glass down. "I have had a visit from Lord Ferrin. He told me to expect a visitor soon, and that this visitor would bring a clue as to my destiny. It is not hard to take that information and see you here and conclude what your business with me is."

"Lord Torval did indicate that you would be an astute one," the old man smiled. "I am glad to see he was right."

"The gods of magic usually are," William smiled. "You have come to ask me to succeed you."

"Indeed. My time on Calthea nears its end. I have but enough time to see my successor through the ritual."

"I have duties. I do not know if my duty to the Blademaster is compatible with taking the mantle of the Dream Weaver about my neck," William's soft voice said. "You know all too well what she will face. I am needed with her."

"Yes, you are," the Dream Weaver nodded. "And I have seen that she is not the last Blademaster that you will serve. You cannot meddle directly in events with the weavings, but you can use your other considerable magic in order to support your Blademasters."

"If I do this, what must I do?"

"You must meet me at the Tower of the White and go through the ritual. If you are, as Lord Torval suspects, the correct one, the magic will accept you. If you are not, you may well cease to exist."

William took a drink of his juice as he mulled over the Dream Weaver's words.

"I must think on this," the younger mage said, his voice barely above a whisper. "My decision affects more than myself, and I must take that into consideration."

"Of course," the Dream Weaver smiled. "But do not take too long. I have little time left."

"I will accompany the Blademaster on her journey to Barandale," William stood. "You will have my answer after."

"I will be at the Tower of the White when you are ready," the Dream Weaver said. He stood and faced the younger mage. "Now that I have met you, I doubt not that you are the correct choice to succeed me as the Dream Weaver. Whether you believe that or not is a different story."

The old man shuffled his way towards the door of the tap room, William following behind. The younger mage stopped where Alana and Colwyn were still standing. The three friends watched the the Dream Weaver go.

Overall, the man had generated more questions than he had answered. Alana knew that that was normal for the Dream Weaver, though. He had been very cryptic when she had known him in Talondale before she left for Ravendale years before.

In a way, it was a comfort to know that the man had not changed.

"I will leave you two now," William said softly. "I am going to go alert Martin and Meryn that they should be ready to leave on a new journey soon. Then I need some time to think about what the Dream Walker said to me."

"What did he say?" Alana asked. "He spoke so softly neither Colwyn nor I could hear."

"It is not for me to say at this time," William said after a moment. "When the time comes for you to know, I will tell you. But that time is not today, I am afraid."

"That's all right, William," Colwyn cut Alana off, knowing she was about to protest. "When you are ready to tell us what is going on, we will listen."

"Thank you, Colwyn," the mage bowed slightly. He turned and started to walk out of the tap room, but stopped and turned back. "It's not that I don't want to tell you. It's that I need to figure out what to do about what he said before I can talk to you about it."

"I can't say I understand, William, but you know Colwyn and I are both here for you when you are ready to talk," Alana smiled at her friend.

"Thank you both," William returned the smile. With that he made his way out of the tap room.

As he opened the door to leave, a burly man in plate armor entered the tap room. The man had clearly been about to open the door himself and quickly covered his surprise at having the door opened as he was reaching for the door.

Colwyn saw the sigil on the man's armor and groaned. He turned away from the door so the man wouldn't see him right away.

"What is it, Colwyn?" Alana frowned at him.

"That man is a soldier from Arvendale," Colwyn muttered. "Lord Dargan must have sent him to speak to me. I cannot imagine what about, however. I am sure that it will mean trouble, however. No messenger from my father can be good news for us."

Colwyn watched as the man walked over to the bar. Albert leaned in to listen to the man's quiet question and then pointed towards where Colwyn was standing. The man nodded and started over to him.

"Lord Colwyn Starseeker, I would speak to you," the man snapped off when he arrived to where he and Alana were standing. The man looked at Alana pointedly. "Alone."

"Alana, I will meet you back at the house," Colwyn put his hand on her arm. "I am sure this won't take long."

"All right," Alana nodded. She started to leave and stopped. She leaned up and kissed him on the cheek. "Don't take too long, though. We have things to discuss."

Colwyn smiled and watched her leave the tap room. The sight of her never ceased to amaze him, nor did the fact that she was his wife. Some men, he thought, were just born lucky.

When she was gone, he turned to the soldier and crossed his arms. "What does my father want?" he asked.

"Lord Dargan bade me bring you a message," the soldier said. The man pulled a sealed letter from a courier pouch that he had tied around his waist. "He requests that you return to Arvendale immediately."

"I see," Colwyn frowned.

He took the letter from the soldier and broke the seal. The soldier waited patiently while Colwyn carefully opened the letter to read it. He recognized his father's graceful even strokes as soon as he opened the letter. The tone of the message was formal and cold. That did not surprise him, as their relationship had been strained over the years.

"Colwyn,
You have been gone from our presence for too long. We bid you return to Arvendale immediately. We require and request your help with your sister.

Your sister, Bella, has refused the marriage that we have arranged for her and has chosen, instead, to fall in love with a member of the palace guard. We find this intolerable.

She refuses to fulfill her duties to the nobility. As this is a situation that you have created, for she is only doing this as she has seen you do so first, we require you to speak to your sister to change her mind.

We require that you return forthwith. The soldier that has brought you this message will bring your reply. We will be greatly displeased if you choose to ignore this message.

Signed by our hand,
Lord Dargan Starseeker
First Lord of the Arvendale Territory.

PS. Your sister has stated that you are the only one that she will speak with on this matter. We cannot stress enough our desire to have you return home to resolve this."

Colwyn read the letter over twice before looking up at the soldier.

"Do you know the content of this message?" he asked softly.

"I know only to expect a reply to bring to your father, Lord Colwyn," the soldier replied.

"Hurry to Arvendale and tell my father that I will return to Arvendale soon," Colwyn said after a moment's thought. "Tell him that I will only be able to visit, but that I will accede to his request."

"Very well," the soldier bowed. "I will tell him. Can I tell him when to expect you?"

"We will leave as soon as we have secured provisions," Colwyn answered, his voice hot. "We will be there and gone before the snows come."

"I will tell him your words," the soldier bowed. Without another word, he turned and left the tap room, his armor jangling as he went.

"Well, that's going to be no end of trouble," Colwyn muttered. He made his way over to the bar. "Albert, we're going to need provisions. You know what we'll need. I'm not yet sure when we're leaving, but it will be soon, I am sure."

"You won't leave without my cooking breakfast for you, will you?" the innkeeper asked.

"Of course not," Colwyn smiled. "I would never think of depriving you of the joy of sending us off. Alana or I will let you know when we're leaving. I would imagine it will be in the next couple days."

"What did that soldier want with you?" Albert asked, unable to control his curiosity.

"He was a messenger from my father," Colwyn said. He drained the last of the ale from his mug. "He was sent here to cause me an inordinate amount of trouble."

"That is what the nobility tends to do," Albert shrugged.

"Even for other members of the nobility," Colwyn laughed. He tossed some coins on the bar to cover the meal he and Alana had just had plus the cost of the provisions that Albert would gather for their journey. "Maybe even especially for other members of the nobility. Thanks again for a wonderful lunch, Albert."

"You're welcome, Colwyn," the old innkeeper smiled.

Colwyn returned the smile then made his way out of the inn.

When he got back to the house he shared with Alana, Colwyn had fairly well calmed his anger down. He was not looking forward to dealing with his father. It was not a situation that would be comfortable for any of them.

Especially not for himself and Alana.

Their marriage would cause a great deal of trouble when they got to Arvendale, but there was no way around that. He touched the pocket of his jerkin where he had the letter from the king. He could only hope and pray to Taelin and Laeyra that the letter would be enough.

He did not know how he could reach his father and get him to acknowledge his marriage without it.

He entered the house and found Alana in the sitting room. She was poring over a map of the Southern Dales. He could tell that she was looking at the route from Ravendale to Barandale, where the Dream Weaver had said they would find a child of the light. He knew that a trip to Arvendale would be out of the way, but not too far out of the way.

"Hi," she said without looking up. "I'm just figuring out our route to Barandale."

"I gave Albert the money for provisions," Colwyn came up behind her and took her in his arms. "They will be ready when we're ready to leave."

"What did that soldier want, Colwyn?" Alana asked as she leaned back into his embrace.

"We need to make a slight detour on our way to Barandale," Colwyn sighed. He gave her a gentle squeeze. "On the bright side, you're going to meet your in-laws."

"We're going to Arvendale?" she turned back to look at him. "Now?"

"I have been summoned," he sighed a second time. This one was a deeper sigh. "I cannot turn down a summons from my father."

"I suppose you can't," she nuzzled her head into his chest. "But it is inconvenient."

"Lord Dargan is never convenient," Colwyn rumbled with a chuckle. "He takes pride in inconveniencing people."

"That's not a nice thing to say about your father," Alana scolded him.

"Why not?" Colwyn shrugged. "It's the truth. Dargan Starseeker thinks of Dargan Starseeker first. It is a lesson I have learned well from him. But only so that I know what not to do when I am the First Lord of the Arvendale Territory."

"So why does he want you to visit now, of all times?" she asked him, leaning her head back in his chest.

"As soon as I figure out the real reason we're going to Arvendale, I will tell you," his voice was quiet.

He knew there would be more to their visit than just what was in the message from his father. Colwyn was not a man that believed in coincidences. It was too much a coincidence that he was being summoned now when so much was going on. The summons had to be a part of everything else, whether Dargan admitted it or not.

It just remained to see where this summons fit into everything.

William wished, more than anything, that Silvestra was there to talk to. The offer from the Dream Weaver was not one to be taken lightly, but he could not decide whether or not to take the offer without considering how it would affect his wife. Nor could he fail to consider how it would affect his duties with the Blademaster.

William knew that most mages, whether they admitted it or not, craved power. He was no exception. What he had been offered, he knew, most mages would have accepted without hesitation.

He thought that the fact that he needed time to think about it may, indeed, show that he was the right person to take the offered power.

If Silvestra had been there, he could have talked things through with her. He knew that she would not be able to tell him what to do. She'd already told him that she could not tell him what he was to become. But she was the only one of his companions that would understand just what it meant to be offered the power he had been offered. She was the only one who could possibly understand the depths of the repercussions that his decision would make for himself and for his companions.

He missed her greatly.

After he had told Martin and Meryn to prepare for a journey, he returned to his house on the outskirts of Ravendale. He went over to his desk and pulled a sheet of parchment from the desk, dipped his quill into the ink and began to write.

"My dearest Silvestra,

By the time that you return from your mission to the Isle of Dragons with Lord Taelin, Alana will have led us off on another journey. I believe she intends to go to Barandale, but I believe that there will be a stop along the way. I am not sure where though.

Albert at the Lucky Minotaur will know where we have gone, and he will have a sack of supplies for you. Go to him and he will direct you to us.

We need to talk. I was given an offer of power this day. And while I know that, in the end, it is my decision to make, you are my wife. And I cannot make such a decision as this without talking to you about it first, as it will affect both of us.

While I understand that you may not be able to help me make this decision, at least you are someone I can talk to about it and someone who will understand the ramifications of the choice ahead of me. The others cannot, as much as I love them.

Hurry back to me, my love. I sense that the coming journey will require your presence. The Blademaster is going to soon face some great challenges and she cannot face them without us or all will be lost.

    Yours until we merge with the magic,
    William"

    He read over the letter once to make sure it said exactly what he wanted it to say before sealing it. He wrote her name on the outside of the parchment and left it where he knew she would find it.

    The mage made his way to his bed to be refreshed for the morning, when they would, undoubtedly, be leaving on another journey.

The Age of Darkness

Chapter VI
The Army of Darkness

his time, the portal had dropped her exactly where she expected it would.

She was glad of that. She would have been happy to make another long trek to get to her destination in service to Thraal.

The portal had dropped her a short way from where the army of undead that had been assembled was massing. She had decided to arrive at a short distance from the army so that she could announce herself properly. She was there to take command of the army. There were protocols to be observed.

Surprising the army by appearing in their midst would get her killed before she could take command.

From where she had arrived, she could not see the army, but she knew they were close. She could hear the sounds of arms and armor being tended to. She knew that over the rise she was facing would be the army. She also knew that there would be a sentry between her and the ridge.

She was counting on that, in fact.

She slowly walked up the path to the ridge, carefully keeping her hands away from her swords so that she would not be seen as the threat that she was.

As she expected a sentry stopped her not too far along the path.

"Who are you?" the sentry demanded.

"My name is Kera Rayden," the Nightstalker said. "I bear a message from the High Priest of Thraal for the commanding general of this army."

"Stand where you are," the sentry called. When she did not move, the sentry, a wraith, glided out into the path and looked her over. "I will take you to the general, Nightstalker. I do not think he will be happy to see you."

"Happy or not, he will see me," Kera snarled as she followed the wraith up the path.

It did not take long before they crested the ridge looking over the army of undead. When Kera first caught sight of the army, her jaw dropped.

"Glorious, is it not?" the wraith guiding her said. "There is no way that the Southern Dales can stand against us."

"No, there isn't," she nodded in agreement. "So long as we eliminate the Blademaster first."

"You think even the Blademaster can stand against this?" the wraith shot her a quizzical look.

Looking at the army, Kera admitted that the wraith had a point. The army stretched on in an endless writhing mass. Kera put their numbers at an easy million. While she could not make out individual types of undead, she did not doubt that there were all types. She would imagine some of the officers were liches. She knew, from what Adouon had told her, that the commanding general of the army was an ancient vampyre named Atreus. The actual army itself was probably made up of wraiths like the sentry, shadows, skeletons, zombies, and the like.

No, she did not know that even the Blademaster could stand against such an army. Still...

"I've had experience with this Blademaster," Kera's soft voice said. "She is not one to underestimate."

"As you say, Nightstalker," the wraith said. "Come. I will take you to General Atreus."

As they walked among the army towards the command tents, Kera got a much better idea of the size of the army. She revised her count. She thought there might be closer to double her original estimate now that she was among them. There was no way that the Blademaster could stand against such an army. But Kera had underestimated the woman once before. She was not about to make the same mistake a second time.

As they made their way through the army, Kera felt like the undead warriors were watching her. It was almost as if they despised having a living being amongst them. From what she had heard about the undead, such a thing would not surprise her. She just made her way through the camp, meeting each gaze with her own steely gaze. Without fail, every time she met the gaze of an undead warrior, they looked away.

It felt good being intimidating, even when she was intimidating the undead.

Soon, though, they came to the command tents. The wraith indicated which one belonged to the vampyre, and led the way in.

"General, this is the Nightstalker," the wraith said when they had both entered the command tents. "She has come from the High Priest of Thraal with a message."

"Yes, I have been expecting a messanger from High Priest Adouon," the vampyre said without turning to face them. "I will hear what the Nightstalker has to say in private. You may go."

The wraith bowed and backed out of the tent.

When the vampyre turned, Kera had to school herself so that she did not react, for the vampyre's features were very jarring. The vampyre had glowing red eyes. The rest of his features were that of a normal enough looking human. But with the red glowing eyes, they made the rest of his face look overly sinister.

Kera thought that even the Blademaster would have second thoughts about facing this monster.

"I see my eyes unnerve you, child," the vampyre said softly. "Do not be afraid. I will not harm you, for I know why you are here and who sent you."

"You already know why I am here?" Kera raised an eyebrow.

"Of course," the vampyre nodded. "You are here to take command of the army of undead at the orders of the High Priest of Thraal."

"And you're not upset that I am taking your command from you?" Kera's other eyebrow shot up.

"Of course not," the vampyre laughed. "You are the counter to the one born of the light spoken of in the prophecy of the War of Souls. If we are to succeed, you must lead us."

"Very good," Kera nodded. "I was afraid I would have to fight you for command. It was not a prospect I relished."

"Nor would I," the vampyre appraised her. "I suspect you would give me quite a fight. I dare say I do not know who would win."

The Nightstalker waved towards the table where Atreus had laid out the map of the Southern Dales.

"Tell me what you have planned for the Southern Dales, General," she said. "We can work on details from there.

Part II
Bella Starseeker

Chapter VII
Preparations

Lana and Colwyn hurried from their house to the Lucky Minotaur. Neither of them would dare to leave Ravendale on a journey without giving Albert and Gwen the chance to send them off with one of Albert's famous farewell breakfasts. Even if the old innkeeper did not enjoy making the farewell breakfasts for the companions, neither Alana nor Colwyn wanted to leave without their bellies being full.

Besides. Even though neither one was overly superstitious, there was no point in tempting fate by changing their patterns.

When they arrived at the Lucky Minotaur, they were met by young Ash White, Gwen's brother, who happily took their horses to the stable to care for them. Ash was always eager to curry favor with the Blademaster and her Protector, for he knew that Colwyn was generous to his friends and to those who helped him.

But Alana knew that, far from just currying favor to earn an extra coin, Ash genuinely liked the couple, and wanted to make sure they were well taken care of.

Alana made sure that the young boy knew that his efforts were appreciated every chance she got.

After tossing a couple gold coins to Ash, Alana led the way into the Lucky Minotaur. She did not see Colwyn press a couple extra coins into Ash's hand, but she knew he did. He always did.

When she entered the tap room of the Lucky Minotaur, she noticed William, Martin, and Meryn waiting for them. She scanned the room and frowned slightly when she saw the High Priestess of Taelin sitting in the corner.

Naomi Mastairs had caused no end of trouble for Alana and her companions since she had taken over as the High Priestess of Taelin after Balaam Otakis was killed in Tornith. Alana did not like the woman, and had done little to hide her dislike of the woman whenever she dealt with her.

She suspected that they were going to have to deal with Naomi Mastairs once again.

She nudged Colwyn slightly to make sure he took note of who was sitting in the corner. When she was sure that he had seen Naomi, she headed over to where the rest of their companions were waiting for them.

Alana and Colwyn took seats next to each other at the table. Alana looked over and saw Gwen coming out with a large tray of food. The young girl smiled at them as she started setting down food on the table.

"You're just in time, Alana," Gwen said. "Albert is in back filling your packs now. He will have Ash put them on your horses when he's done. He has a pack for Silvestra too, even though she isn't joining you until partway through your journey."

"Albert is thoughtful as always," Alana returned the young woman's smile. "Please convey our gratitude for everything he has done for us."

"I will," Gwen nodded. "I'll be back out with the rest of your food shortly."

Alana nodded her thanks. She waved to the food on the table, telling her companions that they should start eating. Colwyn spooned some eggs and spiced potatoes onto Alana's plate, since that was always what she wanted most when they had one of Albert's farewell breakfasts. She was glad that she had a husband that was thoughtful and knowledgeable of her likes and dislikes.

It certainly made it easier on her.

She had just taken a bite of potato when Colwyn nudged her elbow. When he had her attention, he pointed. She followed where he was pointing and groaned inwardly. The High Priestess of Taelin had started walking towards the companions' table.

Alana could feel her appetite diminishing.

It did not really matter what Naomi wanted this time. Alana was in no position to do anything for the Temple of the White. Not with the preparations they needed to make in order to be ready to lead the forces of the Southern Dales in the War of Souls.

"I would speak with you, Blademaster," the High Priestess said when she arrived at the table. "You will come with me to the Temple of the White so we can discuss matters."

Alana put her fork down and looked over at Colwyn. Her husband shrugged his shoulders and mouthed "Up to you." at her.

"No, I don't think so," Alana said softly. "Anything you need to say to me, you can say in front of my companions. Make it quick, though. We are getting ready to leave."

"You're not going anywhere," Naomi snarled. "You have duties to the Temple of the White that you must attend to."

"No, I do not," the Blademaster shook her head. Her companions all knew that the tone of voice that she had just used meant danger for the person it was directed at. Unfortunately, Naomi seemed oblivious to the dangerous ground she was treading on.

"Yes, you do," Naomi insisted. She crossed her arms across her chest. "You have caused a great deal of trouble in your short time as the Blademaster and you must stop running around willy nilly and go back to simply serving the Temple of the White for the good of all."

Alana stood from her chair and turned to face Naomi. She took a step towards the High Priestess so that they were directly face to face. Alana was a bit taller than Naomi, so the Blademaster looked down on the smaller woman. The High Priestess looked back at her defiantly.

"Let me make this clear to you, Naomi," Alana's soft voice cracked dangerously. "The Blademasters, and there will be more than just one when we complete the journey we are about to start, do not serve the Temple of the White."

"You serve Taelin," Naomi reminded her.

"No," Alana said. "We honor Taelin and we honor Laeyra. We serve the people. And we serve the balance. We do not serve the Temple of the White. And we do not serve you."

"You lie," Naomi growled. "You lie about your service. You are not fit to be a Blademaster. I will see you stripped of your office."

"See, there is where you are mistaken," Alana smiled. As with her tone, it was a dangerous smile. "There is a High Priestess of the Blades that oversees all things with regards to the Blademaster. You are not her."

"I know all about Solara Moonfire and the Temple of the Blades," Naomi shot back. "She feels you were a mistake too."

"That may be, but she also knows that I am doing as Taelin would wish."

"You are directly responsible for the Dark God returning to Calthea," Naomi snapped. "You are directly responsible for the war that is coming."

"And if we do not lead the forces of the light in the war that is coming, the Southern Dales will be crushed," Alana returned. "What would you have me do, Naomi? Cower in the Temple of the White while you figure out what to do and let everyone die?"

"I would have had you serving the Temple of the White so that this war would have been avoided!" Naomi yelled. "You should never have gone to Willowdale and emptied out the city."

"You would have the people of Valendale suffer and die in servitude?" Alana narrowed her eyes.

"Better that they die than everyone in the Southern Dales be at risk."

"It is you who is unworthy of your position, Naomi. I will pray that Lord Taelin shares his wisdom with you. For now, though, you should go back to the Temple of the White. War is coming. You will be safe there."

"Martin, you are recalled to the Temple," Naomi snapped at the priest. "Since the Blademaster no longer wishes to serve the Temple of the White, she will receive no help from the Temple."

"Martin stays," Alana smiled. "I like him."

"Martin returns to the Temple," Naomi said. "I mean it. You will no longer receive any help from the Temple of the White, Blademaster."

"I will stay with the Blademaster," the young priest spoke from where he was sitting. "If she is going to keep the people of the Southern Dales from falling into darkness, she will need all the help she can get. You should be ashamed of yourself for your treatment of her, High Priestess."

"Very well, since you choose to defy me also, your name shall be stricken from the rolls, Martin. You will no longer be welcomed among the priests at the Temple of the White. You will no longer receive support from the Temple. When you return from this little journey, you will remove your belongings from the Temple. You will need to find another place to live as you will no longer be able to live at the Temple." The High Priestess turned to face Alana. "This is your doing. Martin will no longer be a priest of Taelin. If Lord Taelin had any sense he would strip his abilities from Martin. This is what happens when people listen to you."

"I rather think that Lord Taelin will be proud of Martin for standing up to you,' Alana smiled. "Good day, Naomi. I hope you stay safe on the pedestal you look down on all the little people from."

Naomi stormed out of the tap room. Alana followed her with her eyes to make sure the woman would cause no more trouble on the way out.

When she was gone, Alana sat back down at the table. Her appetite gone, she pushed her plate away.

"When you are all finished, meet me out by the stables," she said softly. "We need to get moving."

She stood, leaned over to kiss Colwyn, and then she walked out of the tap room herself.

Chapter VIII
Homecoming

hey were still a half a day out from the city of Arvendale when Colwyn called a halt for the evening. He did not say a word as he unsaddled the horses and brushed them down. Alana kept glancing up at him as he went about caring for the animals. She knew that something was bothering her husband, but he had closed himself off. It hurt her, but until he felt like telling her what was bothering him, she wouldn't push the issue. She knew how he was. Pushing him would only cause him to close up even further.

Alana worked on getting dinner ready while Colwyn finished currying the animals. She made a simple dinner of beans and rice with some of the dried meat they had. It would not be the tastiest meal that she had ever cooked for the companions, but it would fill them. As she worked, she watched the rest of the companions work on getting the camp set up. William was setting out the bedrolls while Meryn and Martin scouted the area immediately around the camp. The companions had done this enough times that no one needed to be told what to do anymore.

She looked up to see that Colwyn had finished with the currying of the horses and was now watching her. He smiled when he saw her watching him back, but it was a smile completely devoid of his usual joy. Something about this trip to Arvendale was truly bothering him. She wished that she knew what it was. But she knew that all she could do was to wait for him to open up about it. Pushing him away wouldn't do any good for either of them.

The five companions ate their dinner in silence. Even the normally gregarious halfling had little to say. Alana did notice that Meryn was still casting occasional hateful looks at William. She knew that the halfling was still upset that he had chosen Silvestra over her, but Alana did not think that she would have to worry about Meryn pulling anything like she did in Willowdale. While she was pretty sure that the halfling had been cured of her desire for revenge against Silvestra for stealing William away from her, she could not be completely sure of it. And she knew that Colwyn would be watching the halfling even more closely than she would be as well.

"I'll take first watch," Colwyn said softly after dinner was finished. He picked up his sword, the one that had been in his family for generations, from where it was lying next to him and walked out to a spot near the camp where he could watch over the camp and all the paths leading to the camp.

It had been the first thing that she'd heard him speak in hours. Unfortunately so, for it was disheartening for her to hear him only speak when it was necessary like that. She watched him go and sighed softly to herself. She settled herself into her bedroll, the one she shared with Colwyn, and tried to get some sleep.

It was two hours into the first watch and Colwyn was thinking about what would happen when they rode into Arvendale the next day. It wasn't going to be a pleasant experience for either him or Alana. At least he knew what to expect. Alana did not. He supposed that he was going to have to talk to her about what she should expect from his father when they got to Arvendale, but he just was not sure how he should broach the situation with her. But he knew that he would have to figure it out and figure it out quickly.

He was musing on this when he heard the soft footfalls coming from the direction of the camp. He gripped the hilt of his sword, tensing slightly, but he relaxed as soon as he saw that it was Alana coming up to join him in his watch. He smiled slightly about how attuned they had gotten to be over the past few years. It was to the point where they could just about read each other's thoughts. And so he was less than surprised to see her coming up to join him when he had just been thinking about her.

He smiled at her again and moved over slightly on the rock that he had been sitting on so that she could sit down next to him. It was the first genuine smile he had given her all day and he knew that she would cherish such a smile. It was the only real comfort that he could give her before they had the conversation that they were about to have.

"Col, I promised myself that I wasn't going to ask you about what's going on, but we will be at Arvendale tomorrow, and I suspect that I am going to need to know what's going on before we get there," she said softly as she sat down next to him on the rock.

"I know," Colwyn put his arm around the woman he loved. "I had just been sitting here trying to decide when I should tell you what you need to know and here you are coming to ask the questions that I should have answered for you from the start. I just hope that we can both handle the answers."

"You've been apprehensive about this journey to Arvendale ever since we first decided to listen to the messenger and come this way," she looked up at him, her big beautiful green eyes searching out the truth in his. "Why the apprehension?"

"My love, how much do you know about the nobility in the Southern Dales?" he asked keeping his voice soft, stroking her hair.

She closed her eyes and leaned her head into his chest with a sigh. "Not all that much," she admitted. "Since we don't know who my birth parents are, no one knows if I am a noble or a commoner. I guess that since it never came up before, I never worried about learning about it."

"And therein lies a big part of the problem," he sighed.

"What is?" Alana opened one eye to look up at him.

"The nature of your birth," Colwyn grunted. He shifted a little so that they would both be a little more comfortable. "Since no one knows if you are a noble or a commoner, you will not be an acceptable mate for me in my parents' eyes."

"But we love each other," Alana protested.

"Doesn't matter to them," Colwyn shrugged. "I'm a noble. More to the point, I am the firstborn son to one of the nine First Lords in the Southern Dales. I am expected to marry another noble. In fact, one was actually arranged for me, but the girl I was supposed to marry and I both refused to go through with the wedding. I guess that that's where the rift with my parents started. I'm afraid that this visit home isn't going to do all that much to heal that rift."

"You think we're going there to make your sister a Blademaster, don't you?" she asked, and he knew that she had been dying to ask that question for days. He had, in fact, been expecting her to ask it for so long that he had long ago figured out the best way to answer it.

"Alana, I don't believe in coincidences," he quirked an eyebrow at her. "I never have. It was no coincidence that the messenger from my father arrived right after the Dream Weaver delivered his message to us."

"You think that the two messages were related?" she raised her own eyebrow back at him.

"Don't you?" he countered.

"I'll admit. The timing does appear to be a bit odd," she mumbled into his chest. "What did the messenger from your father want anyway? You never told me what he said."

"Apparently, little sister is taking after her brother," the young nobleman laughed. "She's refused to go through with her own arranged marriage. Apparently, she's in love. The message did not say with whom she was in love, but apparently she told my father that I was the only person she would discuss the situation with. As a result, my father has requested that I come to Arvendale and straighten out my wayward sister. As he put it, I put the seed of rebellion into the mind of his younger child. As a result, I must force her to toe the line and become the dutiful daughter that she is supposed to be."

"But if you are right and your sister is a Blademaster..." Alana trailed off.

"Then an arranged marriage won't work. Yes, I'm all too aware of that," Colwyn nodded. "And my father will not be happy if I defy him in this. But what can I do? This is a sacred calling and there is far too much at stake. You heard the Dream Weaver. If we are to survive the coming darkness, we will need all the help that we can get. Getting that help has to take precedence of family concerns. No matter what the personal consequences might be."

"What do you mean, Col?" she looked up at him with concern in her eyes.

"There will come a time when I will no longer be able to adventure with you, my beloved." Colwyn closed his eyes and sighed a deep and long sigh. "I am the heir to the title of First Lord of Arvendale. It is a duty that one day I will have to assume. I thought I could run from my duty, but I cannot. What will become of us when that happens?"

"Well, then I will have no choice but to turn in my blades and become the First Lady of Arvendale," she smiled up at him. "Did you think it would be any different? You are my husband, Colwyn. Whatever you face, we face together as husband and wife."

"And if I am right and my sister is to be a Blademaster, then we will deal with that together as well," he smiled back at her.

"How will you know for sure if she is, Col?" she snuggled closer to his chest. "This is something we would need to be completely sure about."

"You'll have to give me the Bladestone," Colwyn said quietly. Alana reflexively reached up to touch the amber stone hanging around her neck. "Lord Taelin said that either of us can use it. And which of us do you think that Bella will trust more to use it on her?"

"You may have a point there,' Alana nodded as she pulled the amulet from around her neck. She handed it up to him. "Just take good care of it, Col. It is the only one we have, and I don't know how we will be able to identify new Blademasters without it."

"I am sure that if it were to come down to it, we would figure out a way to find them without the Bladestone, Alana," Colwyn chuckled. "But, just the same, I will take good care of it."

"That's all I ask," she smiled up at him. She was silent for a few minutes, just enjoying the feel of his body around her. Finally she said, "So. What can I expect to happen when we get there tomorrow, Col?"

Colwyn idly chewed on a piece of dried meat that he had brought with him on watch. After a few moments of silence, he sighed softly and told her what she wasn't going to want to hear.

"Your lack of noble status is not going to sit well with my parents," he said finally. "In point of fact, they will not even recognize our marriage as valid more than likely."

"I'm pretty sure that a marriage that was ordained by both Lord Taelin and Lady Laeyra is as valid as it possibly could be," she replied hotly.

"I'm not saying it isn't. You know how I feel about our marriage," he stroked her hair calmingly and lovingly. "But my parents are nobles. They can't see past their own wants and needs. The fact that you are not provably of noble blood means that you are not good enough for me in their eyes. They'll try to continue to match me with a woman that they'd find acceptable. Repeatedly. And they will fail. Repeatedly."

"We'll just have to show them that you and I are meant to be together," she smiled up at him.

"I think that it will take divine intervention for that to happen," Colwyn sighed deeply.

When morning broke, it found Colwyn and Alana bathing together in a nearby stream. Colwyn had suggested that they should at least look the part when they rode into Arvendale, he and Alana especially. He suggested that they bathe and wear their finery for the final ride in, suggesting that it might not look all that appropriate if they were to ride into Arvendale in travelling clothes and covered in several days worth of trail dust.

Alana had agreed, although her agreement had been without any real enthusiasm. She loved her armor and did not want to wear anything else. To that, Colwyn had just smiled and suggested that she wear her armor under her dress. That had done the trick, and any resistance she had had to wearing her finery had crumbled completely. Besides, getting to share a bath with Colwyn was always fun in her eyes.

After they finished bathing and dried off, Colwyn pulled on his under breeches before strapping on his elven chain mail. When she noticed him doing so, she looked at him curiously, chuckling softly to herself, for it had been a trial to get him to wear armor in the first place.

"Are you expecting trouble, Col?" she asked as she put on her own armor. "I didn't expect you to put on armor too."

"I'm always expecting trouble," he grunted. He pulled on the mail shirt. "That's part of the reason that you and I have been able to stay alive as long as we have. We both do."

"But we're going to your family's home," she frowned. "Surely, we'd be safe there if we were safe anywhere."

"My father may be well loved in Arvendale, but he is still a noble," Colwyn sighed. He pulled on the mail pants and fastened the two halves together. "Nobles have enemies. Sadly, it's not uncommon for enemies of a noble to strike at the heir to get to the father."

"Better to be safe then," Alana nodded. "But won't they be suspicious of your wearing armor?"

"By the time anyone knows that I am wearing armor, it will be too late. It will mean that they tried to attack me and that the armor stopped the attack."

Alana nodded and slipped the hunter green travelling dress over her shoulders. Colwyn smiled and nodded at her. It was amazing to him that, after all they had been through, she could still turn his head in that dress. He was glad that she was wearing the dress for more reasons than one.

"There's one other thing that you really need to hear, Alana," he said softly as he pulled on his breeches. "Since no one besides me in the party has standing as a noble, I will be the only one allowed to wear a weapon. You will have to leave your swords on your horse. That's the other reason I wanted you to wear that dress. Hide as many knives as you can in your dress. I don't want you going in there without weapons. You just can't wear them openly."

Alana sighed. "All right. I don't like it, but I will do as you ask. Is there anything else I should know?"

"Yes," Colwyn grunted. He pulled the white silk shirt over his head. "I want you to keep an eye on the halfling. I think I can keep her out of the dungeon, but I don't want any of the tableware finding its way into her pouches."

"Of course," Alana laughed. "I think that didn't even need to be said, Col."

"Let's get back to the others. We need to get moving."

They crested the rise overlooking the city of Arvendale when Colwyn called a stop. He stopped himself and sat in the saddle looking down at the city that he had once called home. Alana rode up close to him and took his hand in hers. He smiled at her then turned in his saddle to look at the rest of his companions.

"This is my home. Or at least it once was," he said quietly. "No matter what happens in the palace, please remember that no matter how dissimilar they are to me, Lord Dargan and Lady Serena are my parents. Please treat them as you would treat me. When we get to the palace, you will need to leave your weapons on your horses. Don't worry. Nothing will happen to them in the royal stables."

When all of his companions nodded, he turned back to Alana and smiled weakly. With that smile, he turned and led the companions down the hill towards Arvendale.

The guards at the guard post at the entrance to the city came out and blocked the road. They motioned for the party to stop. Colwyn held up his hand and he and the others reined their horses in.

"Identify yourselves," the lead guard at the gate said.

"What is your name, soldier?" Colwyn demanded.

"Swordsman Stran Tharlos," the guard replied. "Now, you identify yourselves, or you turn those horses right around and leave. If you can't follow the instructions of the guard at the gate, we don't want you in Arvendale."

"Well, Swordsman Stran Tharlos, is Victor Tram still the Captain of the Guards?" Colwyn demanded, his voice getting hotter with the treatment he was getting.

"He is," the guard nodded. "Now. Last chance. Identify yourselves or leave. Last time I will say it."

"Go get Victor," Colwyn ordered, his voice quiet. "We'll wait for him. He, I am sure, still has a good head on his shoulders."

"Don't let them enter," the guard said to the other guards at the gate. "I will go get Captain Tram. He'll straighten this arrogant popinjay out."

"Popinjay?" Colwyn chuckled softly. He watched the guard rushed off to the guard barracks. "New guards. Guess they don't know me."

"I don't think you're a popinjay," Alana smiled at him.

Colwyn rested his hands on the horn of his saddle while he waited. He thought back to all of the lessons in weaponship that he had had with Victor Tram and smiled. He knew this part, at least, would be a pleasant experience. It didn't take long for the swordsman to run to the guard barracks and come back. When he did come back, he had the captain of the guards following behind him. Colwyn recognized Victor Tram immediately, and the easy smile that Alana knew and loved was back on her husband's face.

"There he is, Captain Tram," the guard said. "This is the popinjay who refused to identify himself. He demanded to see you instead. He was rather rude about it, no less."

"Come down from your horse, sir and let me see your face," the captain of the guards ordered.

Colwyn swung his leg over the saddle horn and dropped to the ground. He walked over to where Victor Tram was standing waiting to see who the demanding popinjay was.

"Time was, a troublesome swordsman like Stran here would be whipped for his treatment of a noble," Colwyn grunted as he walked over. Then he smiled broadly at his old friend. "It's good to see you, Victor. Still teaching young upstarts how to fight?"

"As I live and breathe!" the big captain of the guards roared. He grabbed Colwyn up in a giant bear hug. "It is good to see you, my boy. You have been gone from Arvendale for far too long. And who are your companions?"

"Victor, allow me to introduce you to William Stonehands," he said. As Colwyn introduced each member of his party, he pointed at them. "He is a Wizard of the White. Behind him is Meryn Switftfoot, a halfling from Barandale. And this is Martin Faolin, a young priest in the service of my Lord Taelin."

"You've forgotten this lovely lady," Victor nodded towards Alana. "Who might she be?"

"May I introduce you to the chosen champion of our Lord Taelin, Blademaster Alana Steeldrake. My wife," Colwyn said with a very broad smile on his face. He turned to face the woman he loved. "Alana, this is Victor Tram, the captain of the palace guards in Arvendale. He is the man that taught me how to fight with a sword. And with my head."

"Then you have my most sincere gratitude, Captain," Alana smiled down at the captain of the guards. "You have taught my husband very well. Indeed, your teachings have saved both of our lives several times over."

"You honor me, Blademaster. But he was an excellent student." The captain bowed low in reverence to Alana, dropping to one knee. There were some who still held the Blademasters in reverence from the olden times. Victor was one of them. He stood stiffly and turned to face his former student again. "What brings you back to Arvendale, old friend?"

"My father sent me a message asking me to come here to speak to my sister about her relationship with the palace guard she has fallen in love with," Colwyn shrugged. "I had nothing better to do at the time so I figured I would come for a visit."

"Ah, yes. Young Cayden Antioch," Victor nodded. "He's a very good man. She could do a far sight worse than him. The problem, of course, is that he is not of the noble blood.

You know how your father feels about that. I dare say you'll likely have much the same problem when you inform him that you and the Blademaster have gotten married, although I know that it is a holy and sanctified union. I am sure that your father will still have quite a problem with your marriage. I am sorry to tell you this, but I am sure you already know this anyway."

"You haven't said anything that Alana and I haven't already discussed, Victor," Colwyn sighed as he walked back to his horse. "Considering the nature of my marriage to Alana, he will have no choice but to recognize it, though. The love of a Blademaster and her Protector is not something that can be torn asunder by mortal man."

"I think that you will have a hard time convincing your father of that, Lord Colwyn," Victor frowned. He followed Colwyn over to his horse and clasped forearms with the young noble. "He's a bit set in his ways, as you well know. Mount up and I will escort you to the palace. Your mounts will be boarded in the royal stables. And for the record, my boy, it is good to have you back here, even if it is only for a visit."

"It's good to be back," Colwyn smiled again as he climbed back up into the saddle. "I never realized how much I have missed Arvendale. Hopefully my duties with the Blademaster will allow me to return home a little more often."

"That would be good, Lord Colwyn," Victor nodded. He grabbed the lead rope for Colwyn's horse and started slowly walking down the path towards the palace. "It will be good for the citizens of Arvendale to know that you are still very much alive and in the picture. Your parents will not live forever."

Colwyn did not respond to that, simply shrugging at his old friend. Victor led the party through the streets of Arvendale. Crowds lined up on both sides of the street as they went past. Some of the citizenry knew who Colwyn was, whilst others needed to be told. Colwyn frowned slightly at that, knowing that he had been gone from his home for far too long. Indeed, it was something that would have to be rectified over the next few years. But as the party rode towards the palace, the crowd broke into a spontaneous round of applause, for those who did remember Colwyn, remembered that the young noble had always been popular with the citizenry of Arvendale.

When they got to the steps of the palace, Victor passed the reins of Colwyn's horse to a guard. He motioned for other guards to take the reins of the other horses. The captain of the guard motioned for Colwyn and his companions to dismount from the horses and led them up the steps to the palace.

"Lord Dargan is taking petitions today," Victor explained to Colwyn. "He has not been doing so every day, so there is a bit of a line. Since you are his heir, though, we will push you to the front of the line to see him. I am sure none of the petitioners will mind. And if they do, they can return on another day when he is taking petitions."

"Thank you, Victor," Colwyn nodded solemnly. "I really do not wish to put this confrontation off any longer than I need to."

"You are expecting a battle then, Lord Colwyn?" Victor raised an eyebrow. "A good attitude for you to have. I will, of course, have your back, should you somehow require it."

"Victor, I am the Protector to a Blademaster as well as the heir to the throne of the First Lord of Arvendale. I am always expecting a battle. Because more often than not, I find myself in the middle of one," Colwyn laughed, a short booming laugh. The laughter died very quickly though. "In this case, though, it will be a battle of wills with my father. There is, honestly, nothing that you can do to help me in this battle."

"I can, and do, wish you luck then," Victor smiled as they stopped at the doors to the great hall. He clasped the young man's forearm. "You will need it."

"Bring the next petitioners in," Lord Dargan's strong bass voice called from inside the great hall.

"Follow me, but do not say anything unless he addresses you first," Colwyn said to the others. "And Meryn, if so much as one piece of tableware is missing when we leave, I will personally take the opportunity to lock you in the dungeons of Arvendale until you rot. And remember, my friends. These people are my family, no matter how different they seem than me. Please treat them as such."

Meryn shrunk behind Martin at the mention of the dungeons. The party followed Colwyn as he strode through the doors into the great hall. Lord Dargan Starseeker, who looked like nothing so much as an older version of Colwyn watched the party approach with an amused expression on his face. He raised his hand and motioned for the party to stop.

Colwyn motioned for the rest of the party to drop to their knees in supplication, but the lord's son, himself, stood tall. He looked his father right in the eyes and nodded slightly in respect. His father returned the nod with a slight smile.

"Hello, Father," Colwyn said. "I have come forth to you as you bade me by your messenger to do. As you have requested, I will speak with my sister. Indeed, though, I make no promises, for you know as well as I how strong willed my sister is."

"We are glad to have you home, Colwyn," Dargan smiled. And for once, Colwyn knew that it was a genuine smile. For all their problems, Colwyn and his father did love each other. "We know that you will do your best with Bella. Will you be staying long, our son?"

"I cannot, I am afraid, Father," Colwyn bowed his head in respect. "I regret that I have duties that will keep me away from Arvendale for some time. Although I will make an effort to shape my duties so that I can visit more often than I have in the past."

"And do your duties involve this bunch of riff raff that you have surrounded yourself with?" Dargan raised an eyebrow. He pointed to Colwyn's companions, motioning for them to rise. "A wizard, a warrior woman, a priest and a halfling? These are hardly the companions that a lord should be surrounding himself with. And certainly not the companions for the heir to the title of First Lord of Arvendale."

"This riff raff, as you call them, Father, have all saved my life at least once each," Colwyn shrugged slightly. "This warrior woman leads us in what we must do. The five of us have been thrust in the middle of a world spanning conflict. Lord Taelin himself tasked us with this conflict. At this moment in time, I cannot leave my duties to this conflict. We are all that stands between Calthea and the darkness that is coming."

"And what of your duties here, Colwyn?" Dargan demanded. "One day you will succeed me as the First Lord here in Arvendale. You have a duty to prepare yourself for that day."

"I also have a duty to ensure that that day comes, Father," Colwyn nodded. He pointed again at Alana, the woman he loved more than life itself. "I have already told Alana that I have duties to the nobility. And when the time comes for me to assume my duties as First Lord, we are in agreement that I will leave my adventuring days behind me. Until then, my duties to Lord Taelin's will must needs come first."

"Step forward young woman," Arvendale's First Lord commanded, motioning for the Blademaster to come forward. "Who are you and what do you think it is that might give you any right to decide when the heir to the title of First Lord of Arvendale might decide that it is time to fulfill his duties?"

"Lord Starseeker, my name is Alana Steeldrake," Alana strode forward. Her stride and her words were both focused with the same boldness that she did everything with. She was, however, very careful in her choice of words in her explanation of who and what she was with regards to Colwyn. "I have been chosen by Lord Taelin and Lady Laeyra as the first in a new line of Blademasters. I have been imbued with the power and the charge of the office of Blademaster in accordance with the Law of the Blades as it was set down in times of old. Colwyn, in accordance with the Law of the Blades, agreed to undergo the Test of the Blades at the Temple of the Blades. He was successful in his attempt at passing the Test of the Blades. As such, he was sanctified before Lord Taelin and Lady Laeyra as my Protector and my husband in a marriage sanctified by the gods themselves."

"We do not recognize this marriage," Dargan thundered. "Colwyn will marry a noble woman and fulfill his duties as is right under the law of the nobility."

"Our marriage is sanctified by the gods," Alana thundered back. "What they have done, you cannot undo."

"Enough!" Dargan shot to his feet. "We will NOT recognize this marriage. We shall provide quarters for your companions, Colwyn. We will speak more of your flaunting of tradition later. For now, you will go to your own quarters to rest. And you will go alone. There will be a dinner tonight. You are all welcome to attend the dinner. Colwyn, I will have your sister come and see you this evening and you will do your best to put this foolishness out of her head." He motioned for the captain of the guards to come forward. "Guards! Escort our guests to their quarters. This... Blademaster is not allowed to be anywhere near my son's quarters this evening. Colwyn, you will have breakfast with me in my quarters in the morning."

The First Lord of Arvendale sat back down on his throne and waved his hand in a gesture of dismissal.

Colwyn and Alana shared a long look before she was ushered out of the great hall by the guards. Victor nodded to Colwyn in silent agreement that he would look after Alana for him. Colwyn sighed and nodded. He headed off to his own quarters slowly, wishing he had not heeded his father's messenger. The weight of the Bladestone hung around his neck, its constant weight reminding him that he had duties. And that not everything was entirely as it appeared to be in Arvendale.

The Age of Darkness

Chapter IX
Bella and Colwyn

Though his quarters had not changed at all since the day that he had left Arvendale for his training in the Elven Woods, Colwyn nonetheless felt not at all comfortable in the opulence of his room in the palace. He had simple tastes, and the small house that he had built for Alana and himself was far more suited to his tastes than the suite of rooms that were his in Arvendale Palace. He could fit his entire house in Ravendale in the living room of his quarters in the palace.

He knew which he preferred.

In the palace that was his childhood home, he was not even being allowed to see the woman that he loved. He knew that this was going to lead to an epic confrontation with his father. It was a confrontation that he was not looking forward to. But it was one he had been expecting since receiving the letter bidding him come to Arvendale. He would be ready for it when it came.

Colwyn went over to the closet and looked inside. The large walk in closet was larger than the living room of his house in Ravendale. As it had been before he'd left for the Elven Woods, the closet was filled with elegant clothes. They were clothes that were fit for a noble.

There was nothing in the closet that he would feel comfortable wearing.

He knew that it would not be acceptable for him to wear his forest garb to the dinner that he and his companions would be forced to attend. It was yet another thing in this trip that he was not looking forward to. He knew that, because they were his guests, Alana and the others would be at the feast as well.

But they would not be allowed to sit at the table that he would be sitting at.

He hated that he would not get to sit with his companions, and even worse, he hated that he would not get to sit with his wife during dinner. Even though he had known what to expect when they arrived in Arvendale, he was nonetheless upset with how Lord Dargan had responded to his companions and how he had treated Alana. He knew that he would have to find a way to get Dargan to recognize his marriage to Alana. It did not matter in the end, though. Their marriage had been sanctified by Lord Taelin himself. There was nothing that Dargan could do to tear that bond asunder, no matter how much he wanted to.

Still, it rankled to be apart from the woman he loved, especially when she was so close by.

But he knew that they would not be in Arvendale for too long. When they left, Alana and Colwyn would be together again. They just had to get through the next couple hours... a day at most. And then they would not have to deal with Lord Dargan's bias against those that were not members of the nobility until the next time that their adventures brought them to Arvendale. Colwyn did think that they would have to get back to Arvendale a little more often, though. As much as he did not want to admit it to himself, Dargan was not going to live forever. Colwyn would need to make sure he was not forgotten, so that when his father did go to his walk with Taelin, the people of Arvendale would be comfortable with his becoming the new First Lord of Arvendale.

It was a position he did not wish to inherit for a number of years yet.

Colwyn rummaged through the closet and selected one of the lesser ostentatious outfits. While he was sure that his father wanted him to wear an outfit that was far more extravagant than the one that he'd selected, Colwyn would not have been comfortable in it.

The outfit that Colwyn had selected was one of his favorites to wear when he was in Arvendale, though. He smiled as he pulled it out of the closet, because he knew that the deep hunter green color of the jacket would match Alana's dress so perfectly. The outfit consisted of a plain white shirt and plain black pants. The hunter green jacket flowed to his knees and was cinched around the waist by a wide black belt. The black pants tucked into plain knee high black leather boots. The boots had a higher heel than he would have normally worn. It was not a practical outfit for his job as Alana's Protector, but it was more than fitting for his role as the heir to the title of the First Lord of the Arvendale Territory. He supposed that it was in that position that he was to function that night, no matter how much he would prefer to just be Alana's Protector.

Appearances had to be maintained, after all.

Even though he felt that his being a part of the nobility was secondary to his role as the Protector to a Blademaster, he did understand the importance of his maintaining an appearance in Arvendale. At least he knew that he would have a good relationship with the King of the Southern Dales when the time came to become the First Lord of the Arvendale Territory. Such a good relationship would only be good for his people.

Colwyn stripped down to his under breeches and started to dress for dinner. He knew that one of the palace guards would come by soon to bring him down to the dining hall. It would be his first chance to see his sister since he arrived in Arvendale. For that reason, he took the chain with the Bladestone and fastened it around his neck. He would know right away when he saw her if his suspicion about Bella being a Blademaster was correct. He still wasn't sure what he was going to do if that turned out to be the case. He knew that his father would not accept that any more than he was willing to accept the fact that Colwyn was married to a Blademaster.

He would figure that out just as soon as he figured out if he needed to. There was no point in worrying about things until he knew for sure that Bella was a Blademaster and that there was, in fact, something to worry about.

Once he was dressed, he looked at himself in the full length mirror that was in his quarters. Even though he was not comfortable in noble clothes, he had to admit that he did look good in them. He was willing to bet that Alana would like what she saw too.

There came a soft knocking on his door. He frowned slightly. If it were one of the palace guards, he did not think that they would be knocking so softly. His curiosity piqued, he went to the door to see who it was, picking up a dagger on the way. It paid to be cautious, even though he was in his father's house. Perhaps, especially since he was in his father's house. Lord Dargan may have been well loved by the people of Arvendale, but the Starseeker family was not without their enemies.

When he opened the door, he relaxed when he saw that it was his sister, Bella. He smiled at her and let her in, putting the dagger down on a nearby table so that he did not accidentally hurt her or himself with it.

"Hello, Col!" she exclaimed as she gathered him up in a big hug. "It is good to see you. What's this I hear about you coming home with a wife?"

"It's true," Colwyn smiled as he returned the hug. "All of it. As you might have imagined, Father was not happy." He pulled away to look at her. "Now come and sit. Let me look at you. It has been some time since I have seen you, Bella. You've grown!"

"I was still a child when you left, Col," Bella said softly as she sat at the table that he had waved her over to. "I am not a child any longer."

"No," Colwyn agreed. "You are no child. You are still as headstrong as I remember, however. Did you really think Father would let you thumb your nose at the noble traditions?"

"You did!" Bella snapped as she stood up to face her brother. "Hell, you came home with a wife."

"And it will be no end of complications for me," Colwyn's soft voice came back. He felt for the Bladestone around his neck. It had started to warm. He was sure that if he had looked at it, the stone would be glowing softly. He sighed deeply, now knowing full well that he was right about why they had come to Arvendale. "As will your palace guard mean no end of complications for you."

Colwyn turned away from his sister and made his way over to look out the window to the courtyard below. Now that he knew that Bella was a Blademaster, he had to figure out what he was going to do about it. There was no doubt in his mind that Bella and her palace guard were going to have to leave with them when they left Arvendale. There was nothing that Colwyn could do about that fact. He just wasn't sure how he could convince his father that it was necessary.

"What is it, Colwyn?" Bella asked as she joined him at the window. She put her hand on his shoulder and leaned against him. "Something is bothering you."

Colwyn looked down at his sister and smiled. It was a sad smile, because he knew what he was committing her to. He wrapped an arm around her and squeezed her close against him.

"This palace guard of yours," he said. "Are you sure how he feels about you? Are you absolutely sure about his feelings for you?"

"I have no doubts, Colwyn," she nodded. "He loves me."

"Would he die for you if he needed to?" Colwyn asked. "This is very important, Bella. You must be absolutely sure about this."

"I am sure, Colwyn," she frowned. "What is going on, Col?" She looked up at him with a worried expression on her face. "You're scaring me."

Colwyn signed softly and pulled the Bladestone from under his tunic. He looked down at it and shook his head. It was glowing with a soft pulsing light. Just as he had expected it would.

"This is called the Bladestone," Colwyn explained to her as he showed it to Bella. "It was given to Alana and myself by Lord Taelin. In one of our hands it will glow just like this when it is in the presence of a woman that is to become a Blademaster."

"What are you saying, Col?" Bella asked, wanting to make sure she was not misinterpreting things. "Are you saying that I am a Blademaster?"

"So it would appear," Colwyn nodded. "I would imagine that this will cause no end of trouble with Father."

"I would imagine you are right," Bella sighed as she slumped against her brother. "But why were you asking me if I was so sure about Cayden?"

"Do you know anything about the Blademasters, Bella?" Colwyn asked his sister. "I am willing to bet that all you know of the Blademasters comes from the old songs and stories."

"That's true," Bella nodded. She pulled away and went back over to the table. She poured herself a glass of water. "Until your Alana came along, there were no Blademasters in our lifetime to know. Why?"

"There is a lot that is not in the songs and stories, Bella," he sighed. He poured himself an ale and took a long pull from the cup. "Did you know, for instance, that every single Blademaster has been married?"

"No," Bella frowned. "That was never in any of the stories of the old Blademasters."

"Nor would it be," Colwyn smiled. The Blademasters would never let the source of their abilities become public knowledge. A Blademaster's power is bound in the love she shares with her husband and Protector. That is why I was asking if you were sure about how your palace guard felt about you. In order to be the Protector to a Blademaster, he must be your true love. And he will have to prove it in a Test where his very life will be at risk."

"And you have taken this Test for your wife?" Bella gasped. "You have put your own life on the line for her like that?"

"Yes, I did," Colwyn gave a solemn nod of his head. "It was not easy. And I almost failed, even though I was the one who was meant to be Alana's Protector. The Test of the Blades is meant to make sure that the Blademaster only marry the right people."

"You have to help Cayden, Col," Bella said with urgency. "I can't bear to not be with him."

"I can give him no help," Colwyn said softly, sorrow for his sister in his voice. "I cannot do anything to aid him or the Test will be invalidated and he will not be allowed to be your Protector. All I can do is explain the consequences of his going with us. If he is to be the one that is your Protector, he must do it on his own."

"But this isn't fair!" Bella protested. "I have only just found Cayden, and now you're saying that there's a chance I will not be able to marry him?"

"You will find that if you do choose to accept the mantle of a Blademaster, that very little in your life will be what you would call fair, Bella," Colwyn sighed again. "The choice is yours whether or not you will accept the calling, but if you do accept it, you accept all that goes with it. And that includes the fact that Cayden will have to face the Test of the Blades.

"You mean I actually have the choice as to whether or not I become a Blademaster?" Bella turned to face him. "It isn't decided?"

"We, all of us, have free will, Bella," Colwyn nodded. He took another sip of his ale. "But if you choose to accept the mantel of the Blademaster, you cannot change you mind later."

"Will it be dangerous?" she asked.

"I will not lie to you," he nodded. "It will be very dangerous. There is every chance that you will not live to see an old age. The Southern Dales are on the verge of war. A great darkness is coming. Those of us that have accepted the call of the light are the first line of defense for the Southern Dales. If we fail, everyone in the Southern Dales will succumb to the darkness. Alana and I are dedicated to the fight. We need all the help that we can get."

"I understand," she nodded. "I am scared, though."

"I would be more worried if this didn't scare you, Bella."

Bella turned away from her brother and went back to look out the window to watch the guardsmen going through their practices. She did not see Cayden out there, but she knew he probably was on duty at that time. No matter how much she wanted to say no to the call and not take the risk of losing Cayden to the Test of the Blades, she knew that she could not. She knew that the responsibility that had been thrust on her must come first. She knew that the responsibility had come to her because Lord Taelin had known that she would accept the responsibility.

She was her father's daughter after all.

"Love is a very complicated thing," she heaved her own sigh.

"It is," Colwyn nodded in agreement. He smiled sadly, knowing that Bella would never know all that he had been through to prove the love he had with Alana. He was happy that she would never have to face that particular part of it.

He was thankful for small favors.

"I can't ignore the call. Not with so much at stake." She turned to face her brother. "But there is something that you must do for me, big brother."

"And that is, little sister?"

"I need you to explain to Cayden what the consequences are for him if he chooses to go with me," she said. He could detect a tear in her voice. "I will not allow him to come with me if he does not know what the risks are."

"Of course," Colwyn nodded. "I will talk to him after the banquet our father is throwing for his wayward son."

"Thank you, Colwyn," she smiled.

"And then I will talk to Father in the morning. I will let him know that you are coming with us and why," Colwyn grunted. He knew that was only going to make the coming confrontation even harder.

"He will not be happy," Bella reminded him.

"I am praying for divine intervention," Colwyn quipped. "Now, let's get down to the banquet hall before he sends guards looking for us."

The Age of Darkness

Chapter X
The Palace Guard

Olwyn fingered the hilt of his sword as he stood in a window of the castle overlooking the courtyard where some of the guards were sparring to keep in practice. Colwyn had no problem picking Cayden Antioch out of the crowd. The young man stood with a bearing that was hard to miss. And looking at the young man, Colwyn had no doubt why his sister had fallen for him.

But simple attraction would not be enough for Cayden.

Colwyn sighed softly to himself as he steeled himself for what he had to do. He slapped his hand against the side of the window and turned away.

Ten minutes later, Colwyn found himself entering the courtyard outside the castle. He leaned against the castle wall and watched Cayden as he went through some practice maneuvers. He watched the young man carefully, happy with what he saw in how the guard handled his weapon. The young man moved with an easy grace.

"Colwyn, my boy. What brings you out to the practice field tonight?" Victor Tram said as he came up to the young noble. "Here for some pointers from your old weapons master?"

"If only I were," Colwyn shook his head. "No, I am out here to speak with this young palace guard that has stolen the heart of my younger sister."

"Ah, yes," Victor nodded. "I figured you would get around to coming out to speak with him. He is why your father summoned you to Arvendale after all."

"Yes, he is," Colwyn smiled at his old weapons teacher. He looked out into the courtyard and nodded towards Cayden. "That him?"

"Yes," Victor nodded. "That's young Cayden Antioch. A fine young man."

"I hope he is, indeed, a fine young man," Colwyn said after a moment. "For Bella's sake."

"Do you really think your father will actually let Bella marry Cayden?" Victor looked over at Colwyn. "You know how Lord Dargan feels about nobles marrying commoners."

"I think that Lord Dargan will have as little choice in accepting this marriage as he will have in accepting mine," Colwyn said softly.

"I see," Victor frowned.

The two men watched as Cayden went through his practice. Colwyn watched the man's movements closely. As Cayden went through the motions of his practice, Colwyn noted how smooth the young palace guard's movements were. Cayden moved with a fluid grace that many swordsmen took years to master.

If he was as good with a blade as he appeared to be, Bella would be in good hands.

"How is he in a fight?" Colwyn asked Victor.

"One of the best that I've trained," Victor shrugged. "You see how fluid he is. He doesn't waste movement in a fight. He is a man who I would always want to have my back in a fight. Does that answer your question?"

"Yes," Colwyn nodded. "But it is not my back that he will have to have in a fight."

"What are you not telling me, Col?" Victor turned to face his former student.

"There is a very good chance that Alana and I will be taking young Cayden with us when we leave tomorrow, Victor," Colwyn said, still watching Cayden's practice. "I will need to talk to him to make sure he is aware of the consequences of his decision. But if he chooses to go with us, as I suspect he will, Cayden will be leaving with us. As will my sister."

"Oh," Victor said. Understanding dawned on the captain of the guard. "Oh!"

"Yes," Colwyn nodded. "That is why I need to be sure."

"I understand," Victor nodded. "I will leave you to it, then. If there's anything you need, please let me know."

"There is," Colwyn turned to face the captain of the guard. "If you could gather supplies for Bella and Cayden, including packs and bedrolls, and gather some supplies to top the rest of our packs off, that would be a great help."

"Consider it done," Victor smiled. "You will have everything you need by the time you are ready to leave in the morning."

"Thank you, old friend," Colwyn returned the smile. He clasped Victor's arm. "For everything."

"You may find that as you get older, helping people brings you a joy all of its own," Victor raised an eyebrow. "And when you do, you will find that no thanks are necessary."

"I have already learned that lesson, Victor," Colwyn's soft voice said. "But I also know that to the person expressing gratitude, it is something that needs to be said even if the person they are thanking does not need to hear it."

"You have learned much in your time away from Arvendale, Colwyn," Victor smiled. "You will do well when it comes time to succeed your father, I think."

"May that day be many, many years from now!"

Victor bowed to Colwyn and hurried off to start collecting the provisions for the party.

Colwyn watched his friend go, smiling slightly at Victor's back. He turned back to watch Cayden practice some more. The young man appeared to take his practice seriously.

Colwyn decided he liked what he saw.

After watching the young man for several more minutes, Colwyn walked out into the courtyard to where Cayden was practicing. The young man noticed Colwyn coming and watched his progress towards him.

Colwyn was pleased that Cayden was so aware of his surroundings. It would serve him well as the Protector to a Blademaster.

"You have been watching me for some time, my lord," Cayden said in a soft voice when Colwyn came up to him. "Is there something I can do for you?"

"I was trying to determine whether or not you were worthy of my sister," Colwyn smiled.

"Lord Colwyn," Cayden bowed slightly. "I had heard that you had returned to Arvendale. I am sorry I did not recognize you."

"It's all right... Cayden, is it?" Colwyn said. He picked up a practice sword and swung it a few times. He frowned in distaste at the balance on the practice sword. "I forgot how bad the balance on these can be compared to a real blade."

"They serve," Cayden shrugged.

Colwyn took a few more swings with the practice sword and then put it down. He saw a rack of bows near by and his face lit up. He picked one up and examined it.

"Do you shoot, Cayden?" he asked.

"Not well, but I put my practice in," Cayden answered. He put his own practice sword down and looked at Colwyn. "Why are you so interested in me?"

"Do you love my sister, Cayden?" Colwyn asked, his gaze capturing Cayden's. "I mean, do you love her with all her heart? Would you die for her if it was called for?"

"I would," the palace guard nodded. He turned away. "But you must know that your father would never allow it. I suspect that is why you are here. Bella refused to talk to anyone but you."

"What if I told you that there was a way for the two of you to be together?" Colwyn's soft voice caught him off guard. "What if I told you that if you accept the offer you are about to be given, with all the risks involved, then my father will not be able to prevent the two of you from being together?"

"I would jump at the chance given me, my lord."

"Well, first things first," Colwyn laughed. "If you choose to leave with us, it's just Colwyn. Not my lord. Not Lord Colwyn. Just Colwyn."

"I will try to remember that, Lo-... I'll try to remember that, Colwyn," Cayden chuckled. "What are the risks you speak of?"

"Bella is a Blademaster. If you choose to go with us, you agree to be bound by the Law of the Blades," Colwyn explained. "You must undergo the Test of the Blades if you are to marry Bella. It will not be easy. You could die. But if you live and fail, you will never be allowed to see Bella again."

"And if I don't fail?"

"Then you and Bella will be bound in the power of the Law of the Blades. You will be her husband and her Protector."

Cayden walked over to a bench and sat down. He looked over at Colwyn and nodded.

"And if I were to choose not to go?"

"Then you would be prevented from ever seeing her again," Colwyn shrugged. "You would be forced to leave the palace guard in Arvendale to prevent the chance that you might see her when she visits the court."

"I see that I have little choice in the matter," Cayden looked away.

Colwyn sat next to the young man and clapped him on the shoulder. He knew what the young man was feeling. He had felt much the same way when the choice had been put to him.

"I know how you feel, Cayden," Colwyn smiled a sad smile. "I was forced to make the same choice. I put my own life on the line for the chance to marry the woman I love. And I would do it again."

Cayden stared off towards the palace. Colwyn knew that he was weighing his choices in his head.

"You leave me little choice, Colwyn," Cayden said after a while. "I could not bear to lose her. You are at least giving me a chance to be with her. I understand the risks, and I would gladly choose to go with Bella."

"I was kind of hoping you would," Colwyn's smile grew. "I don't know you beyond what Victor has told me and what I have seen of you practicing. But from what I have seen, my sister is in good hands."

"I thank you, Colwyn," Cayden smiled. "You have given me a chance for something I never thought I would be able to have."

"Don't waste the chance given, Cayden," Colwyn stood. "Chances for true love do not come often. Make the most of it."

"I will."

Colwyn started to walk back into the palace but stopped and turned.

"Be ready to leave tomorrow," Colwyn ordered. "Victor is preparing supplies for you. But we will be riding hard and fast to get to our next stop in this journey in time. We want to be back in Ravendale before the snows fall."

"I understand," Cayden nodded as he stood. "I will go start packing now. I will be here when you're ready to go."

Chapter XI
Colwyn and Dargan

he next morning found the First Lord of Arvendale alone in his quarters. He had requested that his son join him for breakfast, but Colwyn had not yet arrived, although, to be fair to the young man, the time set for breakfast was still an hour away.

Dargan Starseeker sipped at his mug of hot spiced wine as he looked out the window of his chambers to the courtyard below. He had hoped that this visit from his son would have started the work towards healing their relationship and get Colwyn to start taking his duties as the heir to the First Lord of Arvendale seriously.

Instead, Colwyn had arrived with a wife. And not even a noble wife.

Dargan sighed softly as he thought about the Blademaster. As a woman, she was fair enough to the eye. He could not get past the fact that she was not of noble birth, though. It was a problem that would have to be resolved soon. He was not sure that anyone would be happy with any resolution for the situation.

He watched out the window as Victor Tram led his guard through morning calisthenics. He was always well pleased with how well Victor kept the guards in shape. He had never once had a complaint about the abilities of the members of his palace guards.

Nor did he have any complaint with how Victor had trained his son how to use a blade. Dargan knew that the fact that Colwyn was still alive was a testament to Victor's teachings.

The First Lord sighed. He could not wrap his brain around how his son could have so flaunted tradition and married without his blessing.

He knew the stories about the Blademasters, and he knew that the marriage between a Blademaster and her Protector was a sanctified and sacred bond. Deep in his heart, he knew that he would have no choice but to accept the marriage between his son and this Blademaster.

He did not have to like it, though.

He turned from the window and started across his chambers to where he would sit and talk with his son over breakfast, but he stopped halfway across the room and stared.

There was someone in his chair.

Dargan did not understand how the old man had gotten into his quarters. He had heard no one enter, and there were guards outside the doors. Had someone tried to enter, they would have raised an alarm.

And yet, there was someone in his chair.

"Your palace is very nice," the old man said. "Very warm and inviting."

"Who are you?" Dargan demanded. "How did you get in here?"

"You should recognize me, Lord Dargan Starseeker," the old man's strong voice said softly in the muted light of the room. "Your son and his wife serve me after all."

"Lord Taelin," Dargan bowed his head in reverence to his god. "We are sorry for not recognizing you. We are honored to have you here."

"Honored to have me here," Taelin stroked his beard. His voice remained soft. In a way, the quiet of his tone was more unnerving to the First Lord than if the god had shouted. "You have a funny way of showing it, Dargan."

The First Lord walked over to the table and refilled his goblet. He sat in the chair that he had set at the table for his son and took a sip of his spiced wine.

"What do you mean?" he asked after he set his goblet down.

"Your son has been bonded to a Blademaster with my blessing," the god shrugged. "And you publicly denounced their marriage. That does not show much in the way of honor to me."

"We were surprised," Dargan shrugged as he picked up his goblet. "Our son has flaunted tradition before. We figured he was doing so again."

"He was not."

"But how can we accept this marriage to a woman not born of the nobility?" Dargan asked.

"Because it is required," the god's voice had turned firm.

Dargan read the tone in Taelin's voice, but could not help but to keep arguing his point.

"Colwyn is the heir to the title of First Lord of Arvendale," Dargan countered. "His duty is here."

"And he will fulfill that duty when the time is right," Taelin nodded. He poured himself a glass of the spiced wine and took a sip. "An excellent vintage."

"And how can he when he is off adventuring with that commoner?" Dargan thundered.

"You would be surprised to know that they have already discussed this very matter." Taelin took another sip of the mulled wine and put his goblet down. "Colwyn takes his duties as your heir as seriously as he takes his duties to his Blademaster."

"He has not shown as much to me."

"Only as you have not been paying attention, Lord Dargan," the god's voice was soft once more. "He has always known that the time will come when he will take your place. As with all children, though, there is a part of him that believes the time will never come."

"But she is a commoner," Dargan grumbled. "How could he marry a commoner?"

"How could he not marry Alana?" Taelin raised an eyebrow. "Do you know that Colwyn was the only one who could have passed the Test of the Blades?"

"They truly love each other then?"

"It is, indeed, true love," Taelin said quietly. "It is one of the truest loves I have ever seen. You should be happy for him. Not too many people are lucky enough to find that."

"We suppose you are right." Dargan drained his goblet. "We were lucky enough that our marriage to Serena ended up being one that blossomed into love. It is good that our son has love at the beginning of his. But we still cannot condone a marriage to a commoner."

"Do you not think that perhaps I may have thought of that?" Taelin raised an eyebrow. "Alana Steeldrake was taken from her home at a very young age and raised as a commoner, but she is as noble of birth as your son is."

"Then who are her parents?" Dargan demanded. "I must know."

"That, I will not tell you. In time, she will discover the nature of her birth, but she must learn that on her own. Until the time that she discovers who here parents were, no one can know. This is a journey she will have to take on her own."

"So then what proof do we have that she is a noble?" Dargan demanded.

"My word," Taelin said in almost a whisper. "I am the Lightbringer. I do not lie. My word shall have to be good enough for you."

"Will it be good enough for the other nobles, though?" Dargan demanded.

"I believe your son is carrying a letter from the King of the Southern Dales blessing his marriage," Taelin shrugged. "If nothing else is, that should be good enough for the other nobles."

"We see," Dargan nodded. He refilled his goblet and took a sip of wine. "You have given us a great deal to think about."

"Here is one more thing to think about," Taelin said. He drained his mug. "When your son comes to talk to you, listen to him. You may not like what he says, but talk to him. Listen to him. Express your displeasure, if you must. But do not deny him what he asks. Know that he is only doing what I have asked him to do."

"We do not understand," Dargan frowned.

"You will," the god smiled. He stood up and stretched. "And now, I am afraid, I must go. There are things that I must do. As much as I would like to see your son again, he does not need my guidance at the moment. He is doing exactly as he must. Know this. I am very proud of him."

"Although we have not told him as much, we are proud of him too," the First Lord said softly. "Perhaps it is something that we need to say."

"Perhaps it is," Taelin smiled at the First Lord. He strode to the center of the room. "Now, I must leave you. Your son will be here soon. Remember my words. Do not interfere with what Colwyn must do."

With those last words, Taelin disappeared in a flash of light. The First Lord of Arvendale was left alone with his thoughts.

Colwyn had gotten up early so that he had time to go see Alana before he was to meet his father for breakfast. It had been the longest they had been apart since his almost betrayal in the Elven Woods.

And neither of them had liked it.

He had confirmed with Victor the night before that she and the rest of their companions were being well taken care of. That was not something that Colwyn was particularly worried about. He knew that Victor would make sure the guards assigned to the companions' quarters would see to their every need.

That did not mitigate how much he missed Alana, however.

And so, he took the opportunity to go see her briefly before he had to face his father.

He knew that his father was not going to be happy that Colwyn was going to defy him yet again, but there was nothing that could be done about it. Even if he wanted to, he could not end his marriage to Alana.

Nor could he force Bella to stop seeing Cayden Antioch. Now that Colwyn knew that Bella was, indeed, a Blademaster, there was little he could do. Bella had to be with her true love.

For the young man's sake, he hoped that Cayden truly was.

He liked the young palace guard. He had seen a spark of keen intellect in Cayden's eyes when he spoke to him. Colwyn knew that Cayden had to be intelligent in order for Bella to fall for him. Like he was, Bella was attracted to intelligence.

The young guard would make a good Protector for Bella if he passed the Test of the Blades. Colwyn knew that he could not interfere with the Test of the Blades or he would give the young man some pointers.

Still, there was one thing he could do for Cayden. He could lend the young man his trap finder stone. Since the Queen of the Forestwalker Elves had given it to him right before his own Test, he did not think it would really count as interference if he passed the stone onto another taking the Test.

Maybe it was skirting the rules, but he did not care. Nor did he think Alana would either.

As he neared the door to the quarters where she was staying, he saw two guards posted outside the door. He did not recognize the guards, and he suspected that they were some of his father's personal guards.

"We can't let you in, Lord Colwyn," one of the guards said as he approached. "Your father has expressly commanded that you not be alone with her."

"I'm not asking to be alone with her," he replied. "One or both of you may come inside to ensure that we do not break my father's commands. I need to speak with her for a few moments, however."

"I suppose if we are in there, you are not alone with her," the other guard nodded. "That would fulfill Lord Dargan's command."

Colwyn pushed the door open, leaving the door open behind him so the two guards could follow him inside.

He smiled when he saw her jump up from where she was sitting when she saw him enter. He gave a slight head tilt to make sure she noticed the guards coming in behind him. She nodded once in understanding.

"Hello, Col," she smiled at him.

"I wanted to see how my father's guards have treated you," he returned the smile. "I was on my way to have breakfast with him. But I wanted to see you first."

"I am glad you did," she said. She sat down at the table and waved for him to take the other seat. "How did it go with your sister?"

"It is as we thought," he sighed, taking the offered seat. He kept his answer cryptic as he did not want the guards to know what they were talking about. "There is no convincing her to not see the guard. My father will just have to understand when I tell him."

"I doubt he will be very understanding," Alana frowned deeply. "He does not seem the understanding type."

"No, he is not, at that," Colwyn barked out a slight laugh. "But it is what it is. All the wishing he could do will neither change what I am nor what my sister is."

"I understand," she nodded. "When do we leave?"

"I wish to leave after I have breakfast with my father, but I suspect it will be later in the day before we can leave," Colwyn said. "Get the others ready, though. We will leave today for certain. We must get to Barandale and then to the Temple of the Blades before the snow starts in earnest."

"At least the winter gives us time to prepare," the Blademaster said. "Thrall cannot send his army to the Southern Dales in the snow."

"We will have time to plan, but I am afraid we will not have that much time," Colwyn sighed. "The army of darkness will press this war just as soon as they can."

"Which is why we need to find this Blademaster in Barandale before the snows hit," Alana nodded. "The sooner we can get some help, the better."

"I agree," Colwyn smiled. "Has the halfling behaved?"

"You scared her mightily yesterday," Alana laughed. "She was almost too scared to eat last night. She managed, though. I daresay this is the first time she's been anywhere that nothing has fallen into any of her pouches."

"Good. My father is far less forgiving than I am," Colwyn's soft voice was tinged with merriment. "I told her she needed to behave herself. I am glad that, for once, she listened."

"She always listens, Col. She just doesn't always follow what we say."

"I know," Colwyn sighed deeply. He looked over at the guards who looked to be getting impatient for the young noble to get on his way. "I have to go, Alana. Get everyone ready. As I said. We will be leaving sometime today."

"We'll be ready when you are," Alana smiled at him.

As hard as it was not to lean over and kiss his wife, he resisted the urge. He knew she would understand why he did not do so. He also knew that she would know that it did not mean that he did not love her any less.

Instead of kissing her, he stood and smiled down at her. It was all he could give her at that moment in time. He hoped it would be enough for her until they could get away from the palace. When she returned the smile, he turned and left the room.

He was not happy that he could not tell her how he felt, but he knew that he did not have to say the words for her to know.

Dargan Starseeker was back at the window looking down at the palace guards that were sparring. From where he was, he could not tell if one of the guards was the one that his daughter had fallen in love with, nor did he care. All he could do was to hope that Colwyn had been able to bring Bella to heed his wishes and go through with the arranged marriage.

One of his children had to respect tradition, after all.

He was hopeful, but he somehow did not think that Colwyn would tell him that he had talked sense into Bella. There was something in what Taelin had said to him that bothered him.

When your son comes to talk to you, listen to him. You may not like what he says, but talk to him. Listen to him. Express your displeasure, if you must. But do not deny him what he asks. Know that he is only doing what I have asked him to do.

He sighed as he took a sip of his spiced wine. *No,* he thought. *Colwyn is going to tell us that he could not talk Bella out of marrying this palace guard. Somehow, we are still going to have to deal with this.*

He turned back towards the door when he heard a soft knocking. It was about the time that Colwyn should be arriving for breakfast, so he expected that it would be his son that would be entering. If it had been someone that was not allowed in the area of the First Lord's quarters, whoever it was would never have gotten close enough to knock on the door.

"Come in," the First Lord called softly.

Colwyn entered the First Lord's quarters and walked over to his father. The two men embraced. Dargan smiled when he realized he had caught his son off guard. No doubt the younger Starseeker was expecting a much colder welcome.

"Colwyn, we may have taken issue with some of your life choices, but you are still our son and we still love you," Dargan said into the younger man's ear.

"I am sorry for not coming home before now, Father," Colwyn said as he pulled away from the embrace. "I admit that I was afraid of this very conversation. But things have changed. I am no longer the young and idealistic noble that left Arvendale years ago running from his duty."

"Yes, you have embraced duty," Dargan nodded. He waved over to the table. "Come and sit, our son. Breakfast will be here shortly. We would like to hear all that has happened since you left our roof. And we would know how you came to be the Protector to a Blademaster."

"It is a long story, Father," Colwyn sighed. "I don't have time to tell the whole story, but there is a great deal of it that you need to know. Some of what has happened will affect the people of Arvendale, so you must prepare."

"We see," Dargan nodded.

Dargan refilled his goblet with spiced wine and offered some to Colwyn. The younger Starseeker declined, instead opting for kava juice. The choice was not lost on Dargan who realized that his son was taking his duties seriously.

It also told Dargan that Colwyn was not just here as his son, but also as the Protector to the Blademaster.

It was an important distinction to note.

Another knock on the door indicated that breakfast had arrived. Colwyn went to the door to let the servants in. Three servants brought trays of food over to the table where Colwyn and Dargan had been sitting. The servants worked quickly, putting the food on the table. Dargan waited until they had finished and had left before indicating that Colwyn should start telling his story.

As they ate, Colwyn told the First Lord about how he left the Elven Woods after completing his training as a ranger. Dargan felt there was a great deal to that story that Colwyn was not telling, but he did not press for details.

If he needed to know the details later, he could always ask.

Colwyn went on to tell of his meeting Alana in Ravendale and how he had stood by her side against the brutes that would have despoiled her honor. Although he did not show it, Dargan beamed with pride at the fact that his son had chosen to protect the woman. It was exactly what he would have wanted his son to do in that situation.

His son went on to tell Dargan about heading to Tornith to learn the fate of the priestess of Taelin who had been sacrified to Thraal. He told of how they had gone to Valendale and discovered the city empty and then spoke of the Temple of the Blades. He glossed over the Test of the Blades, but Dargan knew that it had been far more dangerous than Colwyn was telling him.

After killing the High Priest of Thraal in Tornith, Colwyn explained, the companions took some time to recover from that difficult adventure before setting off to discover what had happened to the people of Valendale. He told of how they had gone to Willowdale to rescue the citizens. That Colwyn had led the citizens of Valendale against the Zeraphim filled Dargan with pride for it meant that the young man had what it took to be a leader.

"And then you summoned me to Arvendale," Colwyn concluded the story. "And so here we are."

Dargan nodded thoughtfully as he chewed on a piece of bacon. The First Lord set his utensils down next to his plate and leaned back in his chair. He studied his son carefully, realizing for the first time since he and his companions had arrived in Arvendale that Colwyn really had changed.

Dargan decided he liked what he saw.

"It has not been easy for you, Colwyn," Dargan declared in a soft voice.

"No, Father, it has not," Colwyn said, a ghost of a smile passing across his face. "But I would not choose to have done anything differently."

"Perhaps it is well that things have happened as they have," the First Lord mused. "We think that these experiences may yet make you a better First Lord when your time comes."

"May that day be many years from now," Colwyn raised his glass in a toast.

"You have grown into a remarkable man, our son," Dargan smiled. "We are proud of the man you have become."

"It has not been an easy road to walk, Father," Colwyn said in a soft voice. He took a sip of his juice. "And there is a great deal of trouble to come for us."

Dargan leaned forward and gazed intently at his son. He knew that he was about to get to the heart of the matter. He was not sure he was going to like the answers to the questions he was about to ask.

"You said that some of what you had to tell us would affect the people of Arvendale," Dargan prompted. "We take it that is the trouble you speak of?"

"You need to read this, Father." Colwyn reached into his tunic and pulled a folded sheet of parchment from a pocket. He slid the parchment across the table. "This is a prophecy that Alana and I found while we were rescuing the people of Valendale."

Dargan picked up the parchment and unfolded it carefully. As he read over the words, he felt his heart hammer, for he knew that this was, indeed, the trouble of which Colwyn was speaking.

"The prophecy of the Great War of Souls

After three hundred years of peace in the world comes the Age of Darkness. The Dark God will return to begin his conquest of the world once more.

In the early days of the Age of Darkness, after the Blademasters have returned to the world of Calthea, the army of the dead shall arise in service to the Dark God. The dead shall rise and wage war across the face of Calthea.

When the twice dead city falls empty for a third time, the storm clouds will gather and the sabres will rattle in their scabbards. The blight of war shall be upon the land and only the one born of the light can lead the charge against the darkness.

The army of the light must uncork the magic of the bean sidhe to turn back the darkness. The one born of the light must lead the legacy of the Blademasters onto the field of battle.

When the soul of the captured bean sidhe wails, the stones of the stronghold of the light will shatter and crumble upon one another. The spirits of the chosen of Taelin will once more take the field of battle in the war against the darkness.

The fire of the sun and the moon will dim and fade to darkness. The one born of the light must walk out from the shadow of the fire of the sun and the moon and lead the chosen of Taelin.

The Twenty Third Law of the Blades will be violated for some of the chosen of Taelin.

If the one born of the light does not lead the charge against the army of the dead, the world will fall into a darkness that will be without end. Only the power of the First Law of the Blades can guide the hand of the one born of the light.

In this battle as in all others the one born of the light will fight, there will be no guarantees. Only by following the wisdom of Taelin and by the luck of Laeyra will the one born of the light prevail.

Should the one born of the light be successful in leading the forces of the light, the world will live in relative peace for a time, but only for a time for the Dark God shall never give up his quest.

If the one born of the light wishes to undo the damage caused by the wailing soul of the captured bean sidhe, she must find the Light of Taelin and use its magic to once more build the stronghold of the light.

In the years after the end of the great war of souls, should the one born of the light in turning back the darkness for a time, she will extend the light three times. But with the third, she will take her place among the spirits of the chosen of Taelin.

So ends the words of the final prophecy of Bahala, the Dream Weaver. With the gifting of this prophecy, I turn the mantle of power of the Dream Weaver over to a new and much younger Dream Weaver. Heed these words, for all that is written here shall come to pass.

May these words one day find their way to the one born of the light. The one who protects her will be able to translate these words for her, although neither will know the meaning behind the words when they find them.

Written by my hand,
Bahala Maranal, the Dream Weaver
Thirty seven years past the Great Purge."

He set the paper down and placed his hands on the table. He steeled his face so that the concern he was feeling did not shine through.

He knew, looking at Colwyn's face, that he had not fooled the younger man.

"Willowdale is referred to as the twice dead city," Dargan said.

"Indeed," Colwyn nodded.

"When you rescued the people of Valendale, Willowdale fell empty for a third time," Dargan continued.

"That is correct," Colwyn confirmed.

"Then this prophecy has been invoked."

"I am afraid so," Colwyn sighed, nodding. "We could not leave the people of Valendale there, though, Father."

"No, you could not," Dargan nodded. "We would have expected nothing less than your doing your very best to rescue those people. We fear for our people, though. War is bad business."

"Yes, it is," Colwyn nodded. He took a sip from his kava juice and sighed. "And this one is going to be worse than normal. It is an army made up almost entirely of undead."

"These are bad tidings," Dargan frowned. "Will you and your Blademaster be ready to lead the fight when the time comes? Based on what we have read in this prophecy, she is to be the one to lead the army of the Southern Dales."

"We will be," Colwyn nodded. The younger Starseeker sighed as he slumped back in his chair. "Becoming ready, I am afraid, has become a part of why we are in Arvendale."

"We though you were here because we summoned you," Dargan frowned.

"That is what brought us to Arvendale," Colwyn nodded. "But in the end, that is not why we are here."

"You are not making any sense to us, Colwyn."

"Let me try to figure out a way to explain in a way that will not upset you further," Colwyn grunted.

"That would be appreciated."

Colwyn pulled a chain from around his neck and handed it to his father. The soft glow of the amber stone faded slightly as the stone left Colwyn's hands. Dargan frowned slightly at the gemstone. He did not understand the importance of what Colwyn was showing him.

"This gemstone was given to Alana and I by Lord Taelin himself," Colwyn began to explain. "He calls it the Bladestone. He gave it to us in order to find other Blademasters to help us in the war that is coming."

"We see," Dargan nodded. He handed Colwyn back the Bladestone. "And this is somehow related to why you are here?"

"While we do not understand the how or the why, the Bladestone glows brighter when it is in the presence of a Blademaster," Colwyn sighed deeply. "Last night, the Bladestone indicated that there was a Blademaster in Arvendale other than Alana."

Dargan looked at Colwyn, realization dawning on him. He knew who the Bladestone had indicated. There was only one person it could have been. The realization did not make him happy.

"Bella," Dargan said softly. "It could only be our daughter."

He hoped he was wrong, but he knew that he wasn't.

"Bella," Colwyn nodded in confirmation. "I have already explained to her what is coming. I've discussed the ramifications of her choice to accept her calling. And I've discussed the ramifications of the choice to go along with Bella to her palace guard."

"Then you were unable to break them apart," Dargan observed.

"In order to be the Protector to a Blademaster, one must be her true love," Colwyn said softly. "I understand that far better than anyone. No one but I could have been Alana's Protector, Father. And if he is, as I believe he is, the one for Bella, no one but Cayden Antioch could be Bella's Protector."

"You're taking Bella with you?" Dargan asked, resigned to the answer that he knew was coming.

"I am afraid I am, Father," Colwyn sighed. He stood and looked at his father. "Believe me when I say that I wish it could have been otherwise. I no more wish for Bella to be in danger than you do."

"We know, Colwyn," Dargan nodded. He stood and came around the table to stand in front of his son. "We also know that there is no way to convince Bella to change her mind once she has herself set on a course of action."

"She is her father's daughter in that regard," Colwyn smiled.

"Indeed she is," Dargan returned the smile. "You both go with our blessing. Where do you head after you leave Arvendale?"

"Barandale," Colwyn said with distaste. "We have been told that there is a Blademaster amongst the halflings of all people."

"You have a halfling as one of your companions," Dargan pointed out.

"She would not have been my first choice," Colwyn winced. "Alana saved her life once, and she has travelled with us ever since. She has saved all of our lives at least once though, so she is, perhaps, not the worst companion to have."

"Well then we are grateful she is one of your companions," Dargan chuckled. "Now, go. We are sure you have preparations to make for the next phase of your journey."

"Thank you, Father," Colwyn smiled. He quickly embraced his father and pulled away. "I will do my best to be safe."

"That is all we ask," Dargan said as he watched Colwyn go.

He turned back to the table and poured another glass of his spiced wine. He took a deep drink from the glass and sighed.

He had preparations of his own to start if the prophecy Colwyn had shown him was any indication of things to come.

Chapter XII
The Rendezvous

It was late afternoon by the time the companions were ready to leave Arvendale. They had spent much of the morning gathering supplies and getting Bella and Cayden ready to travel with the party.

Victor Tram had been a great help. The captain of the guard had been able to provide packs and bedrolls for the two newest members of Alana's companions. He had also been able to gather fresh supplies for all of the companions for the next part of their journey.

By the time that Victor had been able to get all of those provisions together, Alana and her companions had gathered all of their gear together and were waiting for Colwyn to bring Bella and Cayden out to join them. Alana had known that the new Blademaster and her Protector would be made fully ready for the journey that was to come. She trusted that Colwyn would get them ready. Knowing that he was the one preparing them for the journey left her less worried about whether or not they would be ready for what was to come over the next few weeks.

She was not sure what she should expect from Bella and Cayden. While Colwyn, having grown up with Bella, knew her well, Alana did not know either of them and thus had no idea what they were like. She had no idea if the new Blademaster or her Protector would fit in the way the rest of her companions had. It worried her despite Colwyn's reassurances that they would be fine.

A lot depended on the new Blademasters that they were searching for. She could only hope that Colwyn was right that they would do well. She hoped that he was not being blinded to any issues just because Bella was his sister.

As they waited for Colwyn to bring out Bella and Cayden, Alana sat off to the side, apart from the others. She had a great deal on her mind and needed to give some things some thought. She worried about the war that was coming. She worried about the people of the Southern Dales that they were supposed to be protecting by leading the forces of light in the war. And she worried about whether or not all of her companions would make it through the war alive. She feared that someone she loved would not make it all the way to the other side of the war alive. Worse, she feared that it would be Colwyn that did not make it.

She could not bear for there to be a life for her without Colwyn.

She could not imagine her life without any of her companions.

In a way, the people that had chosen to travel with her had all become her family. Even Martin, who was still very new to the party, relatively speaking, had become a part of her family. And while Bella was Colwyn's sister, she could not help but wonder how the woman would fit into that family. She trusted Colwyn implicitly, though. He was convinced that Bella was one of the Blademasters that they were meant to find, and she did not doubt that he was correct about that fact.

She wished that she had some kind of reassurance that the young woman knew how to handler herself with a sword. If she had that reassurance about Bella, she would not have worried.

She would leave it up to her husband and Bella's Protector to make sure that the young woman was ready.

Alana took the time while she was waiting for Colwyn to arrive with the newest Blademaster to go over what they would be doing next. She knew that the next phase of their journey would take them to Barandale. Alana knew little about the territory of Barandale. She knew it was where the halflings came from. Other than that, she had nothing to go by. At least they had a guide to Barandale. Meryn had grown up there, after all. But Alana had no way to know where to begin.

Alana had no idea what a halfling Blademaster would be like. The natural curiosity of the halflings would cause no end of trouble. Colwyn was right about that. She also wasn't sure how the High Priestess of the Blades would react to having a halfling as a Blademaster. It would mean that whoever it was would have free reign of the Temple of the Blades.

The thought amused Alana.

But it did not change the fact that Alana had no idea where to look for a halfling Blademaster in Barandale. They could not just wander the streets of the city waiting for the Bladestone to react to someone. That would take forever, and time was of the essence.

Meryn had once told her that there was a Council of Elders that ran the day to day decisions of the government in Barandale. While the First Lord reported to the King in Ravendale, it was the Council of Elders that ruled. She thought that maybe the Council of Elders might be able to help them in their search.

It was a plan, even if she wasn't sure just how good a plan it was. But at least she had a place to start.

She saw William coming slowly over to her. It was that that caused her thoughts to turn to the silver dragon. Silvestra had been gone for quite a bit of time. She hoped that the dragon woman had succeeded in her mission to help Taelin convince the dragons that they needed to help the Blademasters by sending some more nathair an aeir a chosnaíonns to help guard the Blademasters on their travels.

She took great comfort in having her own nathair an aeir a chosnaíonn around after all.

But even more, she wanted Silvestra back because she knew just how much William missed her. She knew all too well how he felt. She had been separated from Colwyn before, and it had been pure torture. Poor William did his best to hide how much he missed Silvestra. But Alana knew. She did her best not to let on just how much she realized how much her being gone hurt him.

She did not think she was doing a good job, though. She suspected that the young mage knew exactly how much she understood. He had not said anything to make her think that, but she still suspected it.

"Alana, when do you think that they will be out so that we can be on our way?" the mage asked her as he came up to her.

"I'd like to think that they'll be out any time now, William," she said. "I have grown tired of waiting to spend time with my husband."

"Something I understand all too well, Alana," William's quiet voice replied. "Silvestra has been goon too long." He turned away from her to look at the steps of the palace, hoping to catch a glimpse of Colwyn and the others that they were waiting for. He turned back when he felt Alana's hand on his arm.

"I understand, William," she smiled sadly at him. "It's not easy to wait for someone that you love. Remember when we were in Willowdale and Colwyn went off to consult the Legacy of the Blademasters? The entire time he was gone was pure torture. In more ways than one, really. So I do understand where you are coming from."

"I know you do," William returned her sad smile with one of his own. "Which is why I can talk to you about it. I just wish she would get back."

"I do too, William," she said. She gave him a quick side hug. "She'll be back soon."

Colwyn had changed his clothes from when he had had breakfast with his father. Gone was his noble finery. Instead, he was back in his comfortable travelling garb. He had kept the chain mail on under the travelling clothes. He knew that he could not be too careful when it came to protecting himself. If he died, there would be one less ring of protection around Alana. And he knew that with her abilities tied into the love that the two of them shared, were he to die she would be even less protected as her abilities would be gone as well.

He could not allow that.

And so, he had the armor on under his travelling clothes, whether he wanted to be wearing it or not.

After changing, he made sure that his pack was ready to go. He knew that time was of the essence and that they needed to leave right away so that they could get to Barandale and then on to the Temple of the Blades before the snows hit. Winter was fast approaching, and Colwyn was worried that they might get stuck somewhere with the snow keeping them from getting home for the winter.

But he was ready to leave, and he knew that Bella and Cayden were also ready. He had made sure that they had everything that they needed for the journey that was about to start for them. Victor had been all too happy to agree to procure supplies for the two of them. The packs were waiting outside with Alana. All that Bella and Cayden needed to do was to change into something comfortable to travel in. Colwyn had made suggestions to Bella as to what she should wear. Cayden already had an idea of what was appropriate for a prolonged journey. He may have been a palace guard, but he was still a soldier in the Arvendale army, and, as such, he had received training as to what to wear on an extended march.

Colwyn slung his pack over his shoulder and left his quarters. As he always did before leaving for the journeys that took him away from Arvendale, he locked the door to his quarters. While he was gone, he did not like it if the palace staff went into his quarters. Once he had tucked the key into a pouch, he picked up his bow, quiver and sword.

He had everything that he needed, so he shrugged and started off.

His first stop was to pick up his sister at her own quarters. Colwyn knew that she was nervous about what was to come. He understood that nervousness all too well. When he had been about to go through the Test of the Blades, he had felt that nervousness himself. He had tried his best to assure her that everything would be all right, but he knew that it was not reassurance that she needed.

She needed to get through the experience and get to the other side of it. Once she did, she would be fine.

While he did not yet know Cayden Antioch as well as he might have liked, Colwyn knew that the young palace guard would help his sister to get through the process of becoming a Blademaster. That was, after all, part of his job as Bella's Protector. And Colwyn had no doubt that the young man would pass the Test of the Blades. There was something about young Cayden Antioch that gave Colwyn confidence in his abilities. Something about his bearing told Colwyn that there was more to Cayden than first appeared.

It did not take long for Colwyn to get to his sister's quarters from his. The First Lord had kept his children's quarters fairly close to each other so that they could watch out for each other.

And so, he found himself knocking at Bella's door in no time.

When Bella opened the door, he was happy to see that she had changed into clothes that were more practical for a long journey on horseback. She had taken his advice as to what to wear, and he was happy for that. He knew that she would be much more comfortable in what she was wearing now than what she normally wore when she was in the palace. He also knew that she would be given armor when they got to the Temple of the Blades.

"I'm ready to go, Col," she smiled nervously at him.

"Scared?" he asked when he saw the look on her face.

"A little," she admitted. "This is all new to me. I'm excited but I'm also quite nervous. What if you're wrong about me?"

"I'm not wrong," he smiled at her. "Alana felt it too. You are a Blademaster. With all that entails, we had to be sure about it before we brought you to the Temple of the Blades. And we are both quite sure about it." He pulled her in close for a one armed hug. "Have I ever steered you wrong, little sister?"

"No, you haven't, Col," she laughed. "I just don't want this to be the first time. It is a big responsibility that you and your wife are asking me to take on. I am not sure I am ready for it."

"It is bigger than you realize, Bella," Colwyn said softly. "There is a great deal that I have not told you. And there is a great deal that I cannot yet tell you. Just know that you have been called because you are needed. And you will not be facing things alone. Alana and I will be with you. As will Cayden."

"Am I really going to get to be with Cayden?" she asked. "Will Father actually accept that? I know he has issues with your marriage to Alana. I cannot imagine that he is any happier about my ending up marrying Cayden."

"Oh, he isn't happy about it at all," Colwyn laughed a hearty laugh. "But the King of the Southern Dales has made it clear that he is to honor my marriage because I am married to a Blademaster. He knows that he must accept your marriage to Cayden for the same reason."

"Have you talked to him about it? He knows that I am leaving with you and Alana?" she asked, clearly afraid that her father would prevent her from leaving.

"He knows you are coming with me," he nodded, giving her a light squeeze. "Lord Dargan is not happy, but he will not stop you from going. I think he is hoping that you will choose not to take on the mantle of a Blademaster. He knows that it is going to be very dangerous for you. Our father would like for at least one of his children to stay safe. He knows that that is not really in the cards for this family, though."

"I guess not," Bella shrugged. She walked quietly for a few steps then added with a bright smile, "At least I get to marry the man I love."

"There is certainly that," Colwyn smiled. He did not add that if Cayden were to fail the Test of the Blades, she would never be allowed to see him again. He did not want to add to her worry right then.

There would be time enough to learn all of the ramifications of her choice to accept her calling in time.

The two of them made their way down to the Great Hall of the palace so they could leave. They walked in silence, each of them lost in their own thoughts. Colwyn thought about the things that his sister had said. He thought long and hard one more time about whether or not he was right about her being a Blademaster. He felt the weight of the Bladestone around his neck, and he knew all too well that he was not mistaken. And if he was not mistaken about her being a Blademaster, then he knew that, despite any moments of self doubt that Bella was feeling, she would be able to fulfill her duties as a Blademaster when the time came.

When they got to the Great Hall, they were surprised to be greeted by their parents. Colwyn, especially, was surprised to see them. He had not expected to see his father again before they left. While he knew that Dargan had accepted the fact that both of his children had been pressed into the service of the Blademaster Corps, Colwyn knew that his father had not been happy about accepting such a thing. As such, he was expecting that their father would simply let them go without seeing them off.

Colwyn was glad that he had been wrong about that.

"Father," he bowed slightly to the First Lord. "I did not expect to see you again before I left. I am glad you are seeing us off, though."

"We could not let our children leave without saying goodbye," Dargan said in a subdued voice. "We may not agree with our children being a part of the Blademaster Corps, but we are proud of both of our children for following the calling of their hearts."

"I promise that I will try to get home more often, Father," Colwyn said softly. "It is, as you have said, important to make sure that the people of Arvendale remember that I am still alive."

"And we look forward to those visits, our son," Dargan smiled broadly at Colwyn. "Know that we are proud of you. Despite all of our sparring with you in the past, we always have been proud of you. Take good care of your Blademaster. If what you have told us about what is to come is true, then much rides on her shoulders. And yours. Be safe, our son."

"I will do my best, Father," Colwyn returned the smile. "I will not leave you without an heir. I have never once forgotten my duty to the people of Arvendale."

"See that you do not, our son," Dargan clapped him on the shoulder before moving over to stand in front of Bella. "Our daughter, Bella. While we wish that you would not go off on your journey, we understand the calling that you have chosen to accept."

"Thank you, Father," Bella bowed slightly at the waist. "While I admit that I am nervous about becoming a Blademaster, I know that it is an important calling. I can only hope that I can bring honor and the dedication known to be in all members of the house of Starseeker to the position."

"You will do very well in your position, we are sure," Dargan smiled at his daughter. "While we are not happy that you are not to marry into the nobility, we nonetheless accept your impending marriage to Cayden Antioch, as we know, much as your brother's marriage is, that the marriage of a Blademaster and her Protector is a sacred bond that is blessed by our Lord Taelin.

"Thank you, Father," Bella's voice was soft, as if she was afraid that Dargan would change his mind if she said anything.

"However, we have a gift for you and for Cayden," Dargan continued. He held his hand out, and one of the pages behind him handed him a long sword in a scabbard. "This long sword is for you. It is one of our own. If you must become a Blademaster and live your life as a warrior woman, then the least that we can do is to make sure that you are armed with the highest quality blade."

"Thank you, Father," she bowed again. This time, she was in awe. The fact that he had given her a blade out of his personal armory drove home just how accepting he really was of her call as a Blademaster in a way that she had not yet come to believe. "I will remember this token of your love for me every time I have cause to use it."

"We have also provided a blade for your Cayden Antioch out of our personal armory. If he is to be your Protector, then we wish to make sure that he is also given the finest blade to use to protect you," the First Lord said quietly. "We gave it to Victor Tram to give to him when he gathered supplies for the two of you."

"Thank you again, Father," Bella said, a tear leaking from the corner of her eye. She leaned forward and gently hugged her father. She knew that she was the only one who could get away with giving Lord Dargan a hug in public. She rarely took advantage of that, but she needed the hug herself, and she felt that he did as well.

"We will miss you, daughter," he whispered into her ear. "Take care of your brother for me. You always had a better head on your shoulders than he did."

"I will miss you too, Father," Bella cried into his chest. "I will do my best to keep both Colwyn and myself safe. You have my word on that." She pulled away from him. "Thank you for being okay with this. Even if I know you really aren't."

"We are not okay with it," Dargain said with a shrug. "But it is what it is."

Colwyn nodded in understanding to his father and then turned to lead his sister outside to where Alana and the others were waiting.

As soon as he stepped out of the doors of the palace, Colwyn saw Alana. He saw her before he saw anyone else, just as he always did. In many ways, he only ever had eyes for her. And this day was no different. He strode purposefully over to her and took her in his arms. Out of the corner of his eyes, he saw Bella rush over to where Cayden was standing amongst the companions. It made Colwyn smile to see his sister with the man that she loved.

"Are we ready to go, Alana?" he asked the woman he loved.

"We were just waiting for you," she smiled at him. "Victor has supplies and horses for Bella and Cayden. We are ready to go whenever you are. The sooner we leave, the better the chance we have of getting to Barandale and back to the Temple of the Blades before winter sets in. You know as well as I do that, at this point in the year, winter can set in at any moment. At least it will give us time to make preparations for the army of darkness before they are able to move on the Southern Dales. We're going to need all the time we can get to get our new Blademasters ready to face the army that the Dream Weaver spoke of."

"Then let's go get mounted up and get on our way." He turned back to look at his father and waved him over. When his father made his way over to where Colwyn and Alana were standing, Colwyn bowed slightly to his father. "Father, it is time for us to be off. We have a long journey ahead of us and we would like to be done before the snows arrive and make such a journey impossible."

"Go with our blessing, Colwyn," Dargan nodded. He turned to face his daughter in law. "We apologize for the way we treated you, Lady Alana Steeldrake. We ask for your forgiveness, and we welcome you to the house of Starseeker. We swear our family to the Blademaster Corps as the Starseeker family did when the Blademasters were among us before."

"Of course, I forgive you, Lord Dargan," Alana said with a merry smile. "You are the father of the man I love. I could not love my husband as I do and not extend that love to his family. I will do all that I can to bring your son home safely when the time comes for him to succeed you as the First Lord of the Arvendale territory. May that day be many years from now."

"We thank you for that," Dargan returned the smile. "And we bid you and your companions a safe journey. You are all welcome beneath our roof at any time."

"Thank you, Lord Dargan," Alana inclined her head in respect.

"Okay, everyone," Colwyn said to all of their companions. "Let's mount up and get ready to head out."

Colwyn led the way over to where the horses were picketed and was started to boost himself up into his saddle when a shadow passed overhead. Colwyn looked up as the palace guard sprung into action, unsheathing swords and readying bows. They looked up as the shadow passed overhead a second time. When Colwyn saw what was causing the shadow, he waved to the archers to stand down. His father saw the motions he was making and add his own instructions to the men.

"Archers, hold," Dargan bellowed. When he saw the tension loose on the bowstrings, he nodded and turned back to Colwyn. "We expect that there is a good reason for your wanting the archers to stand down."

"She is a friend," Colwyn said softly. "Each Blademaster is assigned a nathair an aeir a chosnaíonn, a dragon that protects her. The silver dragon coming in for a landing now is Alana's nathair an aeir a chosnaíonn."

William looked up at that. He looked to where the silver dragon was gracefully circling the courtyard in preparation to land. The smile that broke across the young mage's face made Colwyn's heart sing with joy. The mage had been so sullen since Silverstra had gone to consult the Council of Dragons. It was good to see the mage smile again.

Everyone in the courtyard stared as the silver dragon continued to circle the courtyard, getting lower and lower with each circle until finally she gently touched down in the middle of the courtyard, kicking up a moderate amount of dust as she landed. As soon as her clawed feet touched the ground, she began to transform herself into her human form, using the dust she had stirred up to hide her form until she could slip her robes over her head.

When she had finished her transformation, she rushed over to where William was waiting for her. He held his arms open wide for her and she fell into his arms, kissing her passionately.

"And she is also William's wife," Colwyn added with a merry laugh.

Silvestra disentangled herself from her husband and walked over to Alana.

"My lady, I have returned," the dragon woman said. "The dragons will send dragons to serve as nathair an aeir a chosnaíonn to our new Blademasters."

"Thank you for securing the help of the Council of Dragons, Silvestra," Alana smiled at her nathair an aeir a chosnaíonn. "It is good to have you back. Can you fly all of us to Barandale now that there are two more added to our company?"

"I will need to take several rest periods along the way, but I can. And I can fly all of you back to the Elven Woods as well," Silvestra nodded. "I will have little energy remaining when we get there, so there will be little I can do to help if there is trouble, but the other dragons should be at the Temple of the Blades by the time we get there."

"Very well," Alana nodded. She turned to the First Lord. "Lord Dargan, we would ask to picket our horses in the royal stables until such time as we come to pick them up."

"Of course," the First Lord nodded. "We shall have them well cared for until your return, Lady Alana."

"Thank you," she bowed slightly to the First Lord. She turned to her companions. "Right, we're going by dragon instead of by horse. When Silvestra's ready, we will go."

Dargan Starseeker watched from the palace steps as the silver dragon launched herself into the sky with his son and daughter on her back. His wife stood by his side, watching as well. They were watching both children ride a dragon out of the city. It was not a new feeling to watch Colwyn leave, but it was the first time Bella had left Arvendale.

Neither Dargan nor Serena were happy to see their children go.

"Are they going to be all right, Dargan?" Serena asked her husband in a soft voice.

"We have done everything for them that we could, Serena," the First Lord said, his voice sounding old. "It is on them to take all that we have taught them as they go out in their duties."

"I worry about them," she said, tears leaking from the corners of her eyes.

"We worry about them, too," Dargan admitted. "But we are also proud of them."

"I am too," she smiled through the tears. "We made two very strong children."

"Indeed we did, Serena," Dargan returned her smile. "Come. We have much we need to do to prepare. Colwyn came with ill tidings of things to come. Arvendale must be ready when the spring thaw arrives."

Part III
Talog Swiftfoot

Chapter XIII
Dragon Flight to Barandale

F they had ridden the horses instead, the trip to Barandale could have taken two weeks. On the far west coast of the Southern Dales, it was as far away from Arvendale as was possible. Alana was relieved to have another option.

Although she had flown a great deal recently already, Silvestra was able to cut their travel time to Barandale to three days. It was yet another advantage to the Blademasters having nathair an aeir a chosnaíonn. She knew that Colwyn, who had first been concerned about having a dragon around, had long since come around to accepting the nathair an aeir a chosnaíonn.

The fact that Alana's current nathair an aeir a chosnaíonn was married to William Stonehands helped immensely.

Alana still mourned the loss of her first dragon, Cobalthaxillius. The great gold dragon had died as he had wished, in battle protecting her. He had finally received the redemption that he had long sought.

While she was happy that he found redemption, she had come to look at the ancient gold dragon as a friend.

She found that she missed him terribly. That she had a new nathair an aeir a chosnaíonn in Silvestra did not mitigate that feeling of loss. She had now lost two companions since becoming the Blademaster. She wondered how many more she would lose before she could lay down her blades.

It was the part of being the leader that she hated. She was responsible for all of her companions' lives, and she did not want to lose a single one of them.

Silvestra flew for four hours before setting down near a stream. They were far away from any settlement and there was no one in sight when they landed, so it was as good a place as any to take a break.

"I need to rest for an hour or so, Alana," the silver dragon rumbled. "Now would be a good time for you all to eat. We can travel a little further tonight. There is a small mountain range not too far away with some caverns that will serve as good shelter for the night."

"Thank you, Silvestra," Alana smiled at her friend.

Silvestra nodded and curled up to rest.

The companions had a quick and cold meal of dried meat, cheese and bread. They did not want to take the time to build a fire since they would only be stopping for an hour or so.

When the dragon rumbled that she was ready, they all climbed back onto her back and flew for several more hours until they got to the mountain range that Silvestra had mentioned. The silver dragon found an unoccupied cavern high on one of the mountains and landed just inside the mouth of the cavern.

"This will be as good a place as any to camp for the night," the dragon said. "We will fly most of the way tomorrow. Where we set up camp will be about a half of a day's walk from Barandale. I think it best if we walk into the city rather than land at the palace as I did in Arvendale."

"Probably wise," Alana nodded.

The companions quickly set up camp. Silvestra curled up right in the mouth of the cavern. A curled up dragon was effective protection for a party of adventurers, but Alana still wanted them to set a watch. It was better to be safe than sorry.

After the companions got settled for the night, Colwyn took the first watch. Halfway through his watch, Alana made her way over to where he was keeping watch not far inside the mouth of the cavern. She had been having trouble sleeping without him in the bedroll with her for a while.

It amazed her how someone could get used to sleeping in the same bed as another person.

As she walked up to him, she marveled once more that she was able to take this man for her husband. It amazed her every time she saw Colwyn how just the sight of him was enough to still set her heart aflutter. It had been that way since the first time she had seen him. She knew that it would be that way every time she saw them even after they enter into the Legacy of the Blademasters.

The smile he sent her way when he saw her coming up to him was enough to take her breath away.

She leaned up and kissed him when she got there. He smiled again and wrapped his arms around her. It was an embrace that always made her feel safe. In a world as crazy as theirs was, it was nice to have someone that made her feel safe.

"Long day," he said into her hair.

"Tomorrow will be too," she shrugged.

"You're sure about our destination?" Colwyn asked.

"You heard the Dream Weaver," she nuzzled her head against his chest. "There is a Blademaster in Barandale. If you have a better idea on where to find one than that, put words to it. Otherwise, we go searching in Barandale."

"But we are seriously going to make a halfling a Blademaster?" Colwyn broke the embrace to hold her at arm's length. He looked deep into her eyes. "Can we really trust a halfling Blademaster?"

"I trust Meryn," Alana pointed out. "If I can trust a sneak thief, I can trust a halfling Blademaster."

"If you say so," Colwyn said. He looked off into the distance, lost in thought.

Alana snuggled herself back against his chest, and started thinking about what they were going to be doing in Barandale.

Alana had known from the moment they had heard that there was a Blademaster in Barandale that Colwyn would have a problem with a halfling Blademaster. He had an innate distrust of the little people. It didn't help that they made such good thieves.

Still, Meryn had saved all of their lives at least once. She thought that maybe Colwyn would cut the halflings a little slack because of that.

Alana was excited about going to Barandale. She had never been to the home of the halflings. Meryn had spoken very little about her home over the years. Alana had been curious about where Meryn had grown up, but it was not in her nature to push.

But now they were going to Meryn's home, so Alana would have many of her questions about the halfling answered. Theoretically. Still, she hoped that Meryn was looking forward to going home. Alana was going to be depending on the halfling a lot while they were in Barandale.

She was sure Colwyn did not like that idea either.

"What are we going to do when we get to Barandale?" Colwyn asked. It was, once again, as if he were reading her mind.

She chuckled to herself at the thought that he could read her mind. He seemed to do it often enough that she wasn't sure whether he actually could or not. Maybe it was part of the bond between the Blademaster and her Protector.

It was something she would have to think about some more.

"Well, I think the best thing would be to talk to their Council of Elders," she purred into his chest. "I'm hoping that maybe they have an idea of where to start looking."

"We're going to have to depend on Meryn to get us in to see them, aren't we?" Colwyn spat out with distaste.

"Yes, we are going to have to depend on Meryn," she nodded. "At least we have someone to help us in Barandale."

"She never talks about home, Alana," Colwyn reminded her. "I rather get the feeling that she's not welcome with her family."

"Well that would be a problem," Alana frowned. "I guess we will just have to talk to her tomorrow and see if it's one we need to worry about."

"I guess."

The night passed quietly as Alana had expected it would. After all, who would attack the party with a large silver dragon sleeping in the mouth of the cave?

When morning came, Silvestra felt refreshed and told Alana that they would be able to go all the way to that night's camp without stopping. Alana had the companions eat a light breakfast rather than the normal breakfast they might have. It would not do for someone to yark while flying. It would be messy for a start.

They flew through the day, heading towards the place that Silvestra had in mind for a camp. While they were flying, Alana thought some more about the thought of a halfling Blademaster.

While she did not see it as a problem, she knew that many in the Southern Dales would.

She suspected that it would come down to her to figure out the best way to deploy a Blademaster that so few would trust. But if this war that was coming was really going to be a war for the entire Southern Dales, then perhaps if the halfling Blademaster were to lead the fight on the western side of the continent, that would solve that.

As the day wore on, they could see Barandale starting to come into view in the far distance. Barandale was smaller than some of the other cities in the Southern Dales, but it was still a good sized city.

Sometime in late afternoon, Silvestra banked off to the right. Alana looked where she was heading and saw several large hills. Silvestra angled for a valley between two of the hills.

The Blademaster trusted her dragon to know where best to rest for the night.

When the dragon landed, the companions slid off her back. They all did their part in getting the camp ready for the night. As they had done many nights together.

With no horses to care for, Colwyn went straight to getting the fire pit set up. Alana set up their bedrolls and joined him at the fire pit so that she could get a stew started.

"We should have biscuits with the stew," Alana decided.

"I can make some biscuits," Colwyn nodded.

The two of them worked on dinner in silence, from time to time watching to make sure the rest of the camp was set up.

When dinner was ready, they called the companions over to the fire and dished out bowls of stew to each of them. A warm freshly baked biscuit went on top of each bowl. The companions tore into their stew. They were all hungry from the long flight. None of them had dared to eat while on Silvestra's back. And Silvestra, who was now in her human form, had expended the most energy as she had been the one doing the flying.

"We should get to Barandale just after midday tomorrow," Silvestra said. "Even if we sleep in a little, which I would like."

"We'll sleep in a little, but only a little," Alana laughed.

"What is our plan when we get there, Alana?" William asked.

"Meryn is going to get us to see the Council of Elders," Alana said, nibbling on a biscuit. "From there we will see what happens. Unless that will be a problem, Meryn?"

"No," Meryn squeaked. "No, that won't be a problem." She scooted next to Martin and tried to make herself smaller.

"Good," Alana nodded. "Normal watches tonight. We'll get up when the sun does. Hopefully we can find the Blademaster in Barandale and be on our way to the Temple of the Blades within a couple days."

The companions nodded and finished their meals in silence. Colwyn looked at Alana as if to say "Did you see how she tried to shrink away when you asked if there would be trouble? There's going to be trouble."

She just shrugged at him. She knew there would likely be some trouble. She expected it. But it did not change that this was where they had to go.

She would worry about it tomorrow.

The Age of Darkness

Chapter XIV
The Council of Elders

s Silvestra had predicted, the companions arrived at Barandale just after midday. It had been a fairly easy walk from their camp to the city gates, and Alana had set a quick pace. No one had complained about how fast they were going. Everyone wanted to be done with the journey as quickly as possible.

Unlike in Arvendale, the companions were not challenged at the gates. Alana supposed that not many people were actually anxious to enter the city gates. Most people could not stand to be around halflings.

A city full of them would be enough to drive most people insane.

There was little that Alana could do about that. They had been told where to find a Blademaster. She was in Barandale. A halfling. It made little sense, but there was a reason they had been directed to Barandale to find another Blademaster. Whether or not finding the Blademaster was the main reason they were going to Barandale remained to be seen.

Alana suspected that, just as the side trip to Arvendale, there was more than met the eye to this trip.

Alana knew, ostensibly, that the main reason for the trip to Barandale was to bring a new Blademaster into the fold. But she did not believe for a second that was the only reason they were returning to Meryn's home city. There was something more to it. She suspected that it had to do with Meryn's family.

Or with Meryn herself.

There was the way that Meryn had shrunk against Martin at the mention of the Council of Elders. That was Alana's first hint that there was more to this journey than first expected. What more, remained the question.

Alana supposed they would find out soon enough.

There was little to be done but to go forward with their plans to speak with the Council of Elders. Alana could think of no other way to start the search for one halfling in a city of them other than to seek the assistance of the Council of Elders. At the very least, the Council would be able to give them some kind of direction to go in.

Alana hoped so at least.

The companions walked though the streets of the city. It was odd to see a city built to such smaller proportions, but as it was a city full of halflings, there was no need for the buildings to be as big as they were in other cities. It made sense, but, by the same token, Alana knew that the rest of the companions, herself included, would not be so comfortable in such cramped quarters.

As they walked through the city, Alana noted that the layout was similar to any of the other Dales she had been in, despite being on a much smaller scale. It made sense. All of the Dales had been designed by the same people, so it only made sense that they would be similar in design.

But it was a comfort to know that they would not get lost moving around Barandale.

It meant that there destination lay more or less in the center of the city. Knowing where they were heading helped. Alana just wished she knew what to expect when they got there.

At least she had a guide.

Even though she was guiding them through the city, Meryn was looking more and more uncomfortable the longer she was in the city. Alana wondered about that. Not for the first time, and probably not for the last time, Alana wondered just what had happened when Meryn had left Barandale years before to make her not want to come home. Alana wondered if whatever it was that had happened would cause a problem for the companions on their search for the Blademaster.

She would have to keep an eye on things.

As they moved through the city, Alana noticed that, while Barandale was indeed laid out in a similar fashion to the other Dales she'd been to, there were some major differences. The residential areas seemed to be blocked off into tight sections. Some of those sections were walled off. It was an odd way of doing things, but Alana had heard that the halflings were a clan oriented people. And so, perhaps the sections were set aside for clans. It was the only thing that she could think of.

But it made some sense. And the bigger sections that had walls around them would be for the bigger clans, if that was the case. It was an interesting way of doing things, and she had not seen it put into practice anywhere else.

Clearly she was going to have to learn more about the way halflings lived if she and her companions were going to have more dealings with them. And if there was a Blademaster coming out of Barandale, it was clear that Alana would, indeed, be having more dealings with the halflings.

It was still strange to Alana that they had gone to the city of the halflings to find a Blademaster. She wasn't sure there was a more odd or controversial choice for a Blademaster than a halfling. And the question begged to be asked. Just how many different types of blades could a halfling Blademaster be a master of anyway? There were likely a great many that a halfling could not hope to even lift.

Alana fought a smile as she thought about what Solara would say when they walked into the Temple of the Blades with a halfling Blademaster. Since such a thing had never been done before, she was sure it would cause a commotion.

Let it, she thought. *It will be good to shake things up a little.*

She knew that some of the members of the Legacy of the Blademasters would be perfectly OK with the thought of a halfling joining the ranks of the Blademasters. She suspected that Raven, for instance, would be wholly amused by it.

But Solara would not be amused. The High Priestess of the Blades would rail against such a thing.

It would be up to Alana to convince Solara that it needed to happen.

That was a battle for another day though. And one that would not happen until Alana could find the Blademaster that was living in Barandale. She hoped that the Council of Elders would be able to point her in a direction to look rather than going through the whole city halfling by halfling.

It took some time to work their way through the city. Even though the city was populated solely by halflings, it turned out to be one of the larger Dales. They passed several clan compounds, including one large compound with high walls near the center of the Dale. Alana watched Meryn closely for some kind of indication as to which compound belonged to her clan, but the halfling gave no such indication.

It was baffling to Alana.

It was something she would have to figure out another time, though. They had arrived at the hall where the Council of Elders met. The Hall of Elders was a small building, smaller than some of the houses they had passed. This surprised Alana somewhat, as she was used to the government center of a Dale being a large sprawling building.

There were guards at the door to the building and they stopped the party when they got there.

"I am Meryn Swiftfoot, granddaughter of Maren Swiftfoot of the Council of Elders," Meryn said to the guards. "I have brought the Blademaster, Alana Steeldrake, to Barandale to speak with the Council of Elders."

"It has been some time since you were in Barandale, Meryn Swiftfoot," one of the guards said. "I will bring your words to the Council of Elders. If they choose to speak to your Blademaster friend, they will summon for you."

"Fair enough," Meryn nodded. "We will wait. I have no doubt that my grandmother will want to speak to Blademaster Alana."

"That's as may be," the guard shrugged. "But protocol demands that even the granddaughter of one of the Council members must wait until summoned."

Meryn nodded again and turned to the companions to make sure they'd heard the instructions to wait. Alana shrugged at her. She'd expected that they would have to wait, so this was no surprise to her.

Alana watched as the guard disappeared into the building. She figured that they were in for quite a wait, so she was surprised when the guard came out mere minutes later.

"The Council says they have been expecting your visit, Blademaster," the guard said. "They will see you immediately."

Alana looked at Colwyn. There was something about the way he'd said that that put Alana on her guard. How could they have known that Alana would be coming? She didn't even know until the Dream Weaver had visited Ravendale.

This trip was intriguing Alana more and more each day.

Alana nodded to the guard and led the way into the building. Although Meryn was the one who lived in Barandale, in this Alana had to be the one to go first. It was Alana's journey that had led them to Barandale in the first place.

Once inside the building, there was no question where they had to go. There was only one direction to go, and it led to a room that must have taken up most of the building.

A long table ran along the back wall of the room, and nine elder halflings sat at the table. It was an imposing sight as any government display Alana had seen. But with each of the halflings being older and slightly smaller than the normal halfling size, there was a part of Alana that could not take the scene seriously.

She was good at hiding the fact that she found the display amusing though.

"Blademaster Alana Steeldrake," the halfling at the center of the table said. "I am Maren Swiftfoot, the eldest of the Elders. Your coming has been expected."

"If I may ask, Lady Maren, how did you know we were coming to Barandale?" Alana asked. "I did not even know we would be coming here until very recently."

"The patron deity of the halflings is our Lady Laeyra," Maren explained. "She came to the Council of Elders two weeks past and informed us that you would be coming to visit. She bade us give you every assistance."

"I see," Alana smiled. It was a warm smile. For all that she sometimes hated her destiny, such as when she felt responsible for starting the War of Souls, she loved being in service to both Taelin and Laeyra. "Lady Laeyra is sacred to me as well."

"We know the Blademasters serve both Lord Taelin and Lady Laeyra," Maren nodded. "It is said that a Blademaster is a child of both."

"So it is said," Alana nodded. "Lady Maren, I have come to Barandale on urgent business. I have been given reason to believe that somewhere in the walls of your city there is a Blademaster."

"Apart from you, you mean?" Maren cocked her head slightly to the right as she looked at Alana.

"We have been sent to Barandale to find this Blademaster," Alana nodded. She sighed. "But other than my companion, Meryn, none of us have been to Barandale and we would not even begin to know where to look. And so I decided we should seek the help of the Council of Elders in the hopes that you might be able to help us."

"I will assist you," Maren nodded. "You will stay in the stronghold of the Swiftfoot Clan as guest friends. Except, of course, for you, Meryn. You need not accept guest rights from me as you belong to the Swiftfoot Clan. Your home is as you left it, you will find."

"Thank you, Grandmother," Meryn whispered.

"Yes," Maren nodded. "I suspect we will talk later."

"Thank you for your hospitality, Lady Maren," Alana bowed slightly. "Even more so, thank you for your help."

"You are welcome, child of the light," Maren smiled. "Come, now. We shall go to the stronghold and talk. The Council of Elders has no more business for today."

The Age of Darkness

Chapter XV
The Swiftfoot Clan

he Swiftfoots were one of the wealthiest families in Barandale. As a result, they lived in a large compound not far from the Hall of Elders. The compound was easily the largest single expanse of buildings in Barandale. A wall twice Alana's height ran around the entire perimeter of the compound.

It had more of a feeling of a palace than a series of buildings for one family.

They had passed the compound on the way to the Hall of Elders. Alana had given little thought to who lived there focused as she was on following Meryn to the Hall of Elders. The halfling had not given the compound so much as a passing look, so Alana dismissed the compound as not currently important.

Of course, now that she knew what the compound was, she was more curious than ever about Meryn's relationship with her family. Clearly there were issues.

Maybe that was why they had come to Barandale.

The party was lead towards the compound by Maren Swiftfoot who had insisted that the companions stay at the compound overnight. The sight of the stooped old halfling shuffling along in front of them might have been amusing had it been anyone but the matriarch of the family of one of her companions. As it was, Alana had a hard time not just picking up the old woman and carrying her.

Alana knew that such an action would be looked upon poorly.

When they got to the gates of the compound, the guards there waved them through. None of them was about to tell the matriarch that she could not enter. And anyone that was with the matriarch was clearly meant to be there as well.

Once they entered the gates, Alana could see just how massive the compound actually was. Along each of the walls were individual buildings. Alana took each of the buildings to be the residence for individual family units of the clan. Alana wondered which of the buildings was Meryn's.

In the center of the compound, surrounded by all of the individual buildings, was an immense courtyard. There was easily enough room for Silvestra to take off directly from the courtyard. Trees lined the courtyard. Near the far end, Alana could make out a small temple to Laeyra.

When they entered the compound, every Swiftfoot was standing just outside their domiciles. The visitors had caused quite a stir by immediately demanding to speak to the Council of Elders when they arrived in Barandale, and everyone wanted to get a good look at them. That was no surprise to Alana, for curiosity was one of the most integral traits of a halfling.

Alana noted that a lot of attention was paid to the fact that Meryn was one of the companions. She knew that the halfling had not been home in some time. She had known Meryn for almost two years and in that time, Meryn had never visited Barandale.

Alana did not know how long it had been before that.

The old halfling shuffled forward and looked around at all of the assembled members of her clan.

"We welcome these visitors to the stronghold of the Swiftfoot Clan," Maren intoned. "Know now that I have extended guest rights to these travelers. Should any harm fall to them, those who perpetrated that harm shall no longer be able to claim rights to the name Swiftfoot. It is so ordered."

Alana relaxed slightly. Offering guest rights was no small thing in the Southern Dales. And the punishment that Maren had named was the easiest punishment. If someone were to harm one of her companions too much, they would likely be executed.

So she relaxed, but not all the way. It would be unwise to completely let down her guard. And she knew that Colwyn would not fully let down his guard either.

Their vigilance is what had kept each other alive for so long.

"Thank you, Lady Maren," Alana said softly. "We thank you for the offer of guest rights and we accept your hospitality."

"Good," Maren nodded. "Now, let us go and discuss the matter of your visit in private."

Maren's house was small, considering she was the matriarch of the clan. Alana was surprised that the matriarch of the clan had one of the smallest houses in the compound. Maren was surprising her in many ways.

Then again, Alana had never given much thought to what the matriarch to a clan of halflings would be like.

Alana had sent the others to where they would be staying for the night. She figured that Alana and Colwyn were the only ones needed for this conversation. She would not even think of trying to send Colwyn with the others.

He'd never let her.

Maren led the way into the small living area and sat down on a small stuffed chair. Alana and Colwyn looked around the living area but there were no chairs that would be big enough for either of them.

Alana shrugged and sat on the floor, crossing her legs. Colwyn, after looking around again, followed suit.

"May I provide you with some nourishment, Blademaster Alana?" Maren asked. "I know it has been a long journey for you."

"Thank you, Lady Maren, but we are fine for now," Alana said.

"Very well," Maren nodded. "Now. Why don't you tell me why it is that you think there is a Blademaster in Barandale?"

"To be honest, we were sent," Colwyn said.

"Sent? By whom?"

"Are you familiar with the Dream Weaver?" Alana asked.

"Of course," Maren nodded. "Ah, he had a weaving that there was a Blademaster in Barandale."

"So he told us," Alana confirmed. "Of course, we had a difficult time imagining a halfling Blademaster when he told us we were to come here."

"There has never been one before," Maren said. "We have never begrudged anyone that."

"Lady Maren, as I am sure you know, many of the people of the Southern Dales have a hard time trusting halflings," Colwyn said. "I will admit that I have had trouble with that in the past myself."

"You are of the nobility, Lord Colwyn," Maren smiled. "That is to be expected. But yes, I would imagine a halfling Blademaster will be difficult for many in the Southern Dales to accept."

"We had trouble accepting it ourselves," Alana admitted. "But in the end, we trust the Dream Weaver. He sent us here. There must be a reason why a halfling Blademaster is needed."

"I think it is the war that is coming," Maren said. She smiled when she saw Alana react to the mention of the war. "Oh, yes. We have heard that war is coming to the Southern Dales. The First Lord has brought that information back to us from the King. But I think that this war may have something to do with why one of us is being called for the first time."

"I can't pretend that whoever becomes a Blademaster from Barandale will be safe, Lady Maren," Alana said in a soft voice. "As you have said. War is coming to the Southern Dales. We have heard tell that the army we will be facing is almost completely made up of the undead. Whoever goes with us may not return."

"In life as in battle, there are no guarantees," Maren shrugged. "I believe it even says that in your Law of the Blades."

"Indeed," Alana nodded. "In life as in battle, there are no guarantees. Victory and defeat teeter on the edge of a thin blade. It is belief in one's self that can make the difference between victory and defeat. A Blademaster must always believe in herself and be willing to seek the help of others in order to claim victory. This is the truth of life and battle. Live or die as you choose." She looked sharply at the older halfling. "It is the Fifteenth Law of the Blades. How have you come to know this one?"

"I did not know the whole law, but I knew the first part, because of the truth of it," Maren shrugged again. "I know you cannot guarantee the safety of whoever goes with you, Lady Blademaster. I also know that whoever from my city is named a Blademaster is being named such because of great need. Even should this woman come from my own clan, I would not hold it against you were she not to make it through the war."

"War is a despicable thing," Alana said softly. "I wish we did not have to fight it, but that way leads to destruction."

"The Dark God has brought this war on," Maren said in a firm voice. "Not you. Never forget that, Blademaster. From what I have seen, the people of the Southern Dales could not have asked for a better champion to lead us in the fight against the darkness."

"Thank you for that, Maren," Alana smiled. She leaned against Colwyn. "I don't always feel like I am the right person to lead this fight. But I know that if I do not lead our armies against the darkness the Southern Dales does not stand a chance."

"Tough to be the Blademaster," Maren grunted.

"Tough, yes," Alana sighed. A tear rolled down her cheek. "At least I have Colwyn by my side."

"Indeed," the old halfling raised an eyebrow. "I would imagine your father, Lord Dargan, is not happy about this, Lord Colwyn."

""We have come to something of an understanding," Colwyn chuckled. "It required divine intervention though."

"I would imagine so!" Maren threw her head back and cackled. The cackle cut off in a cough and the old halfling had to stop to catch her breath. "Lord Dargan is a good man. Stubborn, but a good man."

"He is," Colwyn nodded.

"So, Lady Alana," Maren turned to face the Blademaster. "Just how do you propose to find the halfling that is to become a Blademaster? Barandale is a fairly large city, after all."

"Lord Taelin gave us a pendant that will glow when we are in the presence of a new Blademaster," Alana shrugged. "Unless you have a better idea, I guess we will wander around tomorrow and see when it starts glowing."

"I may have an idea as to who the Blademaster hiding in Barandale might be," Maren said after a few moments of thought. "But I will keep my counsel as to who it is. If I am correct, you will likely find her before this night is over."

"You think it's someone from your clan, then?" Alana raised an eyebrow.

"I think it possible, yes," Maren nodded. "But I can say no more than that until and unless she reveals herself."

"I understand," Alana gave a sage nod. "It is often that way with us."

"Indeed," Maren smiled. "You will find it is that way often with nobles as well. Wouldn't you agree, Lord Colwyn?"

"Such has been my experience, yes," Colwyn nodded. He worked his way up from sitting on the floor. Reaching down, he helped Alana stand up as well. "If you will excuse us, we should probably wander around the courtyard for a while and see if we can discover which clanswoman of yours is a Blademaster."

"Of course," Maren nodded.

Alana and Colwyn started towards the door, moving slowly as they had been sitting in a cramped position for a while. They'd just gotten to the door when Maren called out to Alana once more.

"Blademaster, one more word, if I may."

"Of course," Alana said turning back to the halfling.

"You have done my clan a kindness," the old woman said. "I know that Lord Colwyn does not so much care for my granddaughter or any halfling for that matter." She put up her hand to forestall any comment from the young noble. "I know it is just the way you were raised in the nobility, Lord Colwyn and I take no offense by it."

"You still have my apology for my attitude, Lady Maren," the noble said softly. "It is not right to judge an entire race based on the actions of some."

"The Lightbringer chooses his Blademasters' Protectors well," Maren smiled. "You are, of course, forgiven, Lord Colwyn." She turned back to Alana. "But you, Lady Alana. You have shown great kindness to my granddaughter Meryn. With no prejudice, you have allowed Meryn to travel with you. Most people in the Southern Dales would not have done so."

"Meryn has saved my life on more than one occasion, Lady Maren," Alana said. "She has more than repaid any kindness I've shown her with the most valuable thing she could give me. Friendship."

"The Lightbringer chooses his Blademasters well too," Maren smiled. "So wise for one so young. Yes, the Southern Dales are in good hands."

It was a peaceful evening, and Alana and Colwyn decided they would sit out under the stars for a while. They planned on sleeping outside. While they had been given accommodations, they would have ended up sleeping on the floor. At that point it was just as well to sleep outside. At least the ground might be softer than the floor of a building.

Maren had come out to speak with them, but instead had just sat on a bench nearby and watched the stars with them.

The peacefulness was broken by the sound of the guards challenging someone at the gate. Whoever it was, though, was allowed to enter the compound and the gates clanged shut behind them.

Alana looked up at the sound of the gates closing. She had thought all of the Swiftfoots were in the compound already, so she was surprised to see another female Swiftfoot coming in. But what was more interesting was the fact that, as soon as this new halfling entered the courtyard, the Bladestone started to warm. It was as if the new halfling was the one they were looking for.

Alana realized with a start that this Swiftfoot really was the one they were looking for.

She stood up and walked over to the halfling that had just entered the compound and went to one knee in front of her. The Bladestone grew hotter the closer she got to the halfling, telling her that she was right.

"You," Alana said in a soft voice. "You're the one we're here for."

Chapter XVI
Talóg

alóg looked at Alana with an amused expression on her face. Even though they had not been introduced, there was no doubt who this woman kneeling in front of her could be. There had been much talk in the city of the Blademaster and her companions. And here the Blademaster was.

Looking right at Talby.

But Talby could not figure out what she was talking about. The woman could not possibly be talking to her, could she? Well, she had knelt down in front of her, but still. Talby was sure she was talking to someone else even with that. But the look on the Blademaster's face told Talby that she was deadly serious.

"You must have me confused with someone else, Lady Blademaster."

"No," Alana shook her head. "No, I do not. What is your name?"

"Talby Swiftfoot," the halfling said. She put her hands on her hips and cocked her head slightly. "I'm afraid I don't know yours either."

"I am Alana Steeldrake," the tall woman said. "I am, as you know, a Blademaster."

"Yes, yes. I know that." The halfling woman grimaced at Alana. She wasn't happy about the situation, but only because she did not know what was going on. "What do you mean that I am the one you are here for?"

"Exactly what I said," Alana shrugged. "Tell me, Talby Swiftfoot. Are you an adventurous sort?"

"I spend more time away from Barandale than I do home," Talby shrugged. "Why?"

"Well, at least I'm not going to change your life too much then," the Blademaster shrugged. She stood and turned to face Maren. "This Talby is the one we are here for."

"You're sure?" Maren asked.

"I am," Alana nodded.

"Will someone tell me what's going on?" Talby demanded.

"Congratulations, Talby," Maren said in a soft voice. "Blademaster Alana is here to take you to the Temple of the Blades where you will become the first ever halfling Blademaster."

Talby stared at Maren and then turned to look at the human woman. She kept looking back and forth between the two of them. There was no way that they could be serious, but neither the halfling woman nor the human woman appeared to be joking.

Talby Swiftfoot? A Blademaster?

Talby supposed that stranger things had happened in life. But a halfling Blademaster? Surely the world was not ready for that! And yet, here they were. Apparently the Blademaster was here to make Talby a Blademaster.

There had to be more to it than that.

For instance, why now? Why, out of all the years of the history of Calthea, did fate conspire to have a halfling become a Blademaster? Talby had heard rumors of war coming to the Southern Dales. Could her being named a Blademaster have anything to do with this impending war?

She wasn't sure she liked the thought of that.

"Why me?" Talby asked.

"I don't know," Alana admitted. "I only know that we were told that there was a Blademaster to be found in Barandale. And I am utterly convinced that it is you that we were sent here to find."

"But why me?" she asked again. "I'm nothing special. Yes, I'm a fair hand with a dagger or sword, but there are others that are better than I."

"That is as it may be, but I am not here for them," Alana shrugged. "I am here for you."

"What will I have to do?" she asked.

"There is a great darkness coming to the Southern Dales, Talby," Alana said. "I won't lie to you. Being a Blademaster right now is even more dangerous than it normally is. You will be leading troops into battle. There is every possibility that none of us who fight will make it to the other side of the war that is coming still alive."

"I see," Talby frowned.

The fact was, she supposed, that she loved to fight. That was probably why the Blademaster had come looking for her rather than any of her kinfolk. She liked to fight. She liked the feel of steel clashing against steel.

But she did not know about fighting in a war.

She looked over at the other members of the Swiftfoot Clan that were starting to crowd around them. Talby heaved a huge sigh. She knew that she would do anything to protect her home. If there was a war coming, she would have to be involved in making sure it did not consume her home and her clan.

Her gaze went back to Alana's. When their eyes locked, she thought she saw that Alana understood her inner monologue. That made it a little easier. But still, there was a great deal of responsibility being dropped on her small shoulders. She wasn't completely sure that she was ready to handle such responsibility.

"A war, you say?" she asked the Blademaster.

"A dark and terrible war, I am afraid."

"Are there any other kinds?" Talby raised one eyebrow. "My understanding is all wars are dark and terrible."

"Well, I won't say you're wrong about that," Alana said, her mouth twitching like it wanted to break into a smile. "But this one... Let's just say this war would be particularly bad for the Southern Dales to lose."

"I see," Talby nodded. "Who exactly are we going to be at war with?"

"The forces of the Dark God."

"Ah."

This explained much to Talby. There was little that she could say in argument to fighting a war against the forces of the Dark God. Even though halflings tended to revere one of the neutral aligned deities, they all knew that little good would come from the Dark God having control of Calthea.

Besides, Talby seemed to recall that Laeyra was one of the gods involved with the Blademasters somehow. Surely that meant that Laeyra would look kindly on her becoming a Blademaster?

The thought that her deity would probably approve was the deciding factor. While she still wasn't the most comfortable with the thought of going to war, she knew that it was what would have to be.

"Very well," Talby whispered. "I will go with you."

"Good," Alana nodded. "Good. We will be leaving tomorrow. Make sure you have everything you need for a long journey. I don't know when you will be returning to Barandale."

"I'll be ready at first light," Talby nodded.

"There's... one other thing," Alana winced. "Do you have a mate?"

"Well I did take Tovar Greythistle's ring of hair, but we haven't married," Talby frowned. "Why do you ask?"

"He needs to come too."

"Why?"

"That is not a matter to be discussed in public," Alana said. "But he must come. Bring him to me and I will explain it to both of you at once."

"I will bring him to where you are staying tonight, then, Blademaster," Talby said.

The house that Talby Swiftfoot lived in with Tovar Greythistle was not far away from the Swiftfoot compound. It was much smaller in size than the compound as well. Then again, it was only home to two halflings rather than a whole clan of them, so it did not need to be all that big.

She liked her little house. It suited her far better than the compound did. She had long thought that the compound had gone to the heads of some members of her clan. Some members of her clan were far too self absorbed for her liking.

Except for her cousin, Meryn.

In a lot of ways she and Meryn were alike. They both spent far more time away from Barandale than they spent inside the compound. She was proud that her cousin had become a companion to the Blademaster. She was sure there was a lot to the story. Talby had seen the hateful looks her cousin kept flashing the silver haired woman in the party.

She could only wonder what that was about.

It would be rude to ask. As much as Talby wanted to know the story behind such hateful looks, she would not ask. If Meryn wanted her to know what was going on, she would tell the story of her own volition.

No matter how interesting a story it might turn out to be.

She also wondered why the Blademaster wanted to see her and Tovar together. She figured that it was probably that she wanted to make sure that he was on board with her becoming a Blademaster.

But the looks that Alana had given her companion when she mentioned that she wanted to speak with the both of them told Talby that there may be more to it than that.

Tovar was an adventurous sort himself. It was part of why she had accepted his ring of hair. She knew that he would always understand her need to get out of Barandale from time to time. It was important to her that her partner understood her. What would be the point of being together if they did not understand each other, after all?

Talby hoped that he would understand why she had to do this.

It was not that Talby wanted to go to war. She wanted to have a family some day, after all. Preferably with Tovar. But from the moment that Alana had started talking to her about becoming a Blademaster, she could feel a calling on her heart.

One did not simply ignore the calling of one's heart.

And so, she would go to war, with or without Tovar by her side. She would rather he went with her, though. It would make it much easier to go through what was to come with him by her side.

And so it was that, by the time she had gotten to the little house she shared with Tovar, she had decided that if he did not go with her on this journey, she would give him back his ring of hair and leave him.

It was not an easy decision to make. And she was afraid that she would have to follow through on the threat to leave him. That would hurt her as much as it would hurt him.

But it was the calling of her heart, and that meant that she had no choice.

She had long known that this day, the day when she would have to give Tovar a painful ultimatum, was coming. She had seen it in her meditations. But she had not seen the wrinkle that she was to become a Blademaster. That part had been a complete surprise. There was a part of her that was convinced that it was nothing more than a sick ruse. What would happen when they got to the Temple of the Blades? Would they get there and the Blademaster tell her it was all a joke?

Talby did not think it would happen that way, though. While some of her companions did not quite look convinced, Alana had looked to be deadly serious about it. She'd have to ask Meryn to confirm, but Alana did not look to be a woman that regularly joked about serious matters such as naming a Blademaster.

As soon as she walked into the house, she could hear Tovar's snoring. That was something that could be a problem. Tovar was loud when he got good and deep in sleep. Although, Talby supposed that Alana was used to noisy sleeping halflings. Meryn had been known to snore a bit on the loud side sometimes too.

Talby went over and kicked the bed. It had the desired effect, startling Tovar awake.

"What the hell?" he demanded.

"Get up, Tovar," Talby smiled sweetly down at him. "Get dressed. You're needed over at the compound. And we have some things to discuss before we go back over there."

"So, discuss," he grumbled as he slumped back in bed.

Talby wasn't having any of it. She yanked him out of bed. He yelped when his back hit the floor.

"Now is not the time for sleeping, love," she giggled. "Now is the time for you to go and get washed up. We're seeing some important people."

"Gah," he grumbled as he got up.

Talby laughed as Tovar stumbled over to the wash basin. She started to sort out what the two of them would need for the journey and began stuffing things in their packs. She wasn't sure how long they would be away from Barandale, so she made sure they had everything they could possibly need.

Alana had indicated that it would be some time before they returned to Barandale after all.

"What's all this then?" Tovar asked in a gruff voice when he turned from the wash basin.

"We, the two of us, are going on a journey, Tovar," she said after sliding an extra knife down the side of her pack.

"I can see that you're packing for the two of us," he grumbled. "Where are we going?"

"My cousin, Meryn, came back to Barandale today," Talby looked up from the packs. "She brought the Blademaster with her. Apparently they came to Barandale to name another Blademater. They named me."

That brought Tovar up short. "You? A Blademaster?"

"Is it really so hard to believe, Tovar?" she asked as she stood from the packs. "You've seen how I fight. You've seen how I can so artfully use any bladed weapon that I can pick up."

"True," Tovar nodded. He rubbed his chin. "But a halfling Blademaster? I don't know that the Southern Dales is ready for that."

"Ready or not, they're getting one." Talby shrugged. "Come with me, Tovar. I need you."

"Of course I'll go with you, Tal," he grunted. "Did you really think I would let you face whatever it is you'll face out there alone?"

"I was hoping not," she fluttered her eyelashes at him. "I would have had to kick you out if you didn't."

"Bah," he muttered. "You'd be lost without me."

"Of course I would," she laughed. "Now, come on. The Blademaster wants to have a word with us."

"Why would she want to talk to me?" Tovar grumbled. "I'm just along for the ride."

"Your guess is as good as mine, but she specifically asked for you to be there, so you'll be there."

"The things I do for the love of you, Talby!"

It was another hour or so before Talby and Tovar made it back to the compound. Talby had insisted that he dress nicely for the Blademaster. Tovar had grumbled some more and finally put on one of his best outfits. She told him he looked fine. He told her that he felt like a fool.

Talby had just been content that he was going along with her to talk to the Blademaster.

The walk to the compound had been short and brisk. The wind coming off of the sea made it even chillier than normal for that time of day, so the two of them did not want to take long to get where they were going.

When they got to the compound, they were met by Meryn. Talby greeted her cousin with a warm embrace. Tovar, on the other hand, just stood next to Talby and glowered. Talby knew that all he wanted was to have this talk with the Blademaster so he could go back to bed.

He'd get his wish soon enough.

They followed Meryn through the compound to the quarters where the Blademaster was staying overnight. Since they were expected, Meryn just led them right in.

The Blademaster was sitting at the desk, writing something on a piece of parchment. Her human companion, whom Talby had learned was named Colwyn, was standing next to her, reading over what she was writing. He pointed to the sheet in places and made quiet suggestions. They both stopped what they were doing when Meryn cleared her throat to let them know that they were not alone.

"Ah, yes," the Blademaster smiled. "Talby. Come in. And you must be Tovar Greythistle."

Tovar simply grunted in response.

"Come and sit," Colwyn said. "We have much to discuss with you two."

"If I'm not needed anymore, I'd like to go clear my head," Meryn said in a soft voice.

"Of course, Little One," Colwyn nodded.

Talby watched her cousin go. There was sadness in Meryn's eyes. Once again, Talby could only wonder what that was all about. She had to fight the urge to chase after Meryn and find out.

That would have to wait. There was something more important that had to be dealt with first.

"You wanted to see us, Lady Blademaster?" Talby said as she turned back to face the human woman.

"More to the point, we wanted to see him," Colwyn said, pointing to Tovar. "It is he who needs to know what he risks by coming with us, after all."

"What do you mean?" Tovar growled. "What risk are you talking about?"

"How much do you love Talby, Tovar?" Colwyn asked. "Are you willing to die for her if you are called to?"

"May it never happen," Tovar nodded. "But yes, I would die for her if I needed to."

"What I am about to tell you does not leave this room," Alana said softly. "Not even the Council of Elders can know what you hear today. Because if word were to get out about the source of the Blademasters power, it would cause no end of trouble for us."

"I don't understand," Talby frowned.

"This is my husband, Colwyn," Alana began. "He is also the source of my power. The bond of love that we share is what powers my abilities as a Blademaster. Because of the importance of the bond of love between a Blademaster and her Protector, we have to make sure."

"What does making sure entail?" Tovar asked. "I assume you won't just take my word for it that I love her."

"It is not that we won't take your word for it, Tovar," Alana said. "This is one part of the Law of the Blades that I wish was changeable, but it is not. You must undergo the Test of the Blades when we arrive at the Temple of the Blades."

"And what does this test involve?" Talby asked. "What are you going to require him to do to prove his love?"

"We can't tell you what the test involves because it changes from person to person," Colwyn said. "But it will test your fighting ability, intellect, and, most importantly, your dedication to Talby. If you fail, you will either be dead or barred from ever seeing Talby again."

"I see," Tovar frowned.

"And now that she has accepted the calling of her heart as a Blademaster, if you choose not to take the Test of the Blades, it will be as if you failed. You would never be able to see Talby again."

"I have little choice then, haven't I?" Tovar grumbled. "Of course I'll undergo this Test of the Blades."

"Good," Alana nodded. "We will be leaving in the morning. Make sure you have everything you need for a long journey packed. As I told Talby, I do not know when we will be back in Barandale, but it will not be until the spring at the very least."

"Talby already has us packed," Tovar shrugged. "We'll be ready."

"Meet us in the courtyard in the morning. We will be leaving from there," Colwyn said. "We will be flying on the back of a dragon to get to the Temple of the Blades before the snows start falling."

"A dragon, you say?" Talby's eyes opened wide.

"Indeed. She is my nathair an aeir a chosnaíonn," Alana smiled. "And my friend. When you have bonded under the light of Lord Taelin and Lady Laeyra, a dragon will choose to serve as your nathair an aeir a chosnaíonn as well."

"Is this a part of the Law of the Blades as well?" Tovar asked.

"It is," Colwyn nodded. "In this case, one that Alana and I do not mind so much. Silvestra is the second dragon to serve as nathair an aeir a chosnaíonn for Alana. The first died giving his live to protect her. The dragons have done all they could to protect us. Just as your nathair an aeir a chosnaíonn will do all he or she can to protect you."

"I see," Tovar said in a gruff voice.

"If there's nothing else, Blademaster Alana, I am afraid poor Tovar was woken up for this," Talby laughed. "I think I need to put him back to bed so he will be ready to go in the morning."

"We will see you in the morning then," Alana chuckled, her eyes twinkling.

The Age of Darkness

Chapter XVII
A Ring of Hair

Mergn wanted some time to herself, so she had gone off away from her companions. She had chosen a small birch tree just outside of the Swiftfoot compound to sit alone and try to gather her thoughts.

So much had happened, and she was not sure she was totally equipped to handle everything that had happened.

First she had lost William. She was still upset by the silver dragon taking him away from her. There was no way she could compete with Silvestra, though, and she knew that Taelin was right that he was not the one for her.

And now, she was being supplanted as the most important member of her family that had journeyed out from Barandale. As a companion to the Blademaster, she had a special prominence in her family that no one else had been able to match.

But now her cousin, Talby, had become a Blademaster and risen to new heights.

Meryn did not begrudge Talby her becoming a Blademaster. She was happy for her cousin. But having a cousin that was a Blademaster put Meryn in an awkward situation. Alana had saved her life and Meryn owed her.

But Talby was family.

In the end, Meryn knew that family won out and she would end up travelling with Talby rather than Alana.

She could only hope that Alana understood.

There was a rustling nearby. Meryn frowned and looked around. If it was another halfling they were making sound on purpose so as not to sneak up on her.

If it wasn't another halfling, though... She could be in trouble.

As it turned out the rustling was another halfling, and one she recognized, even though she had not seen him in many years.

"Odway?" she gasped in recognition. "Odway Thistlethumb?"

"It's been a long time, Meryn," the newcomer said. "I was not sure you would remember me."

"How could I forget my oldest friend?" Meryn laughed. She ran over and gave him a hug. "How have you been, Odway?"

"The same as always," he smiled at her. There was no trace of the sadness that she expected to see in his eyes upon seeing her again. "I am a full priest of Laeyra now."

"I am proud of you, Odway!"

"I have kept to my studies and worked hard," he nodded. "I hoped that I would one day see you again. And here I find you. Under the exact same birch tree where I saw you last."

She should have known that it was the same birch tree...

Meryn sat under the birch tree. She was happy that she was finally going to be leaving Barandale, but she was sad as well. She did not think Odway would go with her. And if he did not, then she did not know if or when she would ever see him again.

Something about the thought of losing him gave her pause. But she would not be deterred from her plans.

She had been waiting to leave Barandale for long enough.

She waited for Odway. He had sent her a message to meet her at their birch tree at sunset. She had gotten there a little early, wanting time to think about various things. She did not know why Odway had wanted to meet her, but she could guess.

He was going to give her a ring of hair.

It was the way that halflings proposed. The man would cut a lock of his hair and present it to his intended. It was a long standing tradition. And Meryn had long hoped that she would one day get a ring of hair. But only if the person who was giving it to her would respect the fact that she was leaving Barandale and go with her.

She did not think that Odway would do that.

It wasn't that he didn't want to go with her, she thought. Although she wasn't sure he actually would want to leave Barandale. He was still a novice in the Blue Temple. Until he ascended to the priesthood, he wouldn't leave the temple. She could understand his commitment. And she respected it.

But it precluded his joining her on her adventures outside of Barandale.

She knew that it would hurt him. There was nothing that could be done for that. She hoped he could forgive her in time for any pain she caused him.

Finally, after what seemed like hours of waiting, Odway came walking up to the birch tree. He sad down next to her and leaned in to kiss her on the cheek. In her mind, that confirmed for her what he wanted to meet her about.

"Hello, Odway," she said in a soft voice.

"Hello, Meryn."

She slowly wrapped her arm around him. She really did love him. She just wasn't sure she could take his ring of hair if she was leaving and he was staying.

"I'm here as you asked me to be," Meryn said. She was on the verge of tears, because she knew what was coming and she was afraid that she would end up breaking Odway's heart. That was the last thing she wanted.

"I am glad," he said. "There is something I wish to give you."

"I know," Meryn nodded. She smiled sadly. "I knew as soon as you asked me to meet you what you wanted."

"You did?" Odway's eyes went wide.

"Odway... I love you," she said. "You know that. But I'm leaving Barandale in the morning. You know that also."

Odway held out the ring of hair to her.

"Take it," he said softly. "Be my wife. Stay with me."

"I can't stay any more than you can leave, Odway," she sniffled. "I'm sorry."

"We were meant to be together."

"But you cannot come with me, Odway!" she wailed. "And I cannot stay! So what are we to do?"

"Don't go, Meryn," he pleaded. "Stay with me. Don't end us like this!"

"I can't!" she cried.

She stood up and ran back to her parents' house. She never looked back to see how much she had hurt him.

It would be seven long years before she would see him again under that same birch tree.

She realized that tears had started to flow down her cheek as she remembered the last time she had seen Odway.

"I never meant to hurt you, Odway," Meryn said. She reached up and ran her fingers along his cheek tenderly. "You knew I was going to leave Barandale."

"I knew," Odway nodded. "But I had hoped that I could change your mind."

"Have you never met me?" Meryn laughed. "Once I set my mind on something, nothing can change it."

"That doesn't mean I couldn't try," Odway smiled.

"Oh, Odway. If only things could have been different."

"They still could be, you know. Different I mean."

"What do you mean?" Meryn looked over at her oldest friend.

"I never gave a ring of hair to anyone else, Meryn," Odway said in a soft voice. "There has never been another woman for me."

"I'm still the same headstrong halfling that left Barandale years ago, Odway," Meryn reminded him. "When the Blademasters leave Barandale, I will be going with them once more."

"I know," he nodded. He pulled her close and held her tight against him. "But I'm not letting you get away from me again. If you will have me, I will go with you."

"Odway Thistlethumb, you don't have any idea what you'd be getting into if you left Barandale!"

"I am a priest of Laeyra, Meryn," Odway reminded her. "Talby is going to need a priest by her side. I know that you will be joining your cousin on her journey. I would go with you. I will offer her whatever help I can on her journey."

"You really never met another?" she asked.

"Not once."

"I fell in love while I was out in the world, Odway," she said softly. "And he shattered my heart. In many ways far worse than I broke yours seven years ago."

"What did he do, Meryn?"

"He told me that he loved me. And then he married another," she sniffled.

Meryn leaned into him and cried on his shoulder. It was the first time she had really let herself cry about losing William since that first night. She felt him wrap his arms around her. It felt good to be held.

It had been some time since someone had held her.

She looked up at him, tears streaming down her face. She couldn't believe how nice he was being to her after what she had done. After she had broken his heart.

"How?" she asked, her voice quavering with tears. "How can you be so nice to me, Odway?"

"Because I never stopped loving you, Meryn." He kissed her forehead. "Do you think I was really going to take no for an answer? I knew that one day you would come back for a visit. And when that day came, I would leave with you."

"You knew that, huh?"

"You couldn't stay away from Barandale forever," Odway squeezed her tight. "I just didn't think it would take seven years. Still, I never lost faith."

"I couldn't take your ring then, Odway," she whispered. "But if you are still willing, I would be happy to wear it now."

"You will?"

"On one condition."

"Name your condition, then," he nodded.

"There is a priest of Taelin that travels with Blademaster Alana," she smiled up at him. "Let's not wait any longer. I don't know when we will get back to Barandale. And I want to have my family there when I get married. Let's marry before we leave Barandale. Let's travel the Southern Dales as husband and wife."

Odway looked down at Meryn with a smile. He leaned down and touched his lips to hers. What started as a simple kiss turned into an expression of heat and passion. The world melted away until it was just the two of them.

When they broke away, Meryn was breathless. Her heart hammered in her chest. It had never felt like that when she had kissed William. And it was then that she knew once and for all that Odway had been right seven years before.

"We were meant to be together," he had said. And now she knew that he was right.

And they would be together now as they should have been seven years before.

"That was..." she trailed off.

"I know," he nodded.

Odway reached into his vest pocket and pulled out a fresh ring of hair that he had made for her. Somehow, he had known that she would say yes this time. Meryn held out her hand and he slipped the ring of hair around the ring finger of her left hand.

It was done. They were going to be married.

Meryn felt like she could fly.

Martin was sleeping when he felt a small hand on his shoulder shaking him. He woke with a start to see Meryn shaking him awake.

"What time is it?" he yawned.

"Just after sunset, sleepyhead, Meryn teased.

"Then I only just fell asleep," the priest of Taelin grumbled. "This must be important."

"It is," Meryn nodded. "I have come to ask you a favor. You have become one of my better friends lately. You were so kind to me after William and Silvestra married. And now, I wish for you to do me a favor."

"Of course, Little One," he nodded. "Name it."

"Before we leave tomorrow, I would have you perform a wedding," she said. "I have come to realize that the person I was meant to be with had been right in front of my eyes my whole life. And I almost threw love away for good."

"Love has a way of fixing mistakes like that," Martin said. "Look at William and Silvestra. They were meant to be together and are married now despite the efforts of many to stop that from happening."

"I understand that now," Meryn nodded. "Will you perform the wedding for Odway and I? I want to be married before we leave so that I can be married in front of my family."

"Of course, Little One," he smiled. "I would be honored to. In the morning, you marry Odway."

"Thank you, Martin!" she squealed. She wrapped her tiny arms around the priest and squeezed.

Martin loved nothing more than seeing two people in love together. It made him happy to no end to see Meryn finally find love.

The Age of Darkness

Chapter XVIII
Blessings and Gifts

The morning dawned sunny on the Swiftfoot compound. The sun filtered down into the courtyard and cast shadows in the grass.

Alana was up early. She had slept well knowing that they would soon be on their way to the Temple of the Blades. She had a good feeling that that they would be able to get to the Temple and then to Ravendale before the snows began to fall. That was good, as it would allow for them to be able to plan for the defense of the Southern Dales with the King and his advisors.

If the defense of the Southern Dales depended on her, she wanted to make sure that the King and his generals were in on the planning. While she knew she would have to lead, it only made sense for her to listen to the thoughts of men who had fought wars and knew the best way to deploy troops.

It would be unwise to not take advantage of their experience.

She was the first of her companions to wake. And while she was itching to get moving, she would let them awake as they would. When they were in the relative safety of a place such as the compound, there was no need to get moving at the onset of morning. There had been no need to set a watch, either, for the compound was as secure as any palace. And the Swiftfoots had provided guards for their guests.

Alana sat herself under a tree in the courtyard. She pulled out all her knives and set them in front of her. One by one, she checked each one, making sure they were all well honed. As they were the tools of her trade, she wanted to make sure they were ready to be used at a moment's notice.

After checking all of her knives and putting them away, she pulled out her twin longswords. She pulled the blades free from their scabbards and checked each edge for nicks from use. When she found one, she used the whetstone from one of her pouches to hone the nick out. It was a time consuming process that she did regularly. It would not do for one of her blades to no longer be useable due to wear and tear.

As she was working on her second longsword, she heard footsteps approaching. She knew who it was without looking up. There was no mistaking her husband's tread. The only thing that surprised her about his approach was that it had taken as long as it had for him to come find her. She guessed he must have slept through her getting out of bed.

She smiled as she thought about how she had tired him out the night before.

"Hello, sleepyhead," she beamed at him.

"Woman, you're going to kill me," he groaned.

"But it will be an exquisite death!"

Colwyn laughed as he sat next to her under the tree. No matter what they'd been through over the past few years, just sitting with Colwyn was enough to make Alana smile. It was amazing how such a simple thing was enough to make her happy.

Alana decided that true love was a wonderful thing. And not for the first time.

"So the halfling left the compound last night," Colwyn said.

"I know."

"Did you know she apparently woke Martin in the middle of the night for something?" he asked.

"Yep."

"Any idea what that was about?" he pressed.

"Can't tell you," she shrugged. She nuzzled up against him. "I've been sworn to secrecy."

"Even from me?"

"If it makes you feel better, Col, I don't know what is going on either. All I know is that we will both know what it was all about before we leave later today." She smiled over at him. "But from the way Martin was dodging the question, I think it is something that will make even your cold heart happy."

"I do not have a cold heart!" he protested.

"When it comes to Meryn, you do," she laughed. She poked him in the ribs with her finger. "You do not like her. Despite how much she has done for all of us."

"I'll admit, the noble inside of me has a very hard time dealing with her," Colwyn admitted in a soft voice. "I'll just go ahead and blame my father for that attitude."

"Your father is a bit of a jerk, actually," Alana shrugged. She looked up at Colwyn with a mischievous grin. "But I like him."

"You like him even though he tried to keep us apart?"

"Well, I didn't like that part," Alana frowned. "But he's a good man. He knows honor and duty. A bit rigid in how he deals with rules and traditions, but... Kind of like our Solara Moonfire in that regard."

"Yes, she does seem to be cut from the same pattern as my father when it comes to strict adherence to a set of rules."

"If only she realized."

"Realized what, Alana?"

"The Law of the Blades is not a rigid code like she thinks it is, Colwyn," Alana smiled her beautiful smile at him. "It's a code to live by, true. But it is far from a rigid set of rules. It is, instead, a set of truisms that, if a person were to follow, will make that person a much better form of themselves."

"You may be the first Blademaster to actually understand that, my child," a soft female voice said from behind them. "This pleases me."

"Lady Laeyra," Alana bowed her head toward the goddess. "You honor is with your presence."

"Bah," the goddess waved off Alana's bowing. "Just once, I'd like someone to just come up to me and give me a hug in greeting rather than all this bowing and scraping that I always get. And I'll tell you something else. My husband doesn't like the bowing either, but he'd never say such aloud."

"I don't know that I could actually initiate a hug to either of you, Lady Laeyra," Alana chuckled softly. "It would feel inappropriate."

"It would only be inappropriate if I had not told you that it would be, Alana," Laeyra boomed out a deep laugh. "At any rate. I am here. You are here. And it seems you have found me a halfling Blademaster. I dare say, the High Priestess of the Blades will not like this one bit."

"She's not the only one," Colwyn muttered.

"I know," Laeyra smiled at Colwyn. "It's all right, Colwyn. I do understand your feelings about halflings. But there is a reason for everything we do, and there is a reason that young Talby Swiftfoot has been called."

"Can you at least tell us the reasons for Talby being a Blademaster, Lady Laeyra?" Alana asked. "Even I was stunned to learn where we were going to look for a Blademaster."

"All I can tell you as that there will one day come a time when a halfling Blademaster will come in very handy," Laeyra said softly. "I can tell you no more than that. Just know that Talby will be needed."

"The Dream Weaver has given us an idea of what is coming," Alana said. "I will take all the help I can get."

"Wise words," Laeyra smiled. "One might think you were a child of the light, my child."

"If I may ask, my lady," Colwyn asked. "Why are you here?"

"I'm here for the wedding of course," Laeyra beamed. "I love a good wedding!"

"But Talby and Tovar won't marry until after Tovar goes through the Test of the Blades," Alana furrowed her brow. "Who is getting married?"

"You don't know?" Laeyra raised a golden eyebrow. She clapped her hands in glee. "Wonderful! It will be a surprise then! I love surprises too."

"Lady Laeyra, I wonder if I might ask you a favor," Alana changed the subject. "There is an issue with your husband's High Priestess. Naomi has stripped our Martin Faolin from the roster of the priesthood of Taelin."

"Oh, I wouldn't worry about that," Laeyra smiled broadly. "My Taelin still recognizes Martin as one of his priests, and in the end, that is what matters. I keep telling him that he is going to have to have words with that High Priestess of his, though. He says that there is a reason Naomi is the current High Priestess. But I don't see it. All I see is no end of trouble coming from her."

"That is all we see too," Alana nodded. "She tried to prevent Colwyn and myself from leaving on our journey."

"Yes, I know," Laeyra nodded. "I was watching. I was very proud of you for standing up to her. And I can tell you that you were right. Taelin is quite proud of Martin. You need not worry about Martin. Taelin will look after him."

"That is all we hope for." Alana looked over at Colwyn who nodded. "Martin has become a good and trusted friend. Even though we do not know him all that well, we are pleased to have him with us. I would have hated to have something happen to him because he chose to follow me."

"And this is why we are proud of you," Layera placed her hand on Alana's arm. "You and Colwyn have surpassed our wildest dreams. The caring that you have shown Martin is just further proof that you were the right choice."

Alana snuggled closer to Colwyn. While she appreciated what the goddess was saying, it was not always as easy as she said.

"There are days, Lady Laeyra, when I do not feel as if I were the right choice," Alana said in a soft voice. "There are days when I wish it had been anyone else."

"Had it been anyone else, the people of Valendale would still be captive in Willowdale, Alana,' Laeyra reminded her. "It is only because you and Colwyn have come to love those people that you went looking for a way to free them."

"And we have brought on a war," Alana said. "The blame for that war has fallen at my feet."

"The War of Souls would have started with or without you, Alana," Laeyra sighed. "It was only a matter of time before it began. The war never ends. Only the battles change. The War of Souls is just a new phase of an old war. It has always been and it will always be. Nothing that you or anyone else can do will change that."

"I don't know if that is comforting or not, Lady Laeyra," Alana frowned.

"It was not necessarily meant to be a comfort."

"Then I suppose I shall have to take it for what it is then," Alana shrugged. She nuzzled closer to Colwyn. "A statement of fact."

Laeyra smiled at Alana. It was a smile tinged with sadness. Alana returned the smile with equal sadness.

She knew that the Twenty Third Law of the Blades meant that even if they managed to survive the War of Souls, the conflagration would just fire up again sometime in the future.

The war never ends. Only the battles change.

It was, in many ways, a depressing way to look at life. But at the same token, knowing that the war would continue gave Alana a sense of strength and purpose. It was a feeling of purpose she would need to get through the War of Souls.

Alana was musing on this when William and Silvestra came into the courtyard. They saw Alana and Colwyn and walked towards them. When they saw Laeyra, they both, as one, dropped to their knees in reverence to the goddess.

"Get up," Laeyra laughed from where she was lounging under a tree not far from Alana and Colwyn. "I'm not here to be bowed to. I'm here for the wedding."

"That's the second time you've brought up the wedding," Alana looked over at the goddess. "Who is getting married?"

"Meryn," William said. "Not sure who she's marrying, but I overheard Martin rehearsing for the ceremony."

"You had to go and ruin the surprise, mage!" Laeyra whimpered. She rolled her eyes. "It's a good thing. There are not many chances when someone gets a second chance with the person they are supposed to be with. Fortunately, Meryn is getting that chance. I hope that it will heal the anger she still feels for you, Silvestra."

"Our little Meryn is getting married?" Alana smiled broadly. "Well, good for her."

"Indeed," Colwyn laughed. "I am happy for her."

"I told you that it was going to be good!" Alana smiled as she poked Colwyn in the ribs. "I told you it would warm your cold cold heart."

"Hey!"

Alana laughed and poked him again. When she looked up, she noticed that even Laeyra was having a little trouble keeping a straight face. That made Alana laugh even harder. She was still chuckling when Martin entered the courtyard. Maren Swiftfoot by his side. Alana could tell that the matriarch of the clan was just learning about Meryn's wedding for the first time.

By the way the old halfling woman was smiling, Alana could tell that it was welcome news.

The matriarch looked up and smiled over at the Blademaster and her companion. Maren hobbled her way over to where they were sitting under. When she got over to the tree and saw Laeyra nearby, she started to bow to the goddess but stopped when Laeyra lifted a hand.

"No, I'm only hear to bless the happy couple," the goddess said.

"And they should be happy for your blessing, Lady Laeyra," Maren nodded. She turned to the Blademaster.

207

"And you, Blademaster. How feel you about young Meryn taking a husband today?"

"I have seen poor Meryn go through a great deal," Alana said softly. "I am well pleased that she has found a cause for happiness in her life. She has been a steadfast friend save for one small misjudgment for which she has already sought and received forgiveness. She deserves this."

"I am glad to hear you say so," Maren nodded. "I have long hoped that she would find happiness, and Odway is a good man. One of yours, I believe, Lady Laeyra."

"He is," Laeyra nodded. "He has served me well. My husband and I have a vested interest in both Meryn and Odway. While he could not be here, he wished for me to pass along his blessing as well."

"A double honor then," Maren bowed slightly at the waist. "All we need now are the happy couple and we can get this wedding underway."

"I think we should wait for Talby and Tovar as well," Alana said. "I think it would do them good to see this before going to the Temple of the Blades."

Maren nodded and hobbled over to a nearby bench. She lowered herself onto the bench and sighed a happy little sigh.

"When you get to be as old as I am, you will welcome the little things such as benches as well, Blademaster," Maren counseled. "It is a sad day when your body no longer chooses to work as well as you might want it to."

"I will keep that in mind," Alana smiled. "But I am like as to die in battle as I am to get old."

Maren shrugged and leaned back on the bench.

It was not too much longer before the four halflings they were waiting for arrived. Talby and Tovar arrived first. Talby looked excited for the journey. Tovar looked bored. Meryn and the halfling that Alana assumed was this Odway that Meryn was to marry followed right behind.

Alana studied this new halfling. He was wearing the blue robes of a cleric of Laeyra. But his features were such that Alana would never be able to describe him. He was plain with very nondescript features. Alana was sure she would forget what he looked like on the journey to the Temple of the Blades.

But he looked happy to be with Meryn. And for her part, Meryn looked to be the happiest that Alana had seen her in months. Certainly since the incident in Willowdale where she had overheard William profess his love for Silvestra.

Yes, this marriage would be a good think for the little sneak thief.

Meryn made her way over to Alana and embraced her friend. Alana smiled and hugged the halfling woman back. It was a firm and warm embrace, and Alana was only too happy to show the woman that much of a comfort.

"I hear you're getting married, Little One," Alana whispered in Meryn's ear. "Know that I am truly happy for you."

"I know, Alana," Meryn said. She pulled away to look at her friend. "But I have a request to make of you that I don't think will make you happy."

"You want to join Talby and Tovar in their travels rather than continue travelling with Colwyn and myself," Alana smiled. Her smile widened when she saw the shocked look on Meryn's face. "Oh, I expected you to ask me that from the moment I knew we were coming to Barandale to find a Blademaster, Meryn. It only makes sense for you to journey with Talby to support her as you have supported me."

"You're not mad?" Meryn squeaked.

"Of course not, Little One," Alana laughed. She hugged her friend again. "Talby is going to need all the help that she can get. And I dare say that there are likely to be few that will stand with her. If I were to not let you go with her, and she was killed for lack of help, I would never be able to forgive myself. All I ask is that you do all that you can to protect her as you have always done for me."

"Of course I will!" Meryn said. "She's family."

Alana smiled and turned to Odway. "And you, sir. I expect that you look after our little Meryn. As she said about Talby, she is family to me. I would be ill pleased if harm came to her under your watch."

"I will look after her, Lady Blademaster," Odway nodded. "You can count on that."

"Good," Alana smiled. She looked over at Laeyra with a look that spoke volumes.

The goddess got the message.

"I have come to bless this wedding," Laeyra said softly as she stood. "My Taelin and I love nothing more than to see two people bound in love. It is why we placed the bond of love as the basis for the powers of a Blademaster. Meryn Swiftfoot and Odway Thistlethumb. My Taelin and I both bless your union. May it be a long and happy one."

"Thank you, Lady Laeyra," Meryn bowed low to the goddess. "May your luck always guide us."

"Martin, if you will, I believe these two should be married now," Laeyra smiled at the priest of Taelin. "I can think of no one better to bind them than a priest of Taelin. And no matter what Naomi Mastairs seems to think, that is exactly what you are."

"Thank you, my lady," Martin bowed to Laeyra. "It has been my honor to serve Lord Taelin. I am glad he sees my service as good."

"He does," Laeyra smiled. "Now get on with it. These two should be married so you can all get on your way."

"One thing before we marry," Meryn squeaked. She walked over to Maren and fell to her knees before the matriarch. "I wish to apologize to you, grandmother. You told me seven years ago that I should marry Odway. I chose not to listen and run away instead."

"It is true that you should have listened," Maren smiled. "But the very young do not always do as they are told. This is also true. There is nothing to forgive, my wild child. You have learned something from this?"

"I have learned that I should listen to my elders," Meryn laughed. "Sometimes they even know what they're talking about."

"Hrmph," Maren grumbled. "Go marry your Odway."

The marriage ceremony was quick. Rather than perform a long and drawn out ceremony, Martin simply proclaimed the two married in the presence of the Lady Laeyra. Alana was happy that it was a quick ceremony,

When two people loved each other as Meryn and Odway obviously did, the long and drawn out ceremony wasn't really necessary.

"Before you leave, there is something I would give you, Blademaster Alana," Maren said. She hobbled over to the Blademaster and gave her an amulet. "This is a pass of the Council of Elders. If you are ever stopped by guardsmen of Barandale, you need simply show this and they will not detain you. It can only be given by a member of the High Council. I give it to you as a pledge to the Blademasters."

"Thank you, Lady Maren," Alana smiled. "May I never need to show it."

"I dare say with war coming, it may be needed," Maren sighed heavily. "Thank you for bringing my wild child home. Now go. You have miles to go before the snows fall."

"Well, Silvestra," Alana smiled at the silver haired woman. "I believe that's your cue. We can't leave until we have a dragon to fly away on."

The Age of Darkness

Chapter XIX
The Army Marches

Kera Ragden paced in her tent.

She knew she could not launch a full scale assault on the Southern Dales until the spring. Even undead would have trouble marching in the snow. But she hated the thought of not pursuing the Blademaster for months.

She had to lead a small attack right away.

"General Atreus," she bellowed.

The red eyed vampyre had been waiting at the side of the tent. She had summoned for him over an hour before, and he had patiently waited for her to make a decision as to what she was going to do.

"Yes, Lady Nightstalker?"

"Is there a priest of Thraal of sufficient learning to be able to generate a portal in camp?"

"Yes, Lady Nightstalker," the vampyre nodded. "I can have one summoned to your tent immediately."

"Very good."

The Nightstalker resumed her pacing. She had the beginning of an idea in her head. She just needed to work it the rest of the way through, but she had the beginnings of a plan.

By the time the vampyre had been able to find the priest, she had finalized the plan.

"Here's what we're going to be doing," she explained to the general. "I need to have you assemble a small force, say 250 soldiers. Make sure there are a couple of mages in the mix. I want to lead them on a raid in the Elven Woods."

"You're going to attack the Temple of the Blades," the vampyre guessed.

"Yes," the Nightstalker nodded. "The Blademaster needs to be eliminated if we are to succeed in our war efforts. Prophecy says that the only chance the Southern Dales have is if she leads the side of light. If she is eliminated before the war starts, she cannot lead them."

"Logical," the vampyre agreed. "I will arrange for a strong force for you."

"Will you be able to keep the portal open long enough to send that large a force through?" she asked the priest that had been summoned.

"I have never done so before, but I should be able to, yes."

"Good," she grinned. "Let me know when you have the troops selected and gathered, General."

While she waited for the troops to be gathered together, Kera went over her plan on the map in her tent. She knew that they could not portal into the clearing with the Temple of the Blades directly. And while she did not know exactly where in the Elven Forest it was, she knew that it was generally in the center of the forest.

She knew that, if they portalled into a clearing on the opposite side of the Temple of the Blades from the city of the Forestwalker Elves, they should be able to avoid the Elves from stopping their progress to the Temple of the Blades.

It would be better if they could avoid the Forestwalker Elves.

She looked over the map of the Elven Woods to try to find a suitable clearing. She found a clearing that she thought would work. It was a good four day journey from that clearing to the Temple of the Blades.

It would not be an easy four days either. There were no trails in that part of the forest. That was good. The Blademaster would not expect an attack

The element of surprise would serve her attacking force well.

Now that she had a plan, Kera lay down on her cot and dozed until it was time to get going. She did not really fall asleep, as she did not want to waste any time when the troops were ready. Now that she knew what she was going to do, she was itching to get going. It was that anticipation of combat that she hungered for.

Even though she knew she was still days away from crashing her blade against the Blademaster's.

It did not take long for General Atreus to gather the troops that would be going together. He let her know that they were outside awaiting her orders.

She yawned and stretched before getting up. As soon as she left her tent, she saw the troops spread out in columns in front of her tent. She smiled in appreciation. While it was not the most fearsome squadron of troops she had ever seen, she knew that it would be more than enough to handle the Blademaster's companions while she killed the Blademaster herself.

She explained the plan to the troops and then told the priest to make ready to initiate the portal.

Kera Rayden was the first one through the portal.

The portal let her out in the middle of a clearing in what appeared to be the Elven Woods. If it was the clearing that she had instructed the priest to send her and her troops to, the Temple of the Blades was a slow four day march to the south.

She moved away from the portal so that she would not block the others when they came through. As they came through the portal, she organized them into their groups and got them ready to move out.

It took twenty minutes for all of her soldiers to come through the portal. She was impressed that the priest was able to hold the portal open for the entire time. She would make sure he was noticed by the High Priest the next time she was in Tornith.

When the troops were all through the portal, she began the slow march to the Temple of the Blades.

The going was as tough as she had expected, as there was even less of a path than she had expected. Her troops had to hack their way through the woods. It made her happy that they had to expend so much effort even though it meant that it might take longer to get to the Temple of the Blades.

There was no way that the Blademaster would be expecting this attack.

All she could do was to keep her troops going hard over the next few days until they were near the clearing for the Temple of the Blades. Once they were overlooking the clearing, they would wait until the Blademaster arrived.

And then the Blademaster would die.

PART IV
The Age of
Darkness

Chapter XX
The Elven Woods

ith three extra riders on her back, Silvestra needed to rest more on the journey from Barandale to the Elven Woods. The journey would have taken two days, much like the trip from Arvendale to Barandale had, but with the extra rest needed, it took a third.

Alana did not begrudge her the extra day. Soon enough, Silvestra would get all the rest she needed, but she had done a great deal since they had left Willowdale and Alana knew that the dragon had just about reached the end of her energy reserves.

The first night was uneventful, and they got underway early on the morning of the second day. They flew steadily through the day until the dragon set down on a plain between Arvendale and the Elven Woods. Alana figured that it would take only a couple hours from where they were to get to the Elven Woods in the morning.

As the companions started to set up camp, Alana watched as Colwyn scouted out the perimeter. If Alana's mental map of the Southern Dales was correct, they were still in the Arvendale Territory. She thought they'd be safe where they were, but she also knew that Colwyn would take no chances with three Blademasters in one place.

Especially when she was one of the three.

By the time Colwyn returned from scouting the area, Alana had gotten a stew started for the companions' dinner. With the extra mouths to feed, Alana had to put more into the stew pot. She frowned at how low the companions were on supplies. But it did not matter. They would be back in Ravendale in just a few days and she was sure that they had enough supplies so as to not worry too much.

Besides. There was still game out there. Colwyn would always catch something if they needed to stretch their supplies. That was just one more benefit to having a ranger for a Protector.

She stirred the pot, stealing quick glances at Colwyn. Every time she glanced over at him, she had to fight the urge to smile. The fact that they had gotten through the visit to his family's home and ended up having their marriage recognized by Lord Dargan amazed her.

She knew it amazed Colwyn too.

When the stew was ready, she dished out a healthy bowlful to each of her companions. There was still a good amount of stew in the pot, and she knew the halflings, at least, would all want seconds. It amazed her that people so small could all have such appetites.

She and Colwyn took their bowls to their bedroll on one side of the fire. They ate in silence, just enjoying each other's company. Alana knew that with all that was going to happen, they needed to take advantage of quiet moments like this when they happened. She knew they would be few and far between once the war started.

Still, she knew her husband well enough to know that something was truly bothering him.

If she had to guess, she would say it had something to do with the Elven Woods. She knew what had happened the last time that he went there, but she doubted that the

Queen would dare to do anything like that in front of her. The Queen had pledged her life to the Blademaster, and Alana knew that she meant every word of that pledge.

"Something bothers you, Colwyn," she said as she put her bowl down. "Talk to me."

"I know why you feel we need to go through the Elven Woods and pay our respects to the Forestwalker Elves, Alana," Colwyn's soft voice replied. "But I do not wish to go into the Elven Woods this time. I would just as soon have Silvestra fly straight to the Temple of the Blades."

"She really hurt you the last time," Alana snuggled close to him.

"She almost cost us everything, Alana," he put his arm around her. "She almost cost the Southern Dales everything. She tried so hard to entice me away from you. And she was using magic to do it."

"But you did not turn away from me, my love," Alana reminded Colwyn.

"There is only so much comfort I can take from that, Alana," he sighed. "I will always have to live with the fact that I came close to losing everything. And I can never forgive her for that."

"You need to, my love," she nuzzled her head against his chest. "There is great power in forgiveness. Don't forget the Second Law of the Blades. True love breeds true forgiveness. Nothing is more powerful than the ability to forgive the one you love. And nothing brings you closer than the forgiveness of your own misdeeds. You once loved Queen Mirian. For both your sakes, you need to find a way to forgive her."

"You make it sound so easy, Alana," he said. He gently kissed the top of her head. "I wish it were as simple as that."

"Oh, it's not simple at all," she looked up at him. "But it is the right thing to do and you will feel so much better when you do."

"I will think on it," Colwyn promised her.

It was not exactly what she had wanted to hear, but Alana would take it. She knew that he needed to give the Forestwalker Elf Queen his forgiveness for what she had done. She also knew that Colwyn was stubborn and would not budge from his stance on something until he was good and ready to.

It was part of why she loved him.

"Come, my love," she smiled up at him. "We have a long day ahead of us tomorrow. We should get some sleep."

"I have mid watch tonight, so that is probably a good idea," Colwyn nodded.

Colwyn slipped out of the bedroll, being careful not to wake Alana. He checked to make sure she was still asleep before he slipped away from the bedroll.

Carefully, Colwyn crept out of the camp to where Cayden was standing watch. Cayden had taken the first watch and Colwyn was his replacement. They all hated the mid watch, because it meant the person on mid watch had to deal with a split sleeping schedule. Colwyn ended up taking it more nights than not, though. As he had not stood the mid watch for several days, he took it before anyone else could offer.

He was glad to have mid watch this night. Alana had given him much to think about when she told him that he needed to forgive Mirian Kovalani. It would not be an easy thing, but he needed to give it a great deal of thought. He expected that it would be a quiet night in this part of the Arvendale territory, so he figured he would get a good amount of time to think.

He would need it.

He was also grateful that by relieving Cayden, he would have an opportunity to talk to the young former palace guard before they entered the Elven Woods. What he had to say to Cayden was best not said so close to the Temple of the Blades.

Although he had promised himself that he wouldn't, Colwyn was about to interfere in Cayden's Test of the Blades.

It would not be a large interference. It was no more help than had been given Colwyn. But Colwyn could not deny his sister this, so he would give Cayden what little help he could. He told himself that it was OK to give the young man what help he was going to give because it was the help he had been given on his own Test of the Blades.

In this, he could not deny his sister.

He found Cayden standing on a rock overlooking the camp and the trail nearby. It was a good location to keep watch from, and Colwyn was pleased that Cayden had chosen such a spot. He was hidden from the trail, but he could easily see and intercept anyone coming up on the camp long before they could even catch sight of the sleeping companions.

He tapped Cayden on the shoulder as he came up on the rock. Cayden turned slightly and nodded when he saw it was Colwyn.

"It is time to switch off, then?" the younger man said.

"I would speak with you a moment before you go back to camp," Colwyn nodded.

"Is there something I can do for you, Colwyn?" Cayden asked.

"No," Colwyn shook his head. He looked off down the trail for several long seconds before turning back to Cayden. "There is something I can do for you."

"Oh?" the younger man said, surprise flowing across his face. "And what is that?"

"What I am about to tell you, no one must ever know that I told you, for it is in direct violation of the Laws of the Blades," Colwyn said in a soft voice. "I give you the aid I am about to give you only because you love my sister. You are a good man, Cayden. I would not want Bella to lose you."

"But Bella told me you could give me no aid or else it would invalidate the Test," Cayden frowned.

"Then my own Test needs to be invalidated," Colwyn shrugged. "The aid I am about to give you was aid that was given me. It is very small aid, to be sure, but it can, and will, save you in the Test."

"If you are sure, Colwyn, I will take any help you can give me," Cayden nodded.

"Are you familiar with ioun stones?" Colwyn asked.

"I have heard of them, but I have never seen one," Cayden nodded. "Why do you ask?"

"I am going to lend you two," Colwyn said. "I expect their return when we get back to Ravendale. And I will be greatly displeased if you die or lose either stone."

"I understand. What do they do?"

Colwyn reached into a pouch and pulled out two stones. He looked carefully at the two stones before handing one to Cayden.

"This is a finder stone," Colwyn explained. He handed the stone to Cayden. "When you get to the start of the Test, you take it in your hand and command it to 'find Bella Starseeker'. And then you release it. It will float around your head and indicate which direction you need to go as you go through the dungeon."

"That sounds simple enough," Cayden nodded. He put the stone in a pouch on his belt. "And the other?"

"This is a trap finder stone," Colwyn said as he handed the other stone over. "When you get to the start of the Test, take it in your hand and command it to 'find traps'. Like the finder stone, it will float around your head. When you are about to walk into a trap, and there is at least one in the Test, it will glow red."

"I understand," he said as he put the stone in the same pouch as the finder stone. "Thank you, Colwyn. I am sure that these will come in handy."

"There's one more thing," Colwyn said.

"What?"

"Search everything you kill," Colwyn suggested. "I can't tell you what you need to find, as I am sure that it will be different from my Test, but I suspect that one of the corpses will hold the key to getting out of the trap when you spring it."

"Why are you helping me like this when it has been expressly forbidden for you to do so?" Cayden asked. He looked uncertain that he should be accepting the help.

"Because," Colwyn smiled. "You make my sister happy. And because I am a hopeless romantic. As I told you when I told you what you were in for, if you chose to go with us, chances for true love do not come often. If I can tip the odds and make sure that this chance succeeds, I doubt that Lord Taelin will mind too much."

"Thank you, Colwyn," Cayden bowed slightly. "It means a great deal that you feel that way."

"Just know one thing," Colwyn clapped him on the shoulder. "If you should break her heart, just know that I will break whatever is left of you after Bella gets a hold of you into little tiny pieces."

"No offense meant, Colwyn," Cayden grimaced. "But if I were to break her heart, I would be far more afraid of Bella than you."

"As you should be," Colwyn smiled. "My little sister has always been able to take care of herself, even before being imbued with the power of a Blademaster. Now that she has that power, I doubt you would survive breaking her heart."

"I swore an oath to the ruling family of the Arvendale Territory, Colwyn," the younger man said softly. "That I am no longer a palace guard in Arvendale changes nothing. You need not worry about my breaking my vows to your sister."

"I know. I just needed to hear it directly from you," Colwyn's smile grew broader. "Were I to think that there was any actual risk of you breaking your vows to Bella, you would not be here now." He clapped the younger man on the shoulder. "Now go. Warm up my sister. It's a cold night."

Cayden tossed a smile at Colwyn and headed back to camp. Colwyn just chuckled as he took his spot for watch and drew his sword so he would be ready if anything came towards the camp.

Nothing bothered the camp during the night, though. As the light of dawn broke over the camp, Colwyn was already up making breakfast for the party. He had not slept well. He would not call himself afraid of facing the Queen of the Forestwalker Elves, but he was apprehensive about it.

He knew that Alana was right. He had to find a way to forgive Queen Mirian. It was important for both of them. But he was not sure he could. He had given Alana's words a great deal of thought while he had been on watch in the middle of the night. The Law of the Blades was clear on what he had to do.

Unfortunately, such a thing was not always as easy as it sounded like it should be.

He had wrestled with the need to give forgiveness for his entire watch, but he had come no closer to being able to grant the Elven woman forgiveness than he had when he started. Colwyn knew that Alana would be disappointed, but there was time yet. He doubted that the Elves would let them go straight to the Temple of the Blades since they were visiting the Elves' city. That was just another reason he had wanted to go straight to the Temple of the Blades. He knew that the Elves would want the new Blademasters to stay in the city overnight.

He looked up when he saw Alana coming over to the fire. She brought a smile to his face as she always did. They were the first two up, but he could see movement in some of the other bedrolls. The smell of breakfast cooking was waking their companions, as he expected it would.

"Morning, Colwyn," his Blademaster said as she rubbed her hands by the fire. "How did you sleep?"

"Not well," he admitted with a shrug. "I don't want to go to the Elven Woods, but you are set on this course, so we'll go."

"If it were just us, I would have no problem just dropping into the clearing with the Temple, Colwyn," Alana smiled a sympathetic smile. "But with two new Blademasters in tow, it is only fair that we stop and talk to the Elves so that they know the new Blademasters. That way if they need to come in through the Elven Woods, they don't run into any trouble with the Elves."

"I understand why you want to go this way," Colwyn shrugged. "And I don't disagree that it's a good idea. I just don't want to see Queen Mirian. It is going to be uncomfortable."

"Did you give any thought to what I told you?"

"I thought of nothing else while I was on watch," Colwyn nodded. He poked the sausages on the fire to check how they were doing. Satisfied with their progress, he set to stirring the pot of beans. "It kept me awake a lot of the night too. I just don't know how I can forgive her. I know I need to."

"This is something I can't help you with, Col," Alana sighed. She pulled her knees up to her chest. "I am sure you will figure it out though."

Colwyn said nothing as he stirred the beans. Really, there was nothing for him to say. Alana was right. This was something only he could figure out. And he knew he would get it figured out in time. He just wasn't sure that he would have it figured out by the time he saw Mirian Kovalani again.

As he served up the beans onto plates for the companions, the rest of their party started to come out from their bedrolls. The smell of the cooking sausages lured them. Colwyn smiled to himself as he watched the halflings eagerly eye the cooking sausages. He plopped sausages on top of the beans on each plate and handed out the food.

He and Alana sat on one side of the fire, Alana snuggled up to his side. The companions ate in silence, warming themselves on the food that Colwyn had made and from the fire that still burnt hot.

It did not take long for the companions to finish their breakfasts. When they were done, the companions wasted no time in packing up their gear. Alana and Colwyn had stressed the need for urgency in getting everything done in time for them to be safely back in Ravendale by the time the snow started falling, and no one wanted to be the cause of their not making that deadline.

The flight from where they camped to the edge of the Elven Woods took three hours. It was not an eventful flight, and Colwyn tried to think about what he would say to Queen Mirian when he saw her. But he could not think clearly with the wind whipping in his face.

When they landed, Silvestra transformed back into her human form to make it easier to traverse the forest.

And then they waited.

It was the waiting that bothered him. He knew that they would be brought to the Elven city soon, but Colwyn hated waiting for Otan to show up to guide the party. Colwyn could have guided his companions to the city, but it would have been considered rude for him to bring others uninvited.

Especially when he was not sure he was welcome in the city himself.

And so he waited even though he did not want to. Colwyn stood at the front of the companions, with Alana by his side, so that Otan would see them first. While he wasn't looking forward to seeing his former teacher, he knew that it would be best if he were the one to greet Otan.

It was a full hour that the companions stood at the edge of the Elven Woods before Otan and his rangers came to see who was waiting for them. The sight of Colwyn at the front of the companions brought a wide smile to Otan's face. Despite himself, Colwyn felt himself smiling in return.

"Is maith a fheiceann tú arís, mo dheartháir," Otan said to Colwyn. "I did not think to see you again after your last visit."

"Alana felt that since we are bringing new Blademasters to the Temple of the Blades, it would be best to go through the Elven city so that the Elves could know them," Colwyn said. "Were it up to me, we would have flown straight to the Temple of the Blades."

"I understand," Otan nodded. "The Queen regrets how much you were hurt by her the last time you were here. She bade me look for you in the hopes that I could convey her wish to see you to apologize. I did not dare to think I would get to deliver the message. And yet, here you are."

"And yet, here I am," Colwyn nodded. "I cannot say that I can promise to forgive her, but I will hear the Queen's words. Lead on to the city, mo dheartháir."

Otan nodded once and then turned back into the woods. Colwyn led the companions after him. The elf set a brisk pace and they made good time. But it was well after midday by the time the city came into view.

Colwyn's apprehension grew as he saw the city in the trees. He felt Alana's hand give his a squeeze and he smiled over at her. But even though she was there by his side, this was one fight she could not help him with.

Otan led the companions to the Queen's house in the city. Once there, he turned to face them.

"The Blademasters and their Protectors may enter. I will bring the rest of you to where you may rest," the elf said.

Colwyn watched as Otan led their companions away. Then he turned to Alana with a raised eyebrow. When she nodded that she was ready, Colwyn knocked.

"You and your companions may enter, Colwyn," Mirian called from inside.

Although he was somewhat unnerved that she knew who it was, he did not let it show as he opened the door and led the way inside. When the others were inside, he closed the door behind them and turned to face the queen.

"Well met," she said as she looked over the two new Blademasters. "As with Blademaster Alana, you two will have free pass through the Elven Woods to the Temple of the Blades. You need not come through the elven city if you wish not to."

"Thank you, Your Majesty," Bella bowed slightly.

Talby said nothing, but bowed her head in respect.

"And you, Lord Colwyn," the queen smiled. "It does my heart good to see you once more. I hope that you and I will have a chance to speak while you are here. You shall all be my guests this evening. I know you want to get to the Temple of the Blades and back to Ravendale before the snow starts, but it will be dark before you get to the Temple if you leave now and it is best for you to not travel in darkness in these woods."

"We, of course, accept your hospitality," Colwyn said. He said nothing about their speaking, however. It was a distinction not lost on the queen.

"I will have Otan show you to where you will stay," the queen nodded once. "We will speak again before you leave. Good night, my friends."

Colwyn knew that he was not off the hook and that he would have to speak to the queen at some point that evening, but he was happy for the respite.

As he led the others out of the house, he began to mentally prepare himself for the battle of wits that he knew would be coming.

The Age of Darkness

Chapter XXI
A Quiet Interlude

olwyn sat in the branches of a tree. He had purposefully chosen one that he had never sat in with Mirian, but he doubted that it would matter. If the queen chose to look for him, she would. Colwyn was resigned to the fact that the queen would probably seek him out. He knew that he would have no choice but to talk to the queen.

He just did not know what he would say to her. When he had been in the forest last, he had told Otan that he forgave Mirian. In his heart, though, he was not sure he had. It troubled him that he might have lied to his friend. There was little he could do about it for the moment, though.

All he could do is go forward and work out how to forgive Mirian for real.

He sighed as he thought about the situation. The more he thought about it, the more he realized that Alana was right. The Second Law of the Blades would have to serve him here. He thought about that for a moment. *True love breeds true forgiveness. Nothing is more powerful than the ability to forgive the one you love. And nothing brings you closer than the forgiveness of your own misdeeds.* He knew the power of the Second Law of the Blades from Alana forgiving him for almost betraying her.

He knew that Mirian needed to feel that power too.

"Thinking deep thoughts, my love?" Alana said as she sat next to him.

He had been so lost in thought that he had not heard her come up behind him. It was a lapse that he could have ill afforded were they anywhere other than the city in the trees. Such a lapse could cost him his life. Or worse, it could cost Alana hers.

"Thinking about forgiveness," Colwyn said in a soft voice. "And of the power of the Second Law of the Blades."

"An important law, that one," Alana smiled.

"So it is," Colwyn nodded. He put his arm around her. "Let me ask you something, Alana. How could you forgive me for almost betraying you like I did?"

"How could I love you like I do and not?" Alana looked up at him. "Besides, you didn't actually betray me, so there really was nothing to forgive. I think you have the harder road to granting forgiveness, though."

"What do you mean?"

"You almost betrayed me," Alana snuggled close to him. "Mirian actually betrayed you."

"It's not easy doing the right thing," Colwyn sighed.

"No, it is not," Alana agreed.

"Hard to be the Protector to a Blademaster."

"Hard to be a Blademaster," Alana smiled at him. "But we have each other, and that makes it a little easier."

"There is that," Colwyn chuckled and squeezed her.

They sat like that for a time, just listening to the sounds of the forest. There was something weighing on Colwyn's heart other than forgiving Mirian, though, and he knew he had to be honest with Alana about it.

"Alana, I think there is something else I might need your forgiveness for," he said after a time.

"What is that?"

"I did something I probably should not have done," he sighed. "I interfered in the natural course of the Test of the Blades."

"You gave Cayden some help, didn't you?"

"I did," Colwyn nodded. "To be fair, I gave him no help that I did not, myself, receive."

"What did you do?"

"I lent Cayden my ioun stones," Colwyn admitted.

"Well, considering you had those to help you through your test, I don't really think that's going to be an issue," Alana laid her head back down against his chest.

"And I told him about the trap."

Alana looked up at him. "You did what, now?"

"I told him that there was a trap that if he was caught in and could not escape, he would fail the Test of the Blades," Colwyn said. "That much, Solara told me, so that's not an issue. But I told him to search everything he kills, and that the key to that trap would be on one of their bodies."

"That may have crossed the line, Colwyn," Alana sighed. "It might invalidate the test for Cayden."

"Then my own test needs to be invalidated."

"What do you mean?"

"When I was in the Test of the Blades, I was told to search the pockets of something I killed on my way to you," Colwyn explained. "When I did, I found a gemstone that was the key to the trap I sprung later."

"So you did not give Cayden any aid you did not receive in your test?"

"I did not, no," Colwyn nodded."

"Then there is nothing to worry about," Alana smiled up at him. "I know you did it out of love for your sister."

"Indeed."

"You're a good brother, Colwyn," Alana's smile grew. "And a good husband."

Colwyn did not respond. He pulled Alana tighter against his side and enjoyed the peaceful closeness. With all the danger and travelling, the two of them got into, they did not always get to enjoy quiet time such as this.

Colwyn promised himself that he would always take the opportunity to enjoy such times as he could. He also told himself that he should give the same advice to his sister and Cayden. Once his sister was installed as a Blademaster, it would be important for them to take the time to love each other and to be happy with each other.

Colwyn smiled to himself as he thought about the wisdom of Taelin to use the love between a Blademaster and her Protector to power the abilities of a Blademaster. The more time he spent as the Protector to Alana, the more he realized just how wise a decision it was to do so.

Although he was enjoying the time he was spending with Alana, he was keeping his senses open. Even though the city in the trees was a safe place for them, he had already let down his guard once. The fact that it was Alana that had surprised him did not make it any better that he had had a lapse in attention.

With his senses attuned to the trees around him, he heard the leaves nearby rustle as someone came near. The human, having been trained by the elves, was in his element in the trees, and was not easy to surprise when he was paying attention.

Colwyn was not surprised when he realized that he sound he heard was the queen softly making her way towards where he and Alana were sitting. The queen, although an elf, did not have the training of one of Otan's rangers. She was not able to walk among the trees in complete silence like the rangers could.

Colwyn turned at her approach. He nodded once in respect towards her. Alana turned to see what he was looking at.

"I never heard your approach, Your Majesty," Alana said in surprise when she saw the queen.

"Colwyn did," Mirian smiled. "He was well trained by my brother."

"Otan was a very patient teacher," Colwyn chuckled.

"Blademaster Alana, I would ask to speak to your Protector alone," the elven queen said softly.

"I will let you two talk," Alana nodded. She stood so she could make her way back to where she and Colwyn were staying. "But know this. Queen or no, if you hurt him again, you will answer to me. I may have forgiven you for trying to tempt him away from me, but I will not allow you to cause him any more pain."

"You have my word that I will not cause Colwyn any further pain," Mirian bowed her head slightly towards Alana. "I know that I have caused him far more pain than anyone else could have the last time he and I spoke."

Alana leaned down and gave Colwyn a deep kiss. She lingered longer than she might have otherwise. The kiss surprised Colwyn, but he was not upset by it. He returned the kiss with passion, not caring that the queen was watching. When they parted, Colwyn had to catch his breath. Alana just smiled at him, then turned to look at the queen, just to make sure she got the message.

"I'll be waiting for you when you're done talking to her," Alana smiled. "Don't keep me waiting too long."

"I won't," Colwyn returned the smile.

He watched the woman he loved walk away. He knew that she trusted him not to do anything with the queen. He also knew that she had nothing to worry about. Colwyn had eyes for no one else. As he had told Cayden, true love was something to embrace when it came along.

"She really did not have to put on such a display for my benefit," the queen said softly. "I am no threat to the bond of a Blademaster and her Protector."

"Oh, she is well aware of that, Mirian," Colwyn laughed. "She just wanted to make sure you were. I trust that her point was well made?"

"Well made but completely unnecessary," Mirian shook her head. "You know that the only reason I tempted you was to ensure your bond to Alana was total. Were she not the one spoken of in prophecy, it would not have been necessary."

"It was not necessary even then," Colwyn grumbled. "I am tired of having to prove my love for Alana. The Test of the Blades was bad enough."

"Alana is special," Mirian reminded him.

"Of that, no one needs to remind me," Colwyn returned. "From the first day I saw her, I have been in love with Alana Steeldrake. A deeper love than I could have ever shared with you, Mirian. It was not for you to try to break that love."

"It was necessary," Mirian repeated.

"It was necessary to cause me pain? It was necessary to risk the safety of the Southern Dales?" Colwyn roared in anger. He had been keeping his temper in check, but the queen's insistence that tempting him was necessary was enough to bring it out. "Why, Mirian? Why was it necessary to risk everything? Tell me why you did it."

"Because if Alana Steeldrake does not lead the forces of the light, all will be lost," Mirian shot back. "And she can only do so with a fully committed Protector by her side. Solara Moonfire knew of our previous relationship and believed that I was the only one who could tempt you away from her."

"You should have known me better, Mirian," Colwyn turned away. "You should have trusted me."

"Neither Solara nor I could leave it to chance, Col," Mirian sighed. "Too much rests on your wife's shoulders to leave anything to chance."

"And so you chose to betray me?"

"We had no choice."

"So you keep saying, Mirian," Colwyn's voice grew soft. "But there is always a choice. You chose to violate my trust. You made a conscious choice to hurt me. Worse, you made a conscious choice to hurt the woman I love. There is no excuse for making such a choice."

"Is there any way you can forgive me for what I did, Colwyn?" the queen asked, her voice weak in the face of his anger. It was the only time Colwyn could remember Mirian showing any kind of weakness.

"I forgive you, Mirian," Colwyn nodded. "But neither Alana nor I can forget what you have done. You swore to give your life to the service of the Blademasters. Betray the Blademaster Corps in any other way, and that debt shall come due. I take no pleasure in saying this, but if we are to lead the forces of the light, we need to know we can depend upon those that have sworn to support us."

"I understand," the queen said. Her voice shook as she fought tears. "It is as you say. The defense of the Southern Dales must needs take precedence over anything. I will never betray the Blademasters again. Nor their Protectors. You have my word on that. On my life."

"Good," Colwyn nodded once. "I am sorry that this is the way it must be, Mirian. As you said yourself, much rides on Alana's shoulders. We know about the army that is coming. We can only stand against it as one."

"I know."

"I will tell Otan what I can about what is coming in the morning when we leave," Colwyn said. "He will need to prepare your people to defend themselves and the Temple of the Blades."

"It will be done," Mirian nodded. "I will leave you now. Go be with your Blademaster, and convey my apologies to her for what I did to her."

Colwyn watched the queen leave. While he had forgiven her, he knew that there was still bad blood between the two of them. He sighed, knowing that the time would come when he would have to deal with it.

The Age of Darkness

Chapter XXII
The High Priestess Speaks

he queen did not come see them off the next morning. It was just as well as far as Colwyn was concerned. He had said all that needed to be said. And he had meant it when he told Mirian that, while he would forgive her for what she had done, he would never forget what had happened.

He knew that he had hurt her by saying that. But Colwyn had never been one to lie in order to spare someone's feelings.

And so when Otan showed up to guide the companions out of the city, Colwyn was not surprised. He was wise enough to not let his lack of surprise show, though. It would have been viewed as an insult to the queen. Colwyn could not afford to alienate the Forestwalker Elves with the Temple of the Blades protected in their woods.

Otan was silent as he led the companions out of the city in the trees. Colwyn watched the ranger for some clues as to how he felt, but Otan had carefully guarded his features.

"I thought that Queen Mirian would have seen us off, Otan," Colwyn said softly when the elven ranger had led them out of the city.

"My sister is not feeling well this morning, Colwyn," Otan sighed. "I fear she is heart broken."

"I never meant to hurt her," Colwyn bowed his head slightly.

"I know, mo dheartháir," Otan smiled sadly at Colwyn. "It would have gone far worse if you had not been honest with her. The queen is strong. She will rebound in time."

"Otan, time is something your people may not have," Colwyn grimaced. "War is coming. The elves need to be ready."

"I know," Otan smiled.

"You... know?"

"When you came to us, we knew the time of the Great War of Souls was almost upon us," Otan nodded. "We have been preparing ever since."

"The army of darkness has assembled, Otan," Colwyn said. "They will launch their war with the spring thaw, we believe."

"So, too, do our mages believe, mo dheartháir," Otan nodded again. "Fear not for us. The Forestwalker Elves will be ready."

"Good," Colwyn nodded. "I don't know what the army of undead is planning, but I suspect the Temple of the Blades will be an important target. It is good to know the guardians of these woods are prepared to defend it."

"We are," Otan nodded. "As we promised Lord Taelin we would be centuries ago."

"Tell Mirian that, when this war is over, I will return to make my peace with her," Colwyn said softly.

Otan pulled Colwyn into an embrace. The human returned the embrace. Despite what the Queen of the Forestwalker Elves had done to him, Colwyn could not bring himself to let his anger with her cloud the way he felt about Otan.

"Go dtí tú filleadh ar an gcathair sna crainn, mo dheartháir," Otan whispered into Colwyn's ear. "Féadfaidh an ádh ar Laeyra agus an eagna Taelin leanann tú."

"Until next we meet, Otan," Colwyn nodded as he pulled away. "May the luck of Laeyra and the wisdom of Taelin guide you and your rangers."

Otan smiled as he backed away into the trees.

Colwyn turned towards the path leading to the Temple of the Blades and started to lead the companions down the path.

When they saw the first flash of marble through the trees, Colwyn cut off the path towards the clearing with the Temple of the Blades. It was slow going, as he had to cut through the dense foliage with his sword. As the companions passed through where Colwyn cut, the forest flowed back together, healing itself from each cut Colwyn made.

Colwyn and Alana had been surprised the first time they had seen the forest heal itself behind them. But they knew now that it was a protection for the Temple of the Blades. Colwyn was amused by the look of shock on his sister's face when she saw the way the forest closed in behind them.

"I have never seen trees that heal so fast," Bella remarked.

"And you'll never see them anywhere else, either," Colwyn smiled. "It's part of the protection around the Temple of the Blades. While it's not foolproof, it makes it harder to get to the temple if there's no path to follow."

"I can understand why that might be good protection," Bella nodded. "I'm not sure I could find this temple without you here to guide me."

"You will find that will not be the case for long, my sister," Colwyn laughed.

It took several hours to cut through to the clearing where the Temple of the Blades was. It was not something Colwyn could rush, as the foliage was thick. He had to be careful where he cut and the companions could only move forward when he had cleared the way. It seemed like it took longer to get through to the clearing this time than it had before.

When he burst through into the clearing, Colwyn dropped his sword and bent forward, putting his hands on his knees. The effort had exhausted him. He knew that there was much to do before he could get some rest though, so he took the moment to catch his breath.

Standing in the middle of the clearing before them was the largest and most ornate temple they'd ever seen. The temple was made of black and white polished marble. High marble parapets gave the temple a palatial feel. Banners from the parapets flapped in the breeze. The banners were all the same, a dark blue background with a stylized gold shield in the foreground. The shield was crossed over at the center by two silver long swords.

As they fanned out around the temple, they saw the same stylized shield and swords inlaid into the walls. These inlays were made of silver and gold. The mottling in the marble seemed to be in constant motion, dancing in a pattern, although the companions could draw no meaning from the dancing.

Bella put her hand on the marble and was surprised to feel that it was warm to the touch, almost as if the marble had the blood of life running through it.

"It feels like the temple itself is alive," Bella said in wonder.

"It does feel that way," Colwyn nodded as he placed his own hand next to hers. "Alana and I both made that observation the first time we were here."

"It is so weird to feel that in a building, though," Bella looked over at her brother.

"The Temple of the Blades is a very different place than any other," Colwyn smiled. "It is a place of pure magic and wonder. And it is now your second home as much as it is Alana's and mine."

"Will I ever get used to this?"

"Maybe one day," Colwyn's smile grew broader. "I'll let you know if I ever do."

Bella smiled at her brother. When he started back towards the front of the Temple of the Blades, she followed him. At the front of the Temple of the Blades, Alana and Colwyn went up the twelve steps to the great twinned oaken doors. When they got to the top of the stairs, they turned to face Bella. Once the halfling Blademaster had joined them, Alana spoke to them.

"You are about to enter the Temple of the Blades," she began. "This is a sacred place dedicated to Lord Taelin and Lady Laeyra. No matter which deities you revered prior to today, once you take the vows of a Blademaster, you are bound in service to them. As you are, so, too, your Protectors are also bound in that service. My own husband gave up his service to the lord of nature, Raeven, to stand by my side as my Protector. This is not something that is lightly asked of you, and this will be your last chance to turn back."

Bella and Talby looked at each other and turned back to face Alana. The looks on their faces gave the Blademaster their answer as well as any words could have.

"Very well," Alana nodded to them. "There are words you must hear before you enter. They are these words engraved by the door. As Colwyn is fluent in the elven language, I will have him translate them for you."

Colwyn smiled over at Alana. He walked over to the gold lettering to the left of the great doors.

"These words were left here for us when the Temple of the Blades was built," he said. "They were left here for all of the Blademasters and their Protectors so that they would understand just what we are getting into by accepting the power and responsibilities of the Blademaster Corps." He turned to the words and read them over before turning back to face Bella and Talby. "Ní mór di a rachaidh isteach anseo chun aghaidh a thabhairt ar ndán di dul isteach le croí glan. Ní mór sí ag troid i gcomhréir leis an idéalacha Taelin agus Laeyra. Ní mór di cloí le Dlí na lanna má ghlacann sí ndán di. Teip ciallaíonn bás."

"What does it mean, Colwyn?" Bella asked.

"It means this. She who enters here to face her destiny must enter with a pure heart. She must fight according to the precepts of Taelin and Laeyra. She must abide by the

Law of the Blades if she accepts her destiny. Failure brings death."

"You said if," Talby said softly. "You mean nothing is determined?"

"You can walk away now if you choose, Talby," Alana said. "No shame will come upon you if you do. But once you accept the mantle of the Blademaster, there is no going back. You must accept all that goes with that decision."

"I understand," the halfling Blademater nodded. "If the Great War of Souls is, indeed, coming, then I cannot turn my back on my duty. Lead on so that we can do what must be done."

"Before we go in, Colwyn," Bella said, stopping Alana just as she was starting to turn. "You told us the words to the left of the door. What about the words written to the right?"

Colwyn smiled at his sister. "The words written there are meant to give hope and comfort whilst the words to the left inform us of our duty. The words say the following. Sí nach bhfuil grá nach bhfuil a fhios Taelin chun é Taelin ghrá." His face radiated with joy and amusement as he watched his sister trying to puzzle through the translation. "It means, she who does not love does not know Taelin for Taelin is love."

"I can see why that might have been left here for comfort," Bella smiled. She looked over at Cayden. "Love is what brought me here, after all."

"You would be wise to remember that," Alana said softly.

"Why?"

"All will become clear when you meet Lady Solara," Alana chuckled. "Come, now. It is time for you four to accept your destiny."

Bella and Talby both nodded. Colwyn looked over at Alana and smiled. The Blademaster pushed open the door and led the companions inside the Temple of the Blades.

They entered a four foot square antechamber, the walls of which were made of the same black and white marble as the outside of the temple. Like the marble on the outside of the temple the mottling in the marble seemed to dance in a pattern. Colwyn had yet to determine the story that the patterns in the marble were trying to tell. The only other door in the room was made of plain oak. The golden shield crossed by silver swords they had seen outside was displayed prominently in the center of the door. As they came further into the antechamber, the oak door swung open of its own accord, inviting them inside.

"The marble is somewhat disconcerting, Colwyn," Bella said in a hushed voice.

"You will get used to it the longer you spend here," Colwyn nodded to her. "It is a part of life here."

"I hope you are right that I will get used to it," Bella whispered. "It's a little creepy."

Alana smiled in reassurance at her sister in law. She walked towards the oak door on the far side of the antechamber and it opened of its own accord, causing Talby to gasp.

"Come," Alana said.

She and Colwyn walked through the door, leaving the others to follow as they would.

The doorway led into what had to be the temple's great hall. Reluctantly and just as carefully, the others followed Alana and Colwyn into an immense square room, one hundred fifty feet to the side. The ceiling cleared forty feet over their heads. Scores of banners hung in thirty feet below the ceiling of the hall. Each banner had a design, some sort of crest, on it. There were two banners that had no design, and those banners hung directly over the altar. One banner was white, matching Bella's armor. The other was a deep red, a rusty color reminiscent of the sash Talby wore about her waist. Alana's hunter green banner hung between the two plain banners and slightly forward towards the front of the altar.

The altar itself was a slab of obsidian. Someone had taken the time to carve a bas relief of women fighting shadowy creatures on the front of the altar. On the top, two plain long swords flanked a plain broad sword. The points of the three weapons were touching, as if pointing at the wall behind the altar.

The High Priestess of the Blades, Solara Moonfire, was kneeling in front of the altar with her head bowed. She made no outward notice of the companions' arrival until after she finished her prayer. When she did, she stood and turned to face Alana and her companions.

"Welcome to the Temple of the Blades," Solara said, her soft voice echoed in the Great Hall. "I have been expecting you to return with other Blademasters for some time, Blademaster Alana."

"The search was long and there were other considerations I had to concern myself with during the search," Alana shrugged. "But I have brought two that the Bladestone has indicated are fellow children of the light."

"Then you have done well," Solara smiled. "As you can see by the banners, we were expecting you to bring two."

"I don't know if I should be surprised or not that you knew how many would be coming," Alana laughed.

"Blademaster Alana, it is tradition that, when there are multiple living Blademasters serving Lord Taelin at the same time, one must be chosen to lead them," Solara began. "As the first of this new line of Blademasters, it falls to you to become the Master Blademaster. You alone are named in prophecy to lead the forces of the light in the Great War of Souls. You were named by Lord Taelin himself as the Master Blademaster. You must lead the Blademasters into battle."

"I understand," Alana nodded. "I accept the responsibility. I fully expected that something like that would be the case."

"Very well," Solara nodded. "Please present the new Blademasters."

Alana turned to her companions and motioned Bella and Talby forward. She turned to face Solara with one of them on each side.

"High Priestess Solara Moonfire, I present to you Bella Starseeker, sister to my own Protector and Talby, halfling of the Swiftfoot clan," Alana announced. "The Bladestone, given to me by our Lord Taelin, has identified both of these women to be Blademasters. They have come here, of their own free will, to accept that destiny."

"Before you came to the Temple of the Blades, no halfling had ever entered these hallowed halls," Solara frowned. "And now you present one to me to become a Blademaster?"

"Lady Solara," Alana started. She was stopped by a small hand on her arm. When she looked down, she saw Talby shaking her head.

"Lady Alana, I appreciate what you would say in my defense," the halfling Blademaster said. "But this is my fight. How can I be a Blademaster if others fight my battles for me?" She turned to the High Priestess of the Blades. "I would have you hear me, Lady Solara."

"Very well," Solara nodded. "Speak your piece."

Talby took a deep breath and stepped forward. She looked over to Tovar for support. He nodded at her, smiling broadly.

"All you see when you look at me is a halfling," Talby began. "And I understand your hesitation. My people do have a reputation as thieves and troublemakers. I do not deny that it is a well earned reputation." Talby pointed to Alana. "This woman came to my people and told us of the war that is coming. No one had bothered to tell us we were in danger.

"Because of this woman, my people can prepare themselves as best they can for the danger that is coming.

"This woman told me of the Bladestone and of how it showed her that I was to become a Blademaster. But she did not force the decision on me. She let me choose my own destiny as everyone should be able to.

"Lady Alana told me of the war that was coming. She told me of the army of undead that would run unchecked over the Southern Dales. She told me all she could of what was coming.

"And then she asked me to accept the destiny she was offering.

"I have come here not for treasure or glory. I come because I believe that I can help fight this war. I believe that it is my duty to fight this war. It may not be very halfling of me, this is true. But it is my choice to be here.

Not Alana's, and not yours. I will fight on the side of light, whether it is as a Blademaster or not."

Talby stepped back to Alana's side. When she looked up at the human Blademaster, Alana was beaming proudly down at her. Alana's look of pride meant a great deal to the halfling.

"I have never heard a halfling speak of duty so eloquently before," Solara said, her voice subdued. "And I am shamed for thinking you unworthy, Talby Swiftfoot. You belong amongst the children of light. And you are welcome here."

"Thank you, Lady Solara."

"Bella Starseeker and Talby Swiftfoot, you have come to the Temple of the Blades of your own free will to accept your destiny," Solara continued. "Are you both ready to accept that destiny and to abide by the Law of the Blades."

"I am," the two new Blademasters said in unison.

"Bella Starseeker, have you chosen someone to be your mate and your Protector?"

"This man, Cayden Antioch, has asked for my hand in marriage," Bella said. "My brother has told him that there are consequences to that decision."

"Very well," Solara nodded before turning to face Talby. "Talby Swiftfoot, have you chosen someone to be your mate and your Protector?"

"This man, Tovar Greythistle, has presented me with a ring of hair as per the custom of the halfling people," Talby shrugged. "I have accepted."

"Cayden Antioch and Tovar Greythistle," Solara addressed the two who would be Protectors. "Being the Protector to a Blademaster is a sacred duty, and it is one that you must agree to of your own volition. Know now, that if you accept, you must undergo the Test of the Blades. If you die during the test or in any other way fail to complete the test, you will be forbidden from ever seeing your Blademaster again. And so I ask you, Cayden Antioch, do you agree to undergo the Test of the Blades and become the Protector to Bella Starseeker?"

"I agree," Cayden nodded.

"And Tovar Greythistle, do you agree to undergo the Test of the Blades and become the Protector to Talby Swiftfoot?"

"I would do anything for Talby," Tovar said softly. "So, yes, I agree."

"It is done, then," Solara nodded. "This night, we will have two Tests of the Blades. May the wisdom of Taelin and the luck of Laeyra follow you both as you undergo the Test of the Blades. Come, I will take you to rooms where you can prepare yourselves while the Tests are readied."

The Age of Darkness

Chapter XXIII
Two Are Tested

In a small room, Tovar Greythistle paced. Solara had taken Talby away a few minutes before and he was anxious to get started with the Test.

Tovar had no doubts that he would pass the Test of the Blades. He had known for years that he would marry Talby. For him, this test was nothing more than a formality to prove what he already knew, that he was Talby's true love. He supposed he understood the need to be sure now that Talby was such an important person.

A Blademaster.

No matter how many times he thought about it, it still amazed him that Talby was a Blademaster. He had never expected that his Talby would become as important to the rest of the Southern Dales as she had always been to him.

He did not like having to prove that he loved Talby like this. But the way was the way as they say. And as Talby was now a Blademaster, there was no other way the wedding between Talby and Tovar could happen.

He had always known that Talby was special. It was why he wanted her to be his wife. Neither Tovar nor Talby was particularly normal when it came to being halflings. Yes, they enjoyed collecting treasures, but for the two of them it was always more about the adventures than it was about the treasures they found.

In retrospect, the fact that the rest of the clan consider them, to a degree, outcasts because of the way they loved adventure had a lot to do with their getting together. There was no one else in the whole city that would want to be with a halfling that eschewed the treasures for the adventure itself.

Tovar could not complain with how things had worked out, however. He could not think of a more perfect partner for him than Talby.

As he waited for Solara, he checked the edge of his short sword. It would be mightily embarrassing to be killed because his sword was too dull to use correctly. Satisfied with the edge, he sheathed his sword again and went back to waiting.

He did not have to wait long before Solara entered the little room.

"Before I take you to the Test of the Blades, there is something I must say to you, Tovar Greythistle," Solara said softly.

"And what is that, Lady Solara?"

"Never before has there been a halfling Blademaster," Solara said. "In all the years that the Temple of the Blades has stood, the only halfling that had entered the Temple of the Blades was Meryn Swiftfoot. I reacted poorly to the thought of a halfling Blademaster."

"It's all right, Lady Solara."

"No, it is not," she shook her head. "Although you are not a part of the Blademaster Corps yet, I am still bound by the Second Law of the Blades."

"What is the Second Law of the Blades?"

"The Second Law of the Blades is this," she explained. "True love breeds true forgiveness. Nothing is more powerful than the ability to forgive the one you love. And nothing brings you closer than the forgiveness of your own misdeeds."

"That is a good law to live by," Tovar nodded.

"Talby has already shown more honor before becoming a Blademaster than one former member of the Blademaster Corps showed in her entire life as a Blademaster," Solara bowed her head. "We would be foolish not to accept help so freely offered in the coming war. As her Protector to be, I ask for your forgiveness for my unkind words."

"I understand where they came from" Tovar said softly. "I understand how halflings are viewed in the Southern Dales. We as a race have a reputation as thieves and cutthroats. It is not a reputation we have gotten unfairly. For the most part, it is true. But Talby and I are different. We aren't in this for what we can get out of it monetarily. We're in it for the adventure. And because, as she said, it is the right thing to do."

"Not many will see it that way," Solara said.

"And we will deal with that when the time comes, Lady Solara," Tovar smiled. "You have already seen how feisty my Talby is. I daresay she can handle herself."

"Indeed, she can," Solara chuckled. She looked at Tovar. "Still, I ask your forgiveness for my treatment of yourself and Blademaster Talby."

"No forgiveness is needed, Lady Solara," Tovar said after a moment. "But if it will ease your conscience, you have it."

"Thank you," Solara bowed slightly to him. "Now, let me take you to the Test of the Blades..."

Cayden was restless. While he had appreciated the fact that he had had some extra time with Bella prior to the start of the Test of the Blades, the waiting did little to calm his nerves. Solara had come for Bella about ten minutes ago, and the waiting to start the test was driving Cayden mildly crazy.

He paced back and forth in the small room, thinking about what he was about to do. It was all he could think about. He tried not to. He tried to calm himself like he always did before a battle, but he was having trouble finding that calm.

There was too much riding on what he was about to do.

He knew the risks he was about to take. Cayden was thankful to Colwyn for being honest about the risks. But Cayden would have agreed to take the Test no matter the risks. There was nothing he wouldn't do for Bella.

He remembered the first time he actually met Bella. He had seen her, of course, regularly as a palace guard. But he had not actually met her until the year before.

It was early in the spring and the snows had just finished melting for the year. Bella had gone to Victor to have a guard assigned to go with her into the city, Lord Dargan had told her that she could not go into the city by herself, but if she could get a guard to go with her, he would allow it.

Victor had assigned Cayden.

Cayden was still very young and he was eager to please, so he took the assignment.

No one could have known that Bella and Cayden would fall in love with each other during the trip into the city. But they had. It turned out that Cayden was a very intelligent young man, completely unlike what the young noble woman had expected from a palace guard.

And she was not what Cayden had expected in a noble woman either. She was not obsessed with elegant dresses and jewelry as most of the minor noble women in Arvendale were. She was more interested in practical items.

By the end of the day, Cayden Antioch was in love.

They had both known that a romance would be forbidden by Lord Dargan, but neither cared. But the very young do not always do as they are told, and their romance quickly blossomed. That they had been able to keep it from her father for as long as they had was nothing short of a miracle.

But Lord Dargan had found out.

And he had reacted just as both Bella and Cayden had expected. He demanded that they no longer see each other. Cayden had been scared of the consequences of refusing his edict, but Bella had been firm. She told Dargan that she would not stop seeing the palace guard and the only person she would talk to about it in the future was her brother Colwyn.

And so Dargan had summoned Colwyn to Arvendale to deal with Bella.

Cayden had expected Colwyn to be a younger version of Dargan but he changed his mind about the younger Starseeker as soon as he arrived with a non-noble wife. Cayden had been in the Great Hall when Colwyn had announced that Alana was a Blademaster and that he had married her in accordance with the Law of the Blades.

As angry as Cayden had seen Lord Dargan when dealing with Bella and himself, it had nothing on the way he looked at his son that day. Cayden half expected that the palace guard was going to be called upon to put Colwyn in the dungeon.

And then had come the private conversation he had with Colwyn.

He had expected Colwyn to be the typical condescending noble, but he was not. Colwyn treated Cayden like an equal. And when Cayden realized that he would be the Protector to a Blademaster, he understood why.

Cayden knew that, when the day came for Colwyn to become the First Lord of Arvendale, many people were going to be caught by surprise by the different style of leadership that Colwyn would bring to the position. It wasn't that Lord Dargan wasn't fair, for he was. But he was not someone that the common people could relate to. And Cayden had never once heard Colwyn refer to himself as we.

And that brought Cayden back to the now.

He did not know what to expect from the Test of the Blades, but he was anxious to find out what he would be facing. He fingered the ioun stones that Colwyn had lent him, thankful that Bella's brother was a compassionate man that cared for his sister.

While his senses were not honed nearly as much as he knew Colwyn's to be, as a palace guard, Cayden had had to make sure his senses were always sharp. So he heard the footsteps coming towards his little room long before Solara arrived.

"It is time, Cayden Antioch," Solara said after entering the little room. "Are you read for your Test of the Blades?"

"I'm not sure I will ever be ready, but it is time, as you say," Cayden said in his soft voice.

"Then follow me."

Cayden followed Solara through the halls of the Temple of the Blades. Although he was curious about his surroundings in the temple, he did not let his eyes wander from the High Priestess of the Blades. He did not know where in the temple she was going, and he did not want to be disqualified from becoming Bellla's Protector simply because he could not find the entrance to the Test of the Blades.

Solara stopped at a door and turned to face him.

"Through this door is your Test. There are three levels to your dungeon, and you will find Bella on the third level down," she explained. "You must kill, or otherwise get past, thc creatures in the dungeons to get to her. The final guardian is the only creature you will have no choice but to kill."

"I understand," he nodded.

"Die or otherwise fail to reach your Blademaster to free her and you will fail the test," she finished. "There is no time limit to your test, but know that the longer you take, the harder it will be to complete."

"I am ready, Lady Solara," he said softly.

"Then your test begins now," Solara nodded. "May the wisdom of Taelin and the Luck of Laeyra follow you as you make your way through the Test of the Blades, Cayden Antioch."

With that, Solara turned away and let Cayden through the door to begin his Test of the Blades.

"You are worried, Lord Colwyn," the voice of the first Blademaster called from behind him. "Is it because your sister is currently in the dungeon awaiting her Protector to be to come and rescue her?"

"It is," Colwyn nodded as he turned to face Raven. "More so because it's my sister."

"I understand," Raven smiled at him. "You are right to be worried for Bella. You know it is not an easy life she has accepted."

"Indeed, it is not," Colwyn sighed. "I wish the Bladestone had not confirmed that we were in Arvendale for her. But I was not surprised."

"I imagine you weren't," she laughed. "I doubt I would have been surprised in your place. It does seem to be the way of things."

"The way of things is awful," Colwyn said. He sat on the bench in the little room. "At least she has a good man in Cayden. I will worry about her less with him by her side."

"That is also the way of things," Raven laughed harder. "That is why Blademasters must marry their Protectors. That love protects them far better than any blade."

"And their loved ones," Colwyn flashed a weak smile.

"And their loved ones," Raven nodded. "Be of good cheer, Colwyn. Cayden has passed the Test of the Blades. He will be your sister's Protector."

"That is good to know."

"I have come to bid you come to the Great Hall. There will be bondings soon. It is right that you and Alana be there to witness them."

"I would not be anywhere else when my sister bonds to her Protector," Colwyn smiled, this time a broad and genuine smile.

The Great Hall had been festively decorated while the companions had been waiting for the tests to be completed. Alana and Colwyn knew that the weddings would take place immediately after the tests were completed, so they were not surprised by the way the Great Hall had been readied for such an occasion.

The white and red banners over the altar had changed while they were gone. The white banner bore the crest of the Starseekers, a single gold star over a tree lined road. The red banner bore a white foot with bird wings attached to the ankle. Colwyn mused that it was as good a standard for the Swiftfoot clan than any.

The High Priestess of the Blades stood before the altar. She smiled at Alana and Colwyn.

"As soon as the new Blademasters and their Protectors-to-be arrive, we shall continue," the High Priestess said.

Colwyn nodded. He took his Blademaster's hand and gave it a squeeze. When she smiled over at him, he felt his whole spirit lift much as he always did. Not for the first time, he marveled about how she was able to lift his spirits with a simple smile.

As they waited, Colwyn watched as the Legacy of the Blademasters slowly filtered into the back of the Great Hall. Raven caught Colwyn's eye and smiled broadly at him. He nodded at her, his own smile on his face.

It was not long before the two Protectors entered the Great Hall. Colwyn looked Cayden over and sighed softly to himself. As a palace guard, Cayden would naturally be more comfortable in armor than Colwyn ever would be. The younger man moved easily in the chain mail. Colwyn felt a slight pang of jealousy about that, but it subsided quickly.

Talby was the first of the two new Blademasters to arrive in the Great Hall. She made her way directly to her Protector, making eye contact only with Tovar. Colwyn doubted that the word radiant had ever described a halfling before, but it was the only word he could come up with to describe how Talby looked in her wedding dress.

He could only wonder how his sister would look in hers.

He did not have to wait long, as Bella arrived soon after Talby.

Where Talby looked radiant, Bella looked regal. It was as if she were born to wear such a magnificent dress. Of course, he mused, she had been as it was the wedding dress of a Blademaster. Her eyes lit up when she saw her brother and she made his way over to him.

"Colwyn!" she squealed with glee. Bella launched herself into Colwyn's arms and squeezed him tight. "I am so glad at least one member of my family can be here for this."

"I would not have missed your wedding for the world, Bella," Colwyn laughed. He put her down. "But perhaps, I am not the one you should be hugging."

"You're probably right," Bella laughed heartily as she pulled away from her brother.

Colwyn put his arm around Alana as he watched his little sister walk over to where Cayden was standing there waiting for her.

"Not so long ago, that was us, Col," Alana reminded him as she lay her head against his side.

"Not so long ago, no," Colwyn gave his wife a little squeeze. "I don't know that Bella is nearly as happy as I was though. I am not sure that is possible."

"Maybe not, but she is happy," Alana said. "You've given her a way to be happy, Col."

"It's not an easy road she is about to travel," Colwyn sighed. "I would have saved her from that if I could have."

"We all have a part to play in what's coming, Col," Alana looked up at him. "You, me, Bella, Talby. All of us have a part to play. And there are some we have not yet found that have a part to play as well."

"When did you get so smart?"

"I'm a child of Taelin, silly," Alana laughed. "Did you not think that would come with the rest?"

"Wise and lucky. It can be an annoying combination."

"But you love me," Alana giggled. "Now hush. Here comes Solara."

And indeed, the High Priestess of the Blades had entered the Great Hall. She strode to stand in front of the altar and turned to face the Blademasters and their Protectors.

"The Law of the Blades is unchangeable," Solara's soft voice reverberated throughout the hall. "And it has guided the activities inside the Temple of the Blades for ages." She turned and looked directly at the two new Blademasters. "It is for you to understand why the Tests of the Blades and these weddings are to happen. This is the First Law of the Blades. You are commanded to love. Love your friends. Love your enemies. Love without reservation. Love without hesitation. Love without condition. Love without expectation of return. If you must fight, then fight with love in your heart. If you must kill, then kill with love in your heart. Never kill or fight with hate or anger in your heart. Hate leads to impotence, but love brings power. This is the law a Blademaster must live by more than any other or else she will be powerless to serve as she should. It is the First Law of the Blades because it is the most important. Live by it, or you will die."

Bella looked over at Colwyn, and he could see in her face that she was realizing for the first time exactly what he had agreed to in order to be bound to his Blademaster. She turned back to Solara and nodded once signaling that she understood.

"These must be marriages entered into by both parties of their own free will," Solara continued. "Blademasters Bella Starseeker and Talby Swiftfoot, do you enter this commitment of your own free will? Do you swear that you are not being coerced in any way into marrying the man who would be your Protector? Would you have entered this commitment outside the bounds of the Law of the Blades?"

"My father would have prevented this marriage had it not been for my being named a Blademaster, Lady Solara," Bella said.

"That is not a concern of the Law of the Blades," Solara shrugged. "Were that not to be a consideration, would you have entered into this commitment outside of the bounds of the Law of the Blades?"

"I would have," Bella nodded. "I love this man. And I am thankful for a way for he and I to be together."

"And you, Blademaster Talby?" Solara turned to the halfling.

"Whether as my Protector or as my husband, I would gladly have chosen to spend the rest of my life with Tovar," Talby smiled.

'Very well," Solara nodded, the corners of her mouth fighting the urge to twitch into a smile. She turned to face the Protectors. "Protectors Cayden Antioch and Tovar Greythistle. Do you enter this commitment of your own free will? Do you swear that you are not being coerced in any way into marrying this woman? Would you have entered this commitment outside the bounds of the Law of the Blades?"

"I would have had it been allowed," Cayden nodded.

"Nothing would have kept me from Talby, Lady Solara," Tovar said.

"The Law of the Blades is satisfied that these marriages are being entered into freely by both parties," Solara announced with a smile. She put a hand on Bella's and Cayden's heads and closed her eyes. "Lord Taelin, these two come before you as Blademaster and Protector, and as man and woman. You have commanded that the power of a Blademaster be bound up in love. Therefore, I demand that you bind this Blademaster's power to her love for this man, her Protector, who has passed the Test of the Blades."

When the binding was complete, she repeated the process with Talby and Tovar. When she was done, she slumped against the altar.

"It is done. Let the world know now that these Blademasters and their Protectors are now bound for life. Let the forces of injustice quake with fear, for two more Blademasters shall go forth in full power and authority granted by Lord Taelin and Lady Laeyra."

"What was that rushing I felt during the bonding, Lady Solara?" Bella asked.

"What you felt was your power binding in your love for Cayden," Solara said. "While you both live, your power is tied to the love you share with Cayden, and cannot be broken so long as he is faithful to you."

"I understand," Bella nodded.

"Bella and Cayden. Talby and Tovar. There is one requirement left in the bonding," Alana said with a twinkle in her eye. "The new Blademasters must kiss their Protectors."

Colwyn did not see if the new Blademasters followed Alana's instructions. He chose, at that moment, to reaffirm his own bonding with Alana with a passionate kiss of his own.

The Age of Darkness

Chapter XXIV
Nathair an Aeir a Chosnaionn

It had been an exciting day at the Temple of the Blades. With two new Blademasters installed and bonded to their Protectors, the Temple of the Blades was full of excitement. The Master Blademaster led the two new Blademasters down to the armory to outfit them in proper armor.

Neither of the Blademasters chose any new weapons from the armory, nor did Cayden. Tovar Greythistle took a new short sword, though. Alana smiled at that. The sword he chose was of immensely better quality than the one he had brought to the Temple of the Blades.

Alana was happy that he recognized the quality of his sword in relation to the weapons afforded him in the armory.

When they were done in the armory, Alana led them outside. The weather was brisk, but the sun was shining. There was little doubt that winter was advancing on. But their current journey was nearing its end. All they needed to do was fly back to Ravendale and they would be able to plan through the winter in relative safety.

Colwyn came up to her side and slipped his arm through hers. She smiled over at him, happy at his touch as she always was. There was a great deal of comfort that she took from his touch.

"We'll be home soon, Alana," he said.

"And then we will have the winter to prepare," Alana nodded.

"We will get through this, Alana," Colwyn said quietly, pulling her close.

"How can you be so sure?" she said as she leaned her head against his chest.

"The two children of Dargan Starseeker in the same fight?" Colwyn raised one eyebrow. "Nothing can stand against that."

Alana laughed in spite of herself. Once again, Colwyn had said just what she needed to hear in order to feel better.

"How is it you always know what to say to me?" Alana looked up at him.

"Sometimes being the Protector of a Blademaster means protecting her from herself, my love," Colwyn smiled. "You've been so worried about your part in the coming war that you've forgotten to take time to laugh. You can't be serious all the time or you'll break."

"I think you might need to keep reminding me of that, Col," Alana smiled. She leaned her head back into his chest. "And thank you."

"Nothing to thank me for," he squeezed her gently. "That's what I am here for."

She smiled into his chest, simply comforted by his touch. She leaned up and kissed him gently on the cheek, drawing a smile from him. Nuzzling her neck back against his chest, she watched as the other Blademasters took similar comfort from their Protectors.

True love was a wonderful thing to behold.

A shadow crossed the clearing, causing Alana to pull away from Colwyn. Colwyn, for his part, tensed. Alana's reaction to potential danger had, as it always did caught his attention and forced him into a state of battle readiness.

Alana was pleased that he got himself ready so quickly.

A second shadow passed over the clearing, and it was clear that Alana had not imagined the first shadow. Now fully alert, Alana drew both of her long swords. The other two Blademasters saw her draw her weapons and they drew theirs. She held up one hand to quiet them from asking her what was wrong.

Alana watched as a third shadow passed over the clearing, this one seemingly smaller than the other two. That meant three distinct potential threats. The Master Blademaster growled slightly, deep in her chest. This was not just a threat to her, but to the Temple of the Blades itself. She could not allow such a threat to go unchecked. The Temple of the Blades had become every bit her home as the little house that Colwyn had built for her in Ravendale.

Alana strode to the center of the clearing and looked up. She could not see what was causing the three shadows that she had seen. Whatever else they were, Alana knew that they were large. And she stood ready to defend the Temple of the Blades against whatever they were.

"Alana, hold," Silvestra said from the steps. "If I am right, there is no threat here."

"I can't take the chance, Silvestra," Alana said without turning to look at her friend. "Until I know what those were, I will stand ready to defend the Temple of the Blades."

"I understand," the dragon woman nodded. "And I applaud your vigilance. But I believe those to be dragons sent by the Council of Dragons to be nathair an aeir a chosnaíonn to Bella and Talby."

"They were certainly big enough shadows to have been caused by dragons, Alana," Colwyn said.

"I'm not standing down until we know for sure, Col," Alana said, still watching the skies.

"I'm not asking you to," Colwyn said as he joined her. "I'm just saying that Silvestra could well be right."

"Better to be vigilant and wrong than to dismiss a potential threat and be killed," Alana shrugged.

She stood at a ready position, the points of her swords gently touching the ground. Her companions all knew how quickly she could respond to a threat from that position. It was a position from which she could respond to an attack almost instantly.

As she watched the sky, the shadows passed over the clearing a second time. While she could not see what was causing the shadows, she did catch a flash of gold as the first one passed overhead. If the lead shadow were a gold dragon, that would go a long way to prove Silvestra correct about the three shadows being dragons sent by the Council of Dragons.

She hoped that would prove the case. She did not think that she or the other two Blademasters were ready to fight monsters the size of dragons.

When the three shadows passed over the clearing a third time, the creatures making the shadows were more visible. And it was clear to Alana that there were three dragons with a large gold dragon in the lead of the three. She relaxed slightly at that knowledge, but not to the point where she put her swords away.

"Everyone up to the steps," she waved to the others. "Give them room to land."

Alana led the way up to the steps, joining the rest of her companions. The other two Blademasters and their Protectors joined Alana and her companions on the steps to the Temple of the Blades. None of them wanted to be trampled by dragons.

The dragons passed over the clearing three more times before they were low enough to land. The first dragon to land was a large gold dragon, and Alana knew that it was the sun shining off his scales that she had seen. As soon as the gold dragon touched down, he morphed into his human form and stood off to the side so as to not be in the way of the other two dragons.

The second dragon to land was a bronze dragon larger than any living dragon Alana had seen. The only dragon that she had seen larger than this bronze dragon had been the undead dragon that had been serving Kera Rayden in Willowdale. She shuddered at the memory of the undead dragon. It had been the undead dragon that had killed her first nathair an aeir a chosnaíonn, Cobalthaxillius. The noble gold dragon died fighting the massive dragon and had earned his redemption. This bronze dragon was nearly as large as that undead dragon had been. He too morphed into his human form and waited for the third dragon to land.

The third dragon was smaller than the other two with luminescent blue scales. Alana had heard of the gemstone dragons that were neutrally aligned, but she had never seen one before. The dragon that had just landed, though, could only be a sapphire dragon. Alana watched in fascination as the sapphire dragon turned into her human form. As a woman, she had hair the same luminescent blue color as her scales had been. It was an odd hair color, but Alana thought it worked for her.

The gold haired dragon man turned and walked over to the steps of the Temple. He dropped to one knee in front of Alana and bowed his head. The other two dragon people followed his example.

"My name is Aurientallus," he said, his head still bowed. "I represent the Council of Dragons. I have brought these two dragons as I was bid by my Lord Taelin to serve as the nathair an aeir a chosnaíonn to the two newest Blademasters."

Alana looked at the three dragon people kneeling in front of her. She looked from one to the other, and then nodded once. Finally convinced that there was no threat, the Master Blademaster sheathed her blades.

"Aurientallus, welcome once more to the Temple of the Blades," Alana smiled at him. "As I understand it, you were once the nathair an aeir a chosnaíonn to a Blademaster yourself."

"Indeed I was," he said as he rose. "I had the honor to be the first nathair an aeir a chosnaíonn. I served Blademaster Raven Windrider, although I was a much younger dragon then."

"And now you have returned to the Temple to bring other dragons to serve as the nathair an aeir a chosnaíonn to Blademasters," she said. "You could have sent anyone to guide them."

"I could have," Aurientallus nodded. "But if I had, I would have missed an opportunity to see old friends. With the war that is fast approaching, I feared to miss such an opportunity lest I never get another."

"I understand." A broad smile lit Alana's face. "Go then, noble dragon. Go and see your Blademaster. I am sure she will welcome your visit. I am sure the dragons and the Blademasters can figure out who goes with whom without you."

"Thank you, Lady Alana Steeldrake," Aurientallus bowed low. "I will speak with you once more before I leave."

Alana nodded and moved aside so that he could ascend the steps to the Temple of the Blades. When he disappeared inside the Temple, Alana turned back to the other two dragons and motioned for them to stand.

"We have two new Blademasters and there are two of you," she said. "This works out well. I would not presume to dictate which of you will go with each Blademaster. I will introduce the two Blademasters and leave it to the two of you to figure out which of them you will travel with if that is agreeable to both of you?"

The two dragon people nodded in agreement and Alana motioned for Talby and Bella to step forward. The dragon people looked at both of the new Blademasters and then walked off a few paces from the Temple of the Blades. They kept their voices low as they talked, so Alana could not hear what they were saying. After a few minutes, the man threw back his head and let out a raucous laugh. He was still chuckling when they approached the Temple of the Blades once more.

"I am Greytonix," the man said. His voice was boisterous and loud. Alana instantly liked him. "You may call me Grey. It would amuse me greatly to serve as the nathair an aeir a chosnaíonn to the smallest Blademaster in the history of the Blademasters. Blademaster Talby Swiftfoot, if you will have me as your nathair an aeir a chosnaíonn, I will be happy to serve you."

"I am honored," Talby nodded to Greytonix. "It will be enjoyable to have you as a companion."

"Thank you, Lady Talby," Greytonix rumbled happily. "This will be very interesting, indeed."

Alana looked at the blue haired woman. The blue haired woman looked amused by everything that was going on. Alana had a feeling that this woman felt superior to Greytonix. And quite possibly that she felt superior to the Blademasters as well. It was just as well that she would be Bella's nathair an aeir a chosnaíonn. This way, Alana could keep an eye on the woman. Alana's first instinct was not to like her, and she hoped she was wrong about that.

"I believe that means you will be traveling with Bella," Alana said to the dragon woman.

"Yes," the blue haired woman nodded. "I will. My name is Timeanalia, but you make call me Nalia."

"I'm Bella," the younger Blademaster piped up. "I am glad to meet you, Nalia."

"I pledge myself to your service as your nathair an aeir a chosnaíonn, Lady Bella," Nalia said softly. She bowed slightly. "May you never come to harm under my watch."

"Thank you, Nalia," Bella nodded to the blue haired woman. "I am sure I will be safe with you traveling with me."

"I think that you and your Blademasters should take some time to get to know each other," Alana said to the dragons. "There is a great darkness coming and a lot may well ride on your protection."

Aurientallus had not been inside the Temple of the Blades since his Blademaster had passed into the Legacy of the Blademasters. It was not that he did not want to visit the Temple. It was more that he did not feel comfortable there.

He wished he had made time to visit before now.

He mounted the steps to the temple, pausing at the entranceway to read over the words engraved on the plaques by the door.

"Ní mór di a rachaidh isteach anseo chun aghaidh a thabhairt ar ndán di dul isteach le croí glan. Ní mór sí ag troid i gcomhréir leis an idéalacha Taelin agus Laeyra. Ní mór di cloí le Dlí na lanna má ghlacann sí ndán di. Teip ciallaíonn bás," he said aloud. *She who enters here to face her destiny must enter with a pure heart. She must fight according to the precepts of Taelin and Laeyra. She must abide by the Law of the Blades if she accepts her destiny. Failure brings death.*

He turned to the other plaque and read that one as well. "Sí nach bhfuil grá nach bhfuil a fhios Taelin chun é Taelin ghrá." *She who does not love does not know Taelin for Taelin is love.*

Having served as the nathair an aeir a chosnaíonn to a Blademaster, he understood these words far better than most. He had seen a Blademaster at the height of her power. He knew what a Blademaster fully engaged in the battle was capable of. He did not think these three new Blademasters knew the full extent of their powers just yet.

But Alana Steeldrake had impressed him. He thought maybe she could reach her full potential. It would be interesting to see what this new Blademaster would do in the middle of the Great War of Souls. He had studied the Dream Weaver's prophecy about the war. While he did not fully understand the prophecy, he had an idea of what some of it meant.

He knew that some members of the Legacy of the Blademasters would not see the other side of the war, although he did not know who of the Legacy of the Blademasters would die a second death.

And so, he chose to take the opportunity to visit the Temple of the Blades when he had the chance. Bringing Greytonix and Timeanalia to the Temple of the Blades gave him the perfect opportunity to visit. It would be good to see his old friends again.

He took a deep breath and took the final step to enter the Temple of the Blades.

The Temple had not changed much in the time he had been away. Only the additional banners for Blademasters that had come and gone after his marked the years since he had visited last.

"Who goes there?" the High Priestess called out as she entered the Great Hall behind him.

"Hello, Solara," he said in a soft voice as he turned to face her. "It has been many years."

"It has indeed, Aurientallus," Solara nodded her head towards him. "Welcome back to the Temple of the Blades."

"Thank you," he smiled. "It has been too long. I thought I should visit my Blademaster before this war starts."

"I believe Raven will like to have a visit," Solara smiled. "If you want, I can call for her."

"No, I think I know where I will wait for her."

Aurientallus bowed slightly to the High Priestess before making his way out of the Great Hall.

Although the dragon had not been in the Temple of the Blades in many years, he still remembered his way around. He slowly walked through the corridors of the temple, remembering his time as Raven's nathair an aeir a chosnaíonn. He had been a much younger dragon then. It had been a rash act, running off to serve Raven.

He had never regretted it though.

And his service to the Blademasters had no doubt played a part in his ascension to the Council of Dragons. He knew that the other gold dragons respected the fact that he had gone willingly to serve the Blademasters when no one else on the Isle of Dragons would have done so.

There had not been so many dragons over the years that had chosen to serve as the nathair an aeir a chosnaíonn to a Blademaster. And some that had served had not returned. Even so, Aurientallus had been the first. And he had gone despite the protestation of the leader of his race of dragons. Eliazar had been against the dragons being assigned to Blademasters.

The dragon smiled as he thought of the consternation he had caused Eliazar by going.

But his time as the nathair an aeir a chosnaíonn to a Blademaster had come and gone. Raven had been a part of the Legacy of the Blademasters for three quarters of a millennium. It was a long time even for a dragon. Gold dragons were the dragons that usually had the longest life expectancies. Some gold dragons, such as Eliazar, reached close to three millenniums in age. At just over a thousand years in age, Aurientallus was just starting to reach what humans would call middle age. It had been a good and quiet life since his Blademaster had passed into the Legacy of the Blademasters.

But now he was being dragged back into the war.

As the Law of the Blades said, the war never ends; only the battles change. He knew that those words were too true. And he knew that this war was just a continuation of the war he had fought by the side of his Blademaster. He was not sure what his part would be in the war that was about to start, but he knew that he would have a part to play.

He knew that, with his Blademaster being put back into the war, he would find himself once more serving as her nathair an aeir a chosnaíonn. He did not mind the thought of that. He was still young enough that he knew he would be able to serve her well. He would do his best to make sure that she would make it through to the other side of the Great War of Souls and return to the Legacy of the Blademasters where she belonged.

The room that Aurientallus chose to wait in was one of many small rooms that peppered the Temple of the Blades. It was just like many other rooms in the temple, about ten feet to a side. Along one wall was a comfortable padded bench. Aurientallus sat on the bench and waited.

He knew that it would not take long for his Blademaster to realize he was in the Temple and come find him.

The room he had chosen had some small significance. Centuries before, he had stood in that very room and pledged the dragons to the service of the Blademasters. And while he knew that some of the dragons did not like that he had done that, it had been the right thing to do.

And so, he figured it was the best place to wait for his Blademaster to come see him.

He did not have to wait long.

Soon after he sat down, the ethereal forms of Raven Windrider and Richard Kale floated through the wall into the room. They looked just the same as they had when they were alive.

"You look well, old friend," Raven smiled as she glided over to where Aurientallus was sitting.

"As do you, my lady," the dragon smiled as he stood and bowed to her. "As dragons were coming to the Temple of the Blades to pledge their service as nathair an aeir a chosnaíonn to the new Blademasters, I decided to accompany them. It has been far too long since I was in the Temple of the Blades."

"Indeed it has," Richard nodded. "We've missed you, Aurientallus. Welcome home."

"You know of the war that is coming, Lady Raven?" the dragon asked.

"Yes," the first Blademaster nodded. "We have been preparing for it. Prophecy says that the Legacy of the Blademasters will take the field again in this war."

"Know that I will be once more by your side when that day comes, my Blademaster," Aurientallus vowed, bowing his head slightly. "As it should be."

"We welcome you to fight by our side one more time, old friend," Raven smiled broadly. "It feels like we have fought this battle before. I would not want to fight this war a second time without you."

"As the Law of the Blades says, my lady," the dragon smiled. "The war never ends; only the battles change."

"So it says," Raven nodded.

The Blademasters and their nathair an aeir a chosnaíonns were getting to know each other in the clearing. Alana and her companions were content to sit on the steps of the Temple of the Blades and watch the other Blademasters getting to know their nathair an aeir a chosnaíonns. It made Alana happy to see other Blademasters.

She tried not to think about the fact that she was responsible for them now. But as the Master Blademaster, she knew that everything that happened to the other Blademasters was her responsibility. It was hard to have the weight of the Southern Dales on her shoulders, but she knew that it was what had to be.

It wasn't just the prophecy of the Great War of Souls that told her she had to be the one to lead them. She could feel it. She could feel the burden of responsibility and she refused to shy away from it.

Alana frowned suddenly. Something wasn't right. She couldn't put her finger on it, but she could feel something off. She looked over at Colwyn and saw that he had tensed. He felt it too.

"There's something just outside the clearing," Colwyn said in a soft voice. "And it is not something that should be here."

"Dangerous?" Alana asked.

"Definitely something malevolent," Colwyn responded after a moment of quiet concentration. "We should make ready for an attack."

Alana opened her mouth to call the rest of the Blademasters' attention to whatever it was that was just outside the clearing.

Before she could say anything she heard the horns.

ChapτeR XXV
Amδush

The waiτinξ was τhe worsτ part.

Kera Rayden had brought her army to a spot not far from the clearing where the Temple of the Blades was. She was waiting for the scouts to come and tell her that the Blademaster and her companions had arrived at the temple.

And then she would attack.

The Nighstalker looked forward to the attack. She relished the chance to end the meddling of the Blademaster before they launched the Great War. Without their champion, the forces of the light stood no chance against her army of undead. The defeat of the Southern Dales would be easy and complete.

And the Nightstalker would have her revenge.

There was a small part of Kera that wondered if her need for revenge on the Blademaster was clouding her judgment, but she kept that part of herself silent. If she was to be successful she needed to have no distractions. Self doubt could only be a distraction.

Distraction while facing the Blademaster would be fatal.

Kera waited, her impatience growing. She wanted to launch the attack, but she would not do so until she knew that her quarry was at the temple. It made no sense to launch an attack on the temple without the Blademaster being there.

She looked over the troops she had assembled for the assault. They stood there waiting, always at the ready. That was the thing about using undead. They did not grow bored, nor did they ever fade from full readiness.

It pleased her to have an army that could attack at a moment's notice.

She heard a rustling nearby her and drew to full attention. After a few moments, one of the scouts that she had sent to monitor the temple appeared.

"Mistress Kera, the Blademaster and her companions have arrived at the Temple of the Blades," the scout reported.

"Very good." She turned to face one of the officers she had brought, a general by the looks of his uniform. "We have about a three hour march from here. We best start."

The army started out towards the clearing where the Temple of the Blades lay. Kera had estimated poorly. While the undead were good at being always ready to fight, they did not fare too well in travelling through a forest. It took more like five hours for the small army to arrive near the clearing.

When they were close enough, she stopped the march and went to scout ahead. She peered through the foliage at the temple grounds. When she saw the Blademaster and her companions standing near the steps to the temple, she smiled wickedly.

She made her way back to where her army was waiting for her and nodded once to the general.

"It's time, general," she said softly. "They are there. It is time to launch the attack. Sound the horns."

The general nodded and made a motion. Mere moments later, loud brass horns sounded, announcing the attack.

Kera led the troops into the clearing for the attack.

When Alana heard the horns, she drew her swords and started down the steps of the Temple of the Blades. Colwyn was by her side, his big sword unslung from his back as he moved.

Both of them had honed instincts when it came to knowing when and where trouble was coming from. Whatever surprise they felt about someone being bold enough to attack the Temple of the Blades vanished the moment they started moving. They did not wait to see if any of the others reacted to the horns.

Alana could only hope that the others would react as quickly.

She did not have time to worry about how the others reacted to the threat, though, as she and Colwyn dove into the fray. All other considerations were gone as she narrowed her focus to the enemies in front of her.

There were a lot of them, and Alana wasn't sure if they could handle so many on their own. But the Temple of the Blades was in danger and Alana felt that she and the others needed to do anything they could in order to protect the Temple of the Blades.

She knew, though, that she had to find a way to survive the confrontation if the Southern Dales was to survive the War of Souls.

She let out a scream as she launched herself towards the attacking undead. She swung her swords as she met the line of undead, taking out two skeletons with her first swing.

She felt the battle rage take her, and she gave into the rage. She let the rage guide her blades, making sure she always protected herself as she attacked.

It was going to be a long and deadly battle.

Bella moved with an easy grace. Cayden had never seen Bella in a fight before, and, for just a moment, he stared in awe as she tore into the skeletons that swarmed into the clearing.

She had moved just as soon as she had heard the horns. While Alana had been the first Blademaster to meet the charge of the undead, Bella had not been too far behind. She would not let her sister in law fight the undead by herself.

What Cayden had not known was that Bella had taken every opportunity to practice with a sword. She had begged Victor Tram for lessons from a young age. It had taken a long time for the captain of the guard to acquiesce to her constant demand for lessons, but he had, in the end.

Bella and the captain of the guard had both known that had her father caught Victor giving Bella swordsmanship lessons, it would not have gone so well for him. Despite the fact that he was Dargan's captain of the guard, Victor had no doubt that Dargan would find him expendable.

But Dargan had not found out about his daughter's training. And she had trained hard. Victor had been impressed with her progress in her studies. They had worked late at night after Lord Dargan had gone to bed, for that was the only way that they could ensure he never found out about the training.

And now that Bella found herself in a life or death battle, she was glad she had been such a good student.

She remembered everything that Victor taught her as she fought. Every block and thrust came from a practice session. Every movement was perfectly choreographed to effectively attack or defend with the smallest amount of energy expended.

It was a beautiful dance that she was in.

She gave herself over fully to the dance, knowing full well that her life was on the line. As she moved, she drowned out everything around her, focusing only on the warriors in front of her.

She silently gave thanks to Victor Tram for teaching her all he could of sword fighting.

Talby was having fun. A Blademaster for scant hours, she relished the opportunity put before her to prove her abilities so soon after forcing the High Priestess of the Blades to accept her as a Blademaster.

She had started with two daggers. It was the way she started every battle she had been in. Talby was not exactly superstitions, but she always believed in using what worked. And this had always worked for her.

Tovar had asked her about it once. He was convinced that there had to be a better way, but Talby had stood fast. While she could have started with better weapons than just two daggers, she was comfortable with the little weapons and knew that it would always be best to start a battle in comfort.

But the daggers never lasted long as her only weapons. Almost always after she dispatched her first opponent in any given battle, she switched out one of her daggers for the sword that the fallen opponent had been using. And on and on. When one of her swords broke, she quickly replaced it as soon as she could.

And so it was that not long after the battle started, little Talby had two swords and pile of undead bodies in her wake.

Alana and Colwyn were fighting back to back. It was a tactic they often used when facing large numbers of opponents. They had fought together often enough that each could anticipate the other's moves.

They fed off each other as they fought, never getting in the other's way, but making sure that they were in position to be able to help the other at a moment's notice if they needed it.

It was that teamwork that they had always counted on over the years, and it had become such an ingrained part of their relationship that neither of them needed to speak to let the other know what was needed.

Alana moved with a fluid grace, each movement exactly what was needed for the moment and nothing more. The sheer number of undead funneling into the clearing told her that she needed to conserve as much energy as she could with each enemy she faced.

She had caught sight of the woman in black leather that she had fought in Willowdale. Ultimately, she knew that she would have to fight the Nightstalker. When she did, she would have the disadvantage, for the Nightstalker had been hanging back while Alana had been fighting since the battle started.

There was nothing that she could do about that though.

All she could do was to keep fighting and hoping for the best.

She dodged one skeleton's thrust while deftly decapitating a second. It was the way the battle had been going since it started. There were simply too many attackers. Every time she cut one down, two more took its place.

And so the battle went. She did not have time to check on the other Blademasters as she fought, but she did try to keep the woman in black leather in sight as much as she could.

So when the Nightstalker started to run all of a sudden, Alana had no choice but to watch where she was going.

Chapter XXVI
Swordfight in the Ramparts

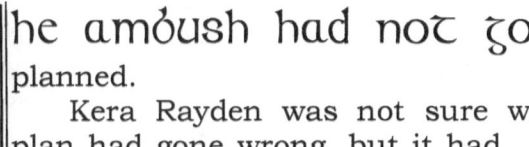he ambush had not gone as planned.

Kera Rayden was not sure where her plan had gone wrong, but it had. She had expected to catch the Blademaster unaware at the Temple of the Blades. There were enough undead soldiers to handle one Blademaster and her companions.

The Nightstalker had not known there would be three Blademasters when she attacked.

Worse, the three Blademasters all had their dragons with them. She had woefully miscalculated the strength of the force she needed.

It angered her to no end that she had miscalculated so badly.

There was little to be done about it, of course. All she could really do was to just hope the attack succeeded. Meanwhile, she needed to get away so she could fight another day.

There was really no place in the clearing where she could open a portal back to where the army was massing. She would have to get away from the battle. As she looked around, she realized that the only place she could get to that would offer the safety to be able to open a portal would be inside the Temple of the Blades itself.

She thought it a fool's errand to run into the heart of the opposition's strength, but there was no choice. She just had to hope she could get to a safe place in the temple before she was caught in there.

She started running for the stairs.

Alana watched the woman in black leather race towards the stairs leading up to the Temple of the Blades. She could not let the Nightstalker get away like she had in Willowdale. It had disturbed her greatly that the woman had gotten away before. She was determined to end the threat the Nightstalker presented once and for all.

"Stay here, Colwyn," she said. "Help the others."

"Good hunting," Colwyn nodded after seeing where Alana was going. "Stop her for good this time."

The Blademaster nodded her head once then started hacking her way towards the Temple of the Blades. The undead were all around, but they were not as skilled in the art of fighting as Alana and her companions were. Still, by sheer numbers, they could easily overwhelm the Blademasters.

It was a sobering thought, and one that Alana chose not to dwell on.

Each swing of one of Alana's swords took out another undead warrior. These undead were far easier to kill than the lich had been. While the lich had been extremely intelligent and cunning, these skeletons and zombies had very little in the way of intelligence. It made them far easier to kill. It also meant that these were the most expendable of the troops available to the Dark God in the War of Souls.

The fact that they would face far tougher completion in the war that was to come was distasteful, but it was something that Alana had to consider if she was going to successfully lead the army of light.

It took Alana some time to fight her way through to the Temple of the Blades. She was far behind the Nightstalker by the time she got there. That wasn't so much of a problem, though, as she saw the Nightstalker enter the Temple, so she knew where the woman in black had gone.

It made it easier to follow the Nightstalker. And she knew that the Legacy of the Blademasters would help keep tabs on where the Nightstalker was so that Alana could successfully confront the follower of Thraal.

When Alana burst through the door into the Great Hall, she surprised Solara. The High Priestess frowned at the sight of a Blademaster with her swords drawn in the Great Hall.

"What is it?" Solara asked.

"The temple is under attack," Alana explained. "The leader of the attack raced into the Temple of the Blades before me. She was dressed all in black. Did you see which way she went?"

"I did not," Solara frowned. "But I have no doubt that the Legacy of the Blademasters are tracking the intruder as we speak."

"I had that thought as well," Alana nodded. "I'll get them to help me."

Alana dashed out of the Great Hall and made her way down one of the corridors of the temple. She had not yet gotten to know the layout of the entire temple, which is something she felt she would need to correct at some point in the near future. She made her way to the room that she and Colwyn tended to use when they were in the temple.

"Raven, I need your help," she called as soon as she entered what she thought of as her room.

It did not take long for Raven to appear in the little room. Raven looked to be upset, but Alana thought that maybe it was just her own feelings projected on Raven. The temple being under attack was as bad as if her own home were being under attack. She thought about that for a moment and realized that the Temple of the Blades was a second home, a realization that made the feeling make more sense.

"What is it, Alana?"

"The temple is under attack, Raven," Alana explained. "The leader of the attack, a woman in all black leather, ran into the temple. I need to find her."

"Wait here," Raven nodded. "I will mobilize the Legacy of the Blademasters, and we will find this woman. It's the Nightstalker that Colwyn told me about, isn't it?"

"It is, yes," Alana nodded.

"Don't worry, Alana," Raven smiled. "We will find her."

Alana nodded and watched as the other Blademaster disappeared through a wall. She knew that Raven would return with the information she needed. She just hoped that it would not take too long.

Alana appreciated the break, though. She had been fighting non-stop since the undead broke through into the clearing. She knew that she would need as much energy as she could tap into to face off against the Nightstalker one on one.

It was not a battle she could afford to lose.

She sheathed her swords and waited patiently for Raven to return with the information she needed. Running through some breathing exercises, she calmed herself and prepared for the fight that was coming.

It was not Raven that entered the room first.

Aurientallus knocked gently on the frame of the open door. Alana smiled when she saw the gold dragon.

"Come in, my friend," she said. "I can use your help as well."

"Raven told me the temple is under attack," Aurientallus nodded. "What can I do to help?"

"I do not wish to ask any more of you," Alana sighed. "You have done so much already by getting the Council of Dragons to send dragons to fight alongside the new Blademasters. But the Blademasters out in the clearing need all the help they can get. They are badly outnumbered."

"Then they will receive some help," Aurientallus shrugged. "Raven is getting you the information you need. The least I can do is go out and help protect the temple."

"Thank you," she bowed slightly to the gold dragon.

"There is no need to thank me, Blademaster Alana," Aurientallus smiled at her. "We all serve the light."

Alana nodded, but he had already turned and made his way out of the room. It helped to have so much support in her bid to defend the Southern Dales, but it still unnerved her some that they looked upon her to lead them in the fight against the darkness.

She still did not feel adequate to the task at hand.

For now, though, all she could do was wait and get herself ready for the next fight.

It was not long before Raven returned.

"We have found the Nightstalker, Alana," she reported. "She is headed towards the ramparts. There is nowhere she can go from there. You'll have her trapped."

"Maybe not trapped," Alana sighed. "She has gotten away from me before. Keep an eye on her to make sure she stays there."

"Several of our sisters are watching her as we speak."

"Good," Alana nodded. "I guess it's time I faced her again."

With that, Alana started her way up to the ramparts.

The undead kept swarming into the clearing. Colwyn looked at the swarming numbers in dismay, but he redoubled his efforts to cut through as many as he could. He worked his way over to where William and Silvestra were sending fireball after fireball into the midst of the undead.

It took what felt like hours to cut through the undead to where his friends were, but eventually he made it. He could see the sweat beading William's brow as he exerted himself by casting spell after spell.

Colwyn knew the mage's energy could not last forever. He and Alana worried about the mage. It was not the first time Colwyn thought about how much power that William was showing more and more. It worried him. The young mage was his friend and he did not want to see William burn out on power. He didn't want to have to wonder, with each spell William cast, if it would be the one that killed William.

While he did not have any magic of his own, Colwyn knew from the elves that using too much magic could kill someone. The magic could overpower him and claim his life.

Colwyn did not want to see that happen to the mage.

It was pretty clear, though, that William seemed to have a good control of the power he wielded. Colwyn took a little comfort from that, but he still worried. He had actually been planning to talk to Silvestra about it at some point. He wondered what Silvestra would think about the worry Colwyn and Alana had for William.

But the middle of a battle was not the time to find such things out.

"How are you two holding up?" Colwyn asked when he had fought to their side.

"We're not going to win like this, Colwyn," Silvestra answered for the two of them. "Something needs to happen to turn the tide of battle in our favor."

"Not sure what we can do but keep fighting," Colwyn grunted as he cut another skeleton down.

"If we keep going at this pace, none of us will be left to keep fighting," Silvestra warned. "Where is Alana?"

"She chased after the Nightstalker," Colwyn said. "That is her fight. This is ours."

"I understand."

They kept fighting side by side. Colwyn understood Silvestra's warning. It was a feeling he had had since the battle began. There were just too many of the enemy and too few of them. But they would go down fighting at any rate.

After a few minutes of furious fighting, there came a loud roar from the direction of the Temple of the Blades. Colwyn turned to face the temple and was shocked to see a giant gold dragon launching himself into the sky over the battle.

The dragon breathed burst of flame after burst of flame down on the undead, being careful not to breathe fire anywhere near the companions.

It was enough to turn the tide. While the other two dragons had been in the battle they had, much like

Silvestra had, remained in their human forms and were raining magic down on the undead.

They had not been as effective as Aurientallus was breathing fire on the undead.

"I think we just had our turning point," Colwyn pointed out.

"I think so too," Silvestra nodded. "Angry dragons tend to make great turning points in battles."

"Indeed," Colwyn smiled.

When Alana burst through the door to the ramparts of the Temple, she drew her swords and skidded to a halt. The Nightstalker stood facing her. The Nightstalker's swords were already out, and she stood in a ready position.

"Blademaster," the Nightstalker snarled when she saw Alana. "It is time to end this, once and for all."

"You are not the first to try, Kera," the Blademaster's soft voice responded. "I do not doubt you will be the last."

Alana raised her swords slightly so that she would be ready for the attack that she knew was coming. She quickly searcher her memory for the last time she and the Nightstalker had fought. She ran though the attack sequence in her head quickly, working out the woman's patterns of attack and defense.

Alana had always had a good memory for attack patterns, but never this clear. She thought perhaps it was an inherent Blademaster ability. It was something she would have to ask Solara or someone in the Legacy of the Blademasters about. But that would have to wait for another time. For now, she had to concentrate on the battle ahead of her.

She waited patiently, willing to let the other woman attack first. For now, the Blademaster was content to let the Nightstalker set the pattern of the fight. Alana was in no hurry. She knew that an opportunity would present itself. She just had to be patient and take the opportunity when it came.

The Nightstalker launched a high attack towards Alana's head. She parried and swiped her other sword towards Kera's side. Kera easily pushed the strike aside.

They circled around each other, neither ready to make the next attack. Alana waited, knowing that the Nightstalker would grow impatient and launch another attack.

Alana was content to wait and conserve her energy. Based on what she had replayed in her mind about the battle in Willowdale, the Nightstalker had a definite weakness in her style. Kera tended to exert herself too much in battle. It was a weakness that Alana could easily exploit by just being patient.

When Kera launched her next attack, Alana was ready. She attacked with both swords, one striking towards Alana's abdomen and the other an uppercut towards her head. Alana stepped back and to the left, letting the blade coming towards her head pass harmlessly overhead. The blade coming towards her abdomen, she caught on her own blade. She twisted her blade slightly, hoping she might be able to disarm Kera. She did not succeed in forcing the other woman to drop one of her swords, but she did successfully block the attack.

"You can't beat me, Blademaster," Kera said as she backed away from Alana. "I am a better fighter than you and I will win in the end."

"I already know your fatal flaw, Kera," Alana said softly. "So long as you let your hate control your actions, you can't win against me."

"Bah, hate is a far stronger motivation than love," Kera hissed. "I am far more powerful than you will ever be, because I have no limitations on me."

"You also have nothing to balance you," Alana said. She felt compassion for the other woman. She hoped that she could reach her and bring her back from the darkness, although she knew it was probably a futile hope. "In all of life, there must be balance. To lose that balance is to invite chaos and death in."

"Chaos and death are all I have left, Blademaster," Kera snarled. "And they are all I need."

The Nightstalker launched another attack, this time swinging both swords furiously, one after the other. Alana had to back up as she defended the strikes. She caught each one on one of her blades, but the furious assault kept her from being able to launch an attack over her own.

She could feel the exertion in her arms, but she knew she had plenty of energy left for the battle. Alana had plenty of untapped reserves of energy should she need them.

She found an opening and kicked out with her right leg. Her boot caught Kera in the stomach, folding the other woman over. The Nightstalker backed up, giving Alana space to breathe.

Alana dropped her swords to a ready position, but did not let down her guard. She knew that Kera was crafty, and she did not want to give the Nightstalker an opening to take her out.

"I can do this all night," Alana said softly. "I can match you blow for blow. You should know that from the last time we fought. You couldn't beat me then and you can't beat me now."

"You talk a good game, Blademaster," Kera snarled. "But you and I both know that this will end with your blood running down my swords."

"Only in your dreams, Kera," the Blademaster smiled. "We both know which of us is the better swordswoman."

"Yes," Kera nodded in agreement. "I am. And I always will be."

"You always will be just talk, Kera," Alana sighed with disappointment. "Renounce Thraal. Come fight by my side. Come to the light. You and I could do great things together. It doesn't have to be this way."

"Yes, it does," Kera said.

She launched another attack. Again, Alana was able to match each attack with a defense of her own. She knew that she would not be able to keep up this defense forever, but she also knew that Kera would make a mistake. When the mistake came, she would have to capitalize on it.

The attack that Kera launched was intricate, and it took all of Alana's concentration in order to match her blows. She knew, though, that if she missed a single attack, it could prove fatal. There was too much riding on her to die in a battle like this.

Soon, an opening presented itself, and Alana launched a quick attack against the Nightstalker. She swung both swords towards Kera's head, hoping to, at the very least, distract Kera long enough to be able to subdue the other woman.

It was just bad luck for Alana. When she launched the attack, Kera shuffled backwards and tripped over a loose stone, falling onto her backside. Alana's swords swished harmlessly several feet over Kera's head.

The Nightstalker cursed and turned to slash down behind her, slicing a hole in the air. Alana knew that the Nightstalker was about to escape again, but she was in no position to be able to stop her.

"We will meet again, Blademaster," the Nightstalker seethed as she launched herself into the hole in the air. "You will not be so lucky next time."

When Kera had made it through the hole, it closed behind her with a soft pop. Alana was alone on the ramparts once more. She slumped slightly from the exertion, but there was no time to rest.

With the Nightstalker gone once more, the Blademaster knew that she needed to go back to the main battle. Alana made her way out of the Temple of the Blades to where her companions were. She looked around at all the bodies and smiled when she realized not one of her companions had been seriously injured.

"Is everyone all right?" she asked Colwyn.

"It was a difficult fight, but we prevailed," Colwyn nodded. "Did you get the Nightstalker?"

"No," Alana sighed deeply. "She got away again."

"I guess it's likely we will see her again, then," Colwyn frowned.

"Very likely," Alana nodded. "I suspect she, like myself, will be a central figure in this war."

"That doesn't surprise me."

"I suspected as much when I first faced her," Alana shrugged.

Alana caught sight of Aurientallus and waved him over to where she and Colwyn were talking. The gold dragon quickly finished the conversation he had been having with Greytonix and made his way over to them.

"What can I do for you, Master Blademaster?" he asked when he got there.

"In light of this attack, I think it would be wise to have a dragon protecting the Temple of the Blades," Alana said. "Do you think that can be arranged?"

"I had much the same thought," Aurientallus nodded. "I will not be returning to the Isle of Dragons until after the War of Souls has ended. I will send word to the Isle of Dragons to send a dragon so that when it comes time for me to take the field of battle at the side of my Blademaster, the Temple of the Blades will remain protected. You need not fear for the safety of the temple while you lead the forces of the light in the war."

"Thank you, noble dragon," Alana bowed her head slightly in respect. "Sometimes, I think we ask too much of the dragons."

"And some of us think you ask not enough," Aurientallus laughed. "Now go. The snows will start falling soon. You should go back to Ravendale and prepare for the war that is soon coming. Don't worry about the Temple of the Blades. It will be safe."

"Thank you, Aurientallus," she smiled at the dragon. She turned to her companions. "Let's go home."

The Age of Darkness

Chapter XXVII
Ravendale

he dragpms landed just outside of Ravendale in the brightness of the early afternoon sun. The landings were soft. The dragons were careful to gently glide in to a landing. Some of the companions were not yet used to flying on the back of a dragon, so they were grateful for the gentle landings.

Alana was the first one off the back of Silvestra. As her feet landed on the ground, she reached up for her pack. Colwyn handed both his and her pack down to her and then joined her.

As soon as everyone was off the three dragons, they shifted into their human forms.

"Bella and Talby, you and your Protectors can join Colwyn and I as we go brief the King," Alana said. She turned to the others. "I know you have various things you need to do. I don't know how long it will take us in with the King, but we will all meet for dinner tonight at the Lucky

Minotaur. If you get there before we do, just wait. We will be along shortly."

"Of course," William nodded.

Alana led the other two Blademasters off to the palace in the center of Ravendale. With the war now definitely on the way, Alana wanted to get started on plans to protect the Southern Dales. She knew they would have the winter, but she wanted to make sure they did not waste the time they were given.

Especially now that she had seen what the troops were like.

It had been a mistake for the Nightstalker to try to attack the Temple of the Blades as she had. Alana understood the strategy, and, had she been by herself, the strategy might had paid off. But there were three bonded Blademasters when the Nightstalker attacked. And their nathair an aeir a chosnaíonn were there too, which made the attack even more foolhardy. Talby and Bella had both held their own against the undead attackers. Alana had been happy to see that.

She was not happy that the Nightstalker had gotten away though.

Alana knew that the time would come when she would face off with the Nightstalker one more time. She vowed that, when that time came, the Nightstalker would not survive the confrontation.

But that was not for her to think about now. Right now, all she needed to focus on was to inform the King as to what was coming and get him to agree to a Council of War. Now that she had gotten a true look at what was coming, she was more determined than ever that the Southern Dales not be unprepared for the army of darkness. There were too many lives at stake. They needed to have a plan in action before the spring came.

Alana would make sure they were ready.

The Prophecy of the Great War of Souls named her as the one that needed to lead the forces of the light if they were to win. She took that responsibility seriously. As she had been named the Master Blademaster by the High

Priestess of the Blades, it was clear that she was not the only one taking the prophecy seriously.

When the six of them arrived at the palace, the guards at the palace gates nodded at her. The King had left standing orders that Alana and Colwyn were to be let in no matter what the hour was. It was a testament to the importance that he placed on the Blademasters that he gave those orders.

"They're with me," Alana said, indicating the other two Blademasters. "The King will want to see them as well."

"Of course, Lady Blademaster," one of the guards nodded. "I will get the King for you. He will meet you in the Council Chambers."

"Thank you, Swordsman," Alana smiled at the guard.

"Of course, Lady Blademaster," the guard bowed to her before hurrying off to summon the King.

Alana led the way to the Council Chambers. She had been in the chambers several times, as had Colwyn. This was different though. It was the first time that the Blademaster was bringing intelligence on the war to the King.

In a way, this visit would change everything.

With the Great War of Souls coming, there could be no half measures. Alana had to lead the troops into battle. And that meant that Alana needed troops *to* lead into battle. The only way that would happen was if the King were to mobilize the armies of the Southern Dales.

She had to hope that her intelligence on the army of darkness was enough to make that happen.

When they arrived in the Council Chambers, they were the only ones there. There were no guards. And, as the Council was not in session, there were no councilors. The fact that there was no one in the Council Chambers was fine with Alana. While she did not expect this to be a battle, the quiet would help her center herself before she met with the King.

She sat at the table and closed her eyes, letting her mind wander as she centered her inner calm. She knew that she had to convey the depth of what she knew so that the King would do what he needed to do.

It was not long before the King arrived to the Council Chambers. When he had heard who was waiting for him, he had rushed to hear what the Blademaster had to say.

Alana looked up when he entered the room and nodded once.

"Your Highness," she said. "I have news."

"I thought you might, Blademaster Alana," the King nodded. "But first, please introduce me to your new companions."

"We have been on a journey to find new Blademasters," Alana said. "In this, we were successful. I present Bella Starseeker, daughter of Lord Dargan Starseeker, and her Protector Cayden Antioch. And this is Talby Swiftfoot, granddaughter of Maren Swiftfoot, and her Protector, Tovar Greythistle."

"A halfling Blademaster!" the King smiled broadly. "What a wonder! I am sure the Council will not approve, but I find it most refreshing."

"When Blademaster Alana told me what was coming, I could not refuse the call," Talby shrugged. "All anyone needs to know is that I am fully dedicated to the defense of the Southern Dales."

"As are we all," King Roland nodded. "Now, tell me of what you've seen."

Alana told the King of the prophecy that the Dream Weaver had given to her about the army of darkness. As she related the text of the prophecy, she shuddered. The red-eyed demon gave her chills, even though she had not yet seen him.

The troops she had seen had been bad enough.

After telling the King about the prophecy, she related the tale of going to Arvendale and Barandale to locate Blademasters and then of the attack at the Temple of the Blades.

The King listened intently to everything Alana told him. She knew that he understood the importance of her report.

"And so, Your Highness, I would suggest that we convene a Council of War as soon as possible," Alana concluded. "We need to take advantage of the time given us to make preparations to protect the Southern Dales."

"I would tend to agree," the King nodded. "Odds are good we have until the spring thaw. The snow should start falling any day now, and has probably already started further north. I doubt that even an army of undead will launch the start of the war in the snow."

"That is what I am hoping," Alana said. "If we can make plans throughout the winter then we will have an advantage."

"I will convene the Council as soon as I can get them all here," the King nodded. "I will summon you when it is time."

"Thank you, King Roland," Alana nodded. "Thank you for taking my report seriously."

"How could I not?" the King raised an eyebrow. "You came to warm me of an impending danger to the Southern Dales. I would be foolish to not take such a report seriously."

"You would be surprised how many people would not take Alana's words seriously, Your Majesty," Colwyn said. "Or how many people would try to have her do anything other than lead the people of the Southern Dales into battle."

"I can imagine," the King nodded. "Your father, Lord Colwyn. How does he feel about Alana's warning?"

"Lord Dargan has begun mobilizing the armies of the Arvendale Territory, my liege," Colwyn said. "Surprisingly, to me at least, he has taken the warning to heart and will do everything he can to ensure that Arvendale is ready. I dare say that you will have his support in the Council."

"Well, there is that at least," Roland stroked his chin. "And has he accepted your marriage to Blademaster Alana?"

"Grudgingly, he has accepted both my marriage and my sister's," Colwyn smiled. It was a sad but genuine smile. "While I am sure that he would like to still fight us both on it, I believe that he had some help in understanding just how important our marriages are. I believe he was convinced by Lord Taelin himself."

"I am glad that he has come around," the King nodded. "Well, I shall not keep you from the dinner that I am quite sure Albert is slaving hard as we speak to prepare for you. A good man, that one."

"We think so as well," Alana smiled broadly. "He has been very kind to us."

"Go and eat," the King commanded. "We will discuss the business of the war soon enough."

Martin slowly made his way to the Temple of the White in Ravendale. He did not want to clear out his small domicile at the Temple, but the High Priestess had made her wishes clear.

He was no longer welcome in the Temple of the White.

His entire life had been dedicated to his service to the Lightbringer, and he was being dismissed from the Tower of the White for fulfilling that duty. There was something greatly troubling about that to him.

But there was little he could do about it. Naomi was the High Priestess of Taelin, and her decision was final. Unless, of course, Taelin himself wished to intervene.

He was not sure that would happen.

In the end, he knew it did not matter. All that mattered was that he was allowed to continue to serve the Blademaster as a priest of Taelin. He knew that his god would still allow that. And that was all he needed.

When he got to the Temple of the White, he spoke to no one. He simply went to his small domicile with his pack to clear it out. It would not take long, as Martin had little in the way of personal belongings. It was the way he preferred it.

When he got to his domicile, he slowly turned around in the center of the room, taking in his home for what he presumed would be his last time. Sighing, he set the pack down and started to fill it with his remembrances from his time in the Temple of the White. As he packed each thing away in his pack, he took a moment to look at it and remember how it had come into his possession. Most of the items were gifts from other priests. Some were things he had purchased.

Nothing in the room was exactly special, but he did not want to leave anything behind.

When he had packed the last thing in his pack, he looked around one more time to make sure he had not missed anything. Sighing, he threw his pack over his back and turned back to the door. He stopped short when he saw who was standing in the doorway.

"Lord Taelin," he bowed slightly to his god.

"Martin Faolin," Taelin crossed his arms. "Why are you leaving my temple?"

"I have been put out from the temple, my lord," Martin said in a soft voice.

"By whom?"

"By High Priestess Naomi, Lord Taelin."

"And why has she put you out?"

"Because I would not forsake the Blademaster and return with her to the Temple of the White when she ordered me to," Martin gulped.

"She did what, now?"

"She told the Blademaster that the Temple of the White would no longer support her and demanded that I return to the temple," Martin explained. He suspected that Taelin actually knew all of this already, but wanted to hear it directly from Martin for some reason. "When I refused she told me to clear out my belongings when the Blademaster and our companions returned from our journey to find other Blademasters."

"And did you find other Blademasters?" Taelin smiled.

"Two," Martin nodded. "One is Lord Colwyn's sister and the other is a halfling from Barandale."

"A halfling, you say?" Taelin raised one bushy eyebrow. "Well, now that will be quite entertaining."

"She has already proven herself to be quite adept with a blade," Martin smiled. "She was actually quite impressive."

"I am sure," Taelin nodded. "Back to what you were saying. Did High Priestess Naomi actually tell the Blademaster that she would receive no more support from my temple?"

"She told Blademaster Alana point blank that she would no longer receive any support from the Temple of the White," Martin said.

"Interesting," Taelin frowned. "And what did the Blademaster say to that?"

"Actually, it was I who spoke up, Lord Taelin," Martin grimaced. "It may not have been my place to, but it needed to be said. I said to Naomi that I would stay with the Blademaster. I told her, 'If she is going to keep the people of the Southern Dales from falling into darkness, she will need all the help she can get. You should be ashamed of yourself for your treatment of her, High Priestess.'"

"I see," Taelin hid a smile. "And what was her reaction to that?"

"I will not forget her words to me," Martin sighed. "She said to me, 'Very well, since you choose to defy me also, your name shall be stricken from the rolls, Martin. You will no longer be welcomed among the priests at the Temple of the White. You will no longer receive support from the Temple. When you return from this little journey, you will remove your belongings from the Temple. You will need to find another place to live as you will no longer be able to live at the Temple.' And then she blamed the Blademaster for it."

"This displeases me," Taelin growled.

"I am sorry for my part in displeasing you, Lord Taelin," Martin bowed his head. "All I have wanted to do is to serve you."

"And you have served me well, my child," Taelin smiled. He put a hand on the young man's shoulder. "Fear not, you have not displeased me. You have done exactly as I would have wished you to. You have supported my chosen one. I could ask no more of you than what you have done. My High Priestess on the other hand..." The god paced back and forth a few times lost in thought. Finally, he turned back to Martin. "Come, Martin. Leave your pack here in your room. We will go have words with my High Priestess. She has defied me for the last time, I think."

Martin gently placed his pack on the floor and fell into step behind his god. He stopped long enough to lock his door. He slipped the key in a pouch and hurried to catch up to Taelin.

The god was in a foul temper, it appeared. Martin, for his part, was glad that it was not directed at him. He did not feel any kind of remorse that Naomi was going to have to deal with an angry Taelin. He supposed he should feel bad for that, but the High Priestess had brought this on herself.

He vowed to himself that he would never do anything to see Taelin's anger directed at him.

Martin followed Taelin to the sanctuary of the High Priestess. The god set a quick pace, and Martin had to scurry along to keep up with him. When they got there the guard at the door tried to prevent their entry.

"Do you know who I am?" the god demanded of the guard.

"Yes, Lord Taelin," the guard gulped. "But the High Priestess has asked not to be disturbed."

"And did she say, 'If the god we all serve shows up, deny him entry?'" Taelin growled.

"N-no, Lord Taelin," the guard paled. "She did not mention you specifically."

"Then get out of my way," Taelin barked. "This young man and I will see my High Priestess now."

"Yes, Lord Taelin," the guard bowed and hurried away from the sanctuary.

It was clear that no one wanted to deal with the god when he was in a bad temper.

Taelin threw open the door, forcing it inwards to crash against the wall. He stormed in, Martin following meekly in his wake.

"What is the meaning of this interruption?" Naomi growled as she stood from where she had been kneeling at the altar. When she turned and saw who had stormed into her sanctuary, she dropped to a knee. "I am sorry, my Lord Taelin. I did not know it was you."

"Get up, Naomi," Taelin barked. "I do not want your bowing and scraping before me when it is clear that you do not respect my wishes."

"My Lord Taelin, I do not know what you mean," Naomi said. She looked behind him and saw Martin standing behind the god. "What is he doing here? He has been put out."

"No," Taelin said in a whisper. "He has not."

"He has defied my wishes," Naomi shrugged. "He has thumbed his nose at the express wishes of the High Priestess. He cannot stay in the Temple of the White."

"What, then, should I do with a High Priestess who thumbs her nose at the express wishes of her god?" Taelin raised an eyebrow at her.

"I have not thumbed my nose at your wishes, Lord Taelin."

"Have you not?"

"No, my lord, I have not."

"I told you before my Blademaster went to Willowdale," Taelin said. "I told you not to go against me when it comes to Alana Steeldrake again. And now I have come to hear that you have withdrawn all support to the Blademaster from my temple."

"Yes, Lord Taelin, I have," Naomi nodded.

"How dare you?"

"How dare she?" Naomi threw back at him. "How dare she refuse her duty to the Temple of the White?"

"Oh, Naomi, how I have failed you," Taelin sighed. "Did you not study the Law of the Blades as I commanded you to do the last time we spoke?"

"I did, Lord Taelin."

"Then how is it that you seem to have completely missed the Twenty First Law of the Blades?" Taelin demanded. "More to the point, how is it that young Martin here understands it more than you, my High Priestess?"

"I don't understand," Naomi frowned. "The Twenty First Law of the Blades?"

"Martin will explain it to you since he clearly has a far better understanding of it than you do," Taelin said in a soft voice. He turned to the young priest behind him. "Martin? The Twenty First Law of the Blades, please."

"The Blademasters only owe fealty to the balance. They serve only the Southern Dales. Their only quest is for the truth. Only in this way can they fulfill their purpose." Martin turned to face the High Priestess. "That is why I could not leave the Blademaster when you commanded me to. I know what she yet faces. And I know that, despite your insistence that she not have it, she and the other Blademasters will need the support of the Temple of the White more than ever."

"But she continues to defy the temple in everything," Naomi protested. "We must not assist her. And if there are more Blademasters than that just compounds the problem."

"Oh, Naomi, you are not making this easy on me," Taelin sighed again. "What did I tell you I would do if you defied me when it came to the Blademasters again?"

"You told me you would put me out of the Temple of the White," Naomi bowed her head.

"And I am afraid that must now happen," Taelin laid his hand on her shoulder. "You may yet one day redeem yourself in my eyes, but it will not be as my High Priestess. Give me the ring of office, Naomi."

Naomi bowed her head even deeper. She pulled the ring off her finger and handed it to her god. She pushed past him to leave the sanctuary.

"Be out of the temple by nightfall, Naomi," Taelin said without turning. "One day, you will have a chance to redeem yourself. I suggest you take it when that day comes."

"Yes, my lord."

When Naomi left the sanctuary, the god turned to Martin and looked at the young man.

"We will need a new High Priest, it would appear," Taelin said.

William was the first to the Lucky Minotaur. He had gotten the dragons settled and then checked on his house. He knew that no one would have entered his home in his absence, but he took comfort in checking that his spell books were all still there.

When he arrived at the Lucky Minotaur, Albert greeted him from the bar in the tap room.

"William!" the old innkeeper cried. "I take it this means that the Blademaster has returned?"

"Indeed," William smiled. "We will be dining here this evening. We will need a larger table than normal. There are seven more of us than when we left."

"I guess I better get some food started cooking then," Albert grunted. "It is good to have you all here tonight, though. The Blademaster is doing her best to keep me in business by herself."

"There are three of them now, actually," William laughed. "Three Blademasters. One of them is a halfling."

"I'll make sure everything is nailed down, then," Albert shook his head, laughing heartily.

William chuckled with the innkeeper and then walked away from the bar so that the old man could start cooking for the companions. The mage started to move some tables together. Gwen came over and helped him. In no time, they had enough tables near the fire put together to accommodate the entire party.

When the tables were together, William pulled out one of his spell books and started to read over a new spell. It was a spell from one of the more advanced spell books he had acquired earlier in the year. And while he was not yet sure it was one he could cast, he was interested in the spell anyway.

The companions started to file into the tap room. As they arrived, they took seats around the table. Meryn and Odway were first, followed by the Blademasters and their Protectors. The dragons filtered in next, Silvestra leaning over and kissing William on the cheek as she sat down next to him.

The only one missing was the priest.

No one had seen Martin since he left for the Temple of the White. No one knew what he was going to do about housing now that he had been cast out from the Temple of the White. They all would help the young priest though.

"It is good for us to be all together tonight," Alana said. "Well, once Martin gets here, we will be at least."

"Will the King convene a Council of War?" William asked.

"Yes," Alana nodded. "He took my warnings seriously and we will be spending the winter planning the defense of the Southern Dales. Unlike some, he takes the warning of a Blademaster very seriously."

"As he should," Colwyn grumbled. "We're trying to keep the Southern Dales from being destroyed by Thraal."

"It may yet be a fight to convince some of the First Lords," Bella piped in. "But at least the First Lord of Arvendale has come to see the truth the Blademaster's concerns. Lord Dargan carries a strong voice in the council chamber."

"It feels odd to depend on Father to support us," Colwyn grimaced. "After the grief he gave Alana and I in Arvendale..."

"Let it go, Col," Alana laughed as she patted his hand. "It's over. You won the battle."

"Never should have been a battle to begin with."

The door to the tap room banged open and the companions turned in one. When they saw the old man lead Martin into the tap room, they all rose at once.

"Lord Taelin!" the old innkeeper called from behind the bar. "It is a great honor that you have chosen to grace my humble establishment."

"Albert Bothain," Taelin smiled warmly at the old man. "You have shown my Blademaster and her companions great kindness over the years. For that you have my gratitude." He turned to the companions. "And they have moved the tables towards the fire. Wonderful."

"Lord Taelin, it is they that have done me the kindness," Albert said in a soft voice. "It has been my great honor to watch Alana become who and what she is. I could be no prouder of her if she were my own daughter. She is an amazing young lady."

Alana blushed slightly at the praise. She blushed even more when Taelin looked over at her with a proud smile.

William hid his face behind his spellbook so that Alana could not see the broad grin. Albert had echoed William's own thoughts on Alana.

"I am proud of Blademaster Alana as well," Taelin said. "And I have news for you from my temple."

"Good news, I hope?" Alana said, regaining her composure.

"Naomi's edict that you shall receive no more support from the Temple of the White has been rescinded," Taelin's smile grew. "Naomi was a mistake, I see now."

"A wise man once told me something about mistakes," William said from his corner. He gently laid his spellbook down and leaned back in his chair. "We all make mistakes. The true test of a person is their reaction to making a mistake. Only by accepting the mistake and doing one's best to make amends can a person keep on the correct path."

Taelin looked at William in surprise. "You quote one of my own Laws of the Blades to me, mage?"

"It seemed appropriate," William shrugged.

"Indeed, it is," Taelin nodded. "Ferrin told you that one, I take it?"

"Yes, he did," Wiliam said. "After I admitted my fear of making my own mistakes."

"Ah," Taelin nodded sagely. "Yes, that would be when he would mention that Law to you. I always liked Ferrin. Always thought he was the wisest of the three gods of magic."

"If I may ask, Lord Taelin, who is your new High Priest if Naomi has been put out from the temple?" Alana asked.

"Ah, yes. That would be important information for you to have, yes?" Taelin smiled. "Young Martin here is my new High Priest."

Alana smiled at Martin. "Good choice, I think."

"I will continue to travel with you for a time, Blademaster Alana," Martin said. "I will see you through the War of Souls before I return to the Temple of the White to coordinate the temple's activities from there."

"Then come join the table, Martin," Alana waved at an empty seat. "Lord Taelin, if I know Albert, there is more than enough food for you to join us."

"I would be delighted my child!" Taelin took a seat at the table and looked around at the people at the table. "You have all made me very proud."

"We all, I think, thank you for that, Lord Taelin," Alana smiled at the god.

"Oh, and Colwyn, I heard what you said to young Cayden when you gave him the two ioun stones to help him in the Test of the Blades," Taelin said as he took a sip of ale. "And you were right. I did not mind that you tipped the scales to help true love survive in this case. But I would prefer if you did not do so again."

"I should have known I would not have been able to do that without your knowledge," Colwyn boomed a deep laugh. "Thank you for not invalidating Cayden's Test because of what I did."

"Why would I?" Taelin raised an eyebrow. "I, too, am something of a hopeless romantic."

The Age of Darkness

Chapter XXVIII
A Look Towards the Future

he maze sat in the branch of a tree in the woods just outside Ravendale. The journey to find the two new Blademasters had been a long one, but even though he had had some time to himself, he had not had a significant amount of time to think about his situation and come to a decision.

If he really thought about it, though, there was no decision to be made. He had known from the moment that the Dream Weaver had made his offer that he was going to the Tower of the White.

He knew that the offer from the Dream Weaver had been what Ferrin had been talking about before the Dream Weaver had arrived in Ravendale.

Knowing that this was the choice that Ferrin had been meaning when he had told William that a choice would soon be coming did not mean that the choice was any easier. William now knew that becoming the next Dream

Weaver was his destiny. He did not, however, know how it would affect his various relationships with his companions.

Least of all, he had no idea how it would affect his marriage.

Even though he knew that Silvestra had long known what his destiny was, he still felt nervous broaching the subject with her.

The thing was that he had already made his decision. He just hoped that the woman he loved could accept that decision.

There would be a great deal to do. He wanted to get to the Tower of the White as soon as possible. If he could get there before the snows fell, that would be better, for that meant he would be able to get back to his Blademaster before the spring thaw. The only way that he thought he would be able to do that would be to have Silvestra fly him there. He would have to talk to her about it.

"You are thinking deep thoughts, my love," Silvestra smiled at him as she sat down next to him on the branch.

He had not heard her climb the tree, so he was very surprised at her sudden appearance. It was, he decided, very pleasant to be surprised by the woman he loved. He hoped that she never stopped surprising him. He reached over and gave her hand an affectionate squeeze.

"You know the choice I have been given," the mage said in a soft voice. "You told me long ago that you knew what I was destined to become. It would seem that the time of my destiny has finally arrived."

"I have wondered why you have been so distant," she nodded. "I should have guessed that the time of your choosing was at hand. You said as much in the letter that you left for me, but I did not make the connection. So let me guess. The Dream Weaver came to tell Alana where she needed to go to find a Blademaster, and, when he did, he also told you that he has chosen you to be his successor. And, further, he has asked you to meet him at the Tower of the White to undergo the ritual to become the Dream Weaver. Have I about summed it up?"

"Yes," he nodded. "Of course, you have known all along what my destiny was. You told me back when we were at the Tower of the White that you knew. You could not tell me back then, of course."

"I could not, no," she sighed. "You know I was prevented from telling you all I knew."

"I know," William smiled at her. He gently squeezed her hand. "I am not mad at you for not telling me something that you could not tell me. That would be unconscionable for me to do."

"So what are you going to do?" she asked. "I know that you have not yet told the Dream Weaver your decision. I know that you have not told anyone what you are going to do. Not even me."

"Will we be okay if I do this?" he asked, finally putting words to the one true worry he had about becoming the Dream Weaver. "Will our marriage survive my doing this?"

"Of course it will, William," she smiled a broad smile at him. "I will always be by your side, no matter what you choose to do. Did you really think that I would change my mind about being with you because you chose to accept your destiny?" She shook her head and swatted him on the shoulder playfully. "I knew what you were to become long ago, my love. I accepted it then. I can do no less now that you have accepted it."

"You are a wonder, Silvestra," he said as he wrapped his arms around her. "What did I do to deserve a woman like you?"

"Oh, you don't deserve me," Silvestra laughed merrily. "I just choose to make you think you do."

"Thanks, I think," William rolled his eyes. He sighed and looked towards Ravendale. "I suppose I need to tell Alana. And then, I think that you need to get me to the Tower of the White before it starts snowing. I don't know how much time it is going to take there, but I think that we both need to be here when the War of Souls starts in earnest in the spring. When Lord Ferrin came to tell me that I would be needing to make a choice about my destiny, he warned me that, once I returned from the Tower of the White, neither of us should stray too far from Alana's side."

"That sounds like wise counsel," Silvestra noted. She started climbing down the tree, but stopped halfway down to look up at him. "Coming?"

They found Alana and Colwyn in the little house they owned on the outskirts of Ravendale just as they expected they would. When Alana opened the door at their knock, she looked less than surprised to see them. William supposed that she had been expecting that he would come see her once he worked things through in his own head.

"May we talk with you, Alana?" William asked her in a soft voice.

"Come in," she nodded. She stepped out of the door and let them enter, closing the door behind them. She motioned for them to take two of the chairs in the small living area. "Have a seat, William. Something has been on your mind of late. I would say that it has been on your mind since before we left for Arvendale. I take it that Colwyn and I are finally going to learn what it is that the Dream Weaver said to you."

"What do you know about the Dream Weaver, Alana?" William began.

"Not all that much," she shrugged. "I knew him a little when I lived in Talondale. But I never got to know him all that well. Why?"

"There is only ever one Dream Weaver," William explained. "Roald Vilas has been the Dream Weaver since the title was passed to him just shy of three hundred years ago. His journey nears its end and he will soon become one with the magic as all mages do. Roald has named his successor."

"You," Colwyn guessed.

"Me," William nodded.

"What does being his successor mean?" Alana asked.

"I must travel to the Tower of the White and submit myself," the mage said. He looked over at Silvestra and then back to Alana. "The magic will decide if I am a fitting successor to Roald. If I am deemed to be such, I will be imbued with the power of the mantle of the Dream Weaver and will return to you."

"And if you are not found to be worthy?" Colwyn asked. "What happens to you then?"

"It depends on what the magic senses in me," William shrugged. "I could be sent from the Tower of the White in disgrace. The worst that could happen is that the magic could consume me and I could cease to exist. If that were to happen, I would, of course, not be returning to you."

"You can't take that kind of risk, William," Alana said. "You are needed here. What of your duties to the Southern Dales?"

"You do not understand, Alana," Silvestra said. "William has no more choice in this than you do in being a Blademaster. I have known for years that this is his destiny. I sometimes wish it were otherwise, for I do not wish him to take the risk either. But it is what it is. He must go. He has no choice."

"I understand," Alana nodded her head finally after looking at William for several long minutes. "When do you leave?"

"Silvestra will fly me over to the Tower of the White as soon as I pack a few things," William responded. There was a resigned note in his voice, as if he were resigned to the worst happening just so he was not surprised if it did.

"When do you think you will be back?" Colwyn asked.

"That is why I am leaving now," William smiled at Colwyn. "The army of Thraal is bogged down for the winter and will not launch their attack on the Southern Dales until at least the spring. I will be back long before they do. If I am not back before the spring thaw arrives, then I will not be coming back."

"Then we shall just have to hope and pray that you will be back before the spring thaw," Alana smiled. She clapped her hands on his shoulders. "Good journey to you, William."

"Thank you, Alana," William stood up. Silvestra stood to join him. "We need to get going if we're going to leave before the snows come."

The Age of Darkness

Epilogue
The Age of Darkness

Lana and Colwyn stood on the front porch to the house they lived in when they were in Ravendale. They were watching William climb onto Silvestra's back and get ready to launch themselves towards the Tower of the White. Alana realized that she had no idea where the Tower of the White was or how long it would take her friends to get there from Ravendale. All she knew was that she missed them mightily already.

She hoped that William would make it through the trials he was about to go through in one piece.

"Do you think he will be okay, Col?" she asked. She wrapped her arms around him and leaned against his chest.

"I am sure he will be fine, Alana," Colwyn smiled down at her. "Our William is a survivor, after all."

"I worry about him sometimes, Col," Alana admitted. "Sometimes I think William takes on more power than he can handle."

"I worry about him, too. But we need to let him actually walk his own path. We cannot walk it for him."

"I know," she sighed. She watched Silvestra launch herself into the air. "Good journey, my friends. Come back to us safely."

The two of them stood there and watched as the dragon flew away, slowly becoming smaller and smaller until she was just a dot in the sky. Soon after, she was not even so much as a dot in the sky.

"He's gone," Colwyn gave her a squeeze. "And we have preparations to make."

"You're right," Alana nodded. "Winter will only hold off the army of Thraal for so long. We need to be ready for them when the spring thaw arrives."

Alana led her husband and Protector back into the house that he had built for her. He closed the door behind them, closing the cold weather out of the house.

In the silence of the early winter morning, the snows began to fall.

Appendix

Every effort has been made to keep things straight for the reader in the story, however, there are a lot of names and concepts. And so, I have provided this handy set of references for you. As the series grows, so too will this Appendix. I hope you all find this information handy.

The Appendix is divided into the following sections:

Deities
(Alignment of the Deity is in Parentheses)
(G = Good Aligned, N = Neutral Algined, E=Evil Aligned)

Ana (*AH-nah*) (N) Goddess of History

Aram (*AH-rum*) (N) God of Balance

Ceres (*SER-ees*) (N) Goddess of Love

Chemish (*KEM-ish*) (E) God of Magic (for evil aligned magic users)

Ferrin (*FER-un*) (G) God of Magic (for good aligned magic users)

Isis (*EYE-sis*) (N) Goddess of Life

Laeyra (*lay-EHR-uh*) (N) Goddess of Luck

Raeven (*RAY-vun*) (G) God of Nature

Ranthos (*RAHN-thos*) (E) God of the Moon

Serrin (*SER-un*) (G) God of the Sun

Taelin (*TAY-lin*) (G) God of Wisdom and Justice, also known as the Lightbringer, the Lord of the Light, and the Bringer of Light

Terra (*TER-uh*) (G) Goddess of Healing

Thraal (*THRAHL*) (E) God of Chaos, often referred to as the Dark God or the Bringer of Chaos

Torval (*TOR-vul*) (N) God of Magic (for neutral aligned magic users)

The Age of Darkness

Vash (*VAHSH*) (E) Goddess of the Seas

Veral (*ver-AHL*) (E) God of War

Xaria (*ZAHR-yuh*) (G) Goddess of Fertility

Zish (*ZISH*) (E) Goddess of Death

Places

The Southern Dales

The Southern Dales are the southernmost region located on the Continent of Calthea on the world of Calthea. Home to many races championed by the gods of good and neutrality, the Southern Dales are a region governed by a king who resides in a palace in Ravendale. Nobles known as the First Lords govern each of the ten territories reporting to the king. The rule fairly, the wisdom of Taelin guiding the leader's hands.

Arvendale – A medium sized city that is deep in the heart of the Southern Dales, on the other side of the Elven Woods from Ravendale and noble seat of the Arvendale territory. Dargan Starseeker, Colwyn's father, is the First Lord of Arvendale, and, although he does not necessarily recognize the fact, Colwyn is the heir to that title

Attendale – A city on the eastern coast of the Southern Dales and the noble seat of the Attendale territory

Barandale – A city on the western coast of the Southern Dales and the noble seat of the Barandale territory. Home to the halflings.

Darcandale – A small city in the northwest of the Southern Dales and the noble seat of the Darcandale territory

Lovendale – A small port town on the southeast coast of the Southern Dales and the noble seat of the Lovendale territory.

Parciandale – A city in the north of the Southern Dales and the noble seat of the Parciandale territory.

Ravendale – The capitol city of the Southern Dales near the center of the Southern Dales and not too far from the Elven

Woods. The noble seat of the Ravendale territory and home of the High Priest of Taelin.

Solvendale – A small town on the southwest of the Southern Dales and noble seat of the Solvendale territory

Talondale – A small merchant city in the southern part of the Southern Dales and noble seat of the Talondale region. Alana's hometown.

Valendale – A town a week's ride south of Ravendale and the noble seat of the Valendale territory. Home to the sage Isaiah.

Willowdale – A city in the far northeast of the Southern Dales. Also known as the Twice Dead City, Willowdale was once the noble seat of the former Willowdale territory, but that area of the Southern Dales has become somewhat vacant. Willowdale is known from time to time to be home to various outlaws and cutthroats

The Elven Woods – A dense forest to the southwest of Ravendale. Home to the Forestwalker clan of elves and the location of the Temple of the Blades

The Temple of the Blades – The ancestral home of the Blademaster. Here, Blademasters learn what they are to become. The Test of the Blades and all Blademaster weddings happen here. In addition, the Temple of the Blades is the location of the Legacy of the Blademasters.

The Wilds

The Wilds are the lands between the Southern Dales and Dracomyr. Each of the town in the Wilds is its own little kingdom, governing over itself. Unlike the Southern Dales or Dracomyr, there is no central council or government for the region.

Vikerin – A small villaige in the Wilds that is home to the largest temples for Taelin and Laeyra in the Wilds.

Dracomyr

Dracomyr is the northernmost part of the continent of Calthea. Dracomyr is home to the shadow creatures and the undead that Thraal loves. The capitol city is Tornith.

The Stonegate Mountains – A mountain range not too far from the Wilds that is home to several large clans of goblins.

Tornith – The capitol city of Dracomyr. The High Priest of Thraal serves in Tornith

Outworld

Outworld refers to places that do not exist as part of the world of Calthea per se.

Limbo – Limbo is a prison where Taelin trapped the essence of the Dark God for several hundred years. It is protected by a multiheaded dragon known as Mahumet

The Isle of Dragons – The Isle of Dragons is home to the dragons of Calthea. The Dragonic Council meets here to oversee law and order for the dragon nation. Although the Isle of Dragons does actually exist as an island on Calthea, it is considered to be part of Outworld as it is inaccessibleto any but the gods and the dragons.

The Age of Darkness

People

Antioch, Cayden – Former Palace Guard in Arvendale, Protector to Bella Starseeker

Bothain, Albert – Proprietor of the Lucky Minotaur

Bunten, Hubert – A brute that occasionally can be found at the Lucky Minotaur

Dalphain, Caiaphas – High Priest of Taelin when the new Blademaster, Alana Steeldrake, is born. Dies of old age

Darkholme, Adouon – High Priest of Thraal after the death of Drakkhous

Delwyn, Merinda – Priestess of Taelin sacrificed to Thraal and beloved of Balaam Otakis

Doilin, Altas – Legate of the Goblins in the Stonegate Mountains

Drakkhous – High Priest of Thraal. Killed by Alana Steeldrake

Greythistle, Tovar – Protector to Talby Swiftfoot

Faollin, Martin – Priest of Taelin assigned to Alana Steeldrake's party

Jana, Deera – An acolyte of Taelin that Alana Seeldrake finds to show some promise

Kale, Richard – Protector of Raven Windrider

Kovalani, Mirian – Queen of the Forestwalker Elves and former lover of Colwyn Starseeker

Kovalani, Otan – Trainer of rangers for the Forestwalker Elves and brother of Mirian Kovalani

Marant, Lilliana – Priestess of Taelin that dies of the wasting sickness in the wilds and beloved of Darius Redwind

Mastairs, Naomi – High Priestess of Taelin after Balaam Otakis dies.

Otakis, Balaam – High Priest of Taelin after Caiaphas Dalphain dies. Killed by Drakkhous in Tornith while protecting Alana Steeldrake

Rayden, Kera – The Nightstalker

Redwind, Darius – Priest of Taelin that becomes Drakkhous after he loses the woman he loves

Sapphire, Crystal – Last Blademaster named before the Great Purge

Starseeker, Bella – A Blademaster. Brother to Colwyn Starseeker

Starseeker, Colwyn – Protector to Alana Steeldrake and heir to the title of First Lord of the Valendale Territory

Starseeker, Dargan – First Lord of the Valendale Territory and Colwyn Starseeker's father.

Starseeker, Serina – Colwyn Starseeker's mother.

Steeldrake, Alana – First Blademaster to be named in over 300 years.

Stonehammer, Roland – King of the Southern Dales

Stonehands, William – Mage of the White that travels with Alana Steeldrake

Swiftfoot, Maren – Leader of the Council of Elders in Barandale. Meryn Swiftfoot's grandmother

Swiftfoot, Meryn – Halfling thief that travels with Alana Steeldrake

Swiftfoot, Talby – Halfling Blademaster. Cousin to Meryn Swiftfoot.

Talon, Isaiah – A sage

Tencis, Olianna – Priestess of Taelin in Tornith

Thames, Mariska – Priestess of Thraal and beloved of Adouon Darkholme

Thistlethumb, Odway – Childhood friend of Meryn Swiftfoot, now her husband

Tram, Victor – Captain of the Palace Guard in Arvendale

Vilas, Arthais – Senior Priest of Taelin in Tornith

Whelan, Marcus – Innkeeper of the White Horse Inn in Valendale.

White, Ash – Stable boy at the Lucky Minotaur. Brother of Gwendolyn White

White, Gwendolyn – Waitress at the Lucky Minotaur. Sister of Ash White

Windrider, Raven – The First Blademaster

The Age of Darkness

Dragons

(Type is in parenthesis)
Good dragons are Gold, Silver, Bronze, Brass, and Copper
Neutral Dragons are Diamond, Ruby, Emerald, Sapphire, and Amethyst
Evil Dragons are, Red, Green, Blue, Black, and White

Alpharin (amethyst) Member of the Dragonic Council

Alpharis (bronze) Member of the Dragonic Council

Calindilarin (undead) Undead dragon in service to Kera Rayden, destroyed during the battle in Willowdale

Centrus (brass) Member of the Dragonic Council

Cobalthaxillius (gold) Nathair an aeir a chosnaíonn to Alana Steeldrake, killed during the battle in Willowdale

Cyrus (green) Member of the Dragonic Council

Eliazar (gold) Leader of the Dragonic Council

Esmertas (emerald) Member of the Dragonic Council

Firegem (ruby) Member of the Dragonic Council

Greytonix (bronze) Nathair an aeir a chosnaíonn to Talby Swiftfoot

Mahumet (multi headed good dragon) Guardian of Limbo

Mintakis (diamond) Member of the Dragonic Council

Onyx (black) Member of the Dragonic Council

Pyrus (copper) Member of the Dragonic Council

Sephiras (sapphire) Member of the Dragonic Council

Shakaaris (red) Member of the Dragonic Council

Silvestra Knightwing (silver) Beloved of William Stonehands and nathair an aeir a chosnaíonn to Alana Steeldrake

Snowfang (white) Member of the Dragonic Council

Talonwing (silver) Member of the Dragonic Council

Timeanalia (sapphire) Nathair an aeir a chosnaíonn to Bella Starseeker

Trakkis (blue) Member of the Dragonic Council

Rick Bentsen

The Prophecy of the Great War of Souls

Tá an tuar an cogadh mór anamacha

Tar éis trí chéad bliain ar fud an domhain a thagann an Aois dorchadais. Beidh an Dia olc ar ais chun tús a conquest an domhain arís.

Sna laethanta tosaigh an Aois dorchadais, tar éis na máistrí na lanna ar ais go dtí saol na Calthea, déanfaidh an arm na marbh chun cinn i seirbhís an Dia olc. Déanfaidh an marbh ardú agus cogadh pá ar fud an aghaidh Calthea.

Nuair a thiteann an chathair faoi dhó marbh folamh ar feadh uair an tríú, beidh an scamaill stoirme a bhailiú agus beidh an claimhte fuaime i gcuid truaillí. Déanfaidh an dúchan cogaidh a bheith ar an talamh agus ní féidir ach an ceann a rugadh ar an bhfianaise an cúiseamh i gcoinne an dorchadas mar thoradh.

Ní mór don arm an solas scaoilte an draíocht na bean sidhe dul ar ais ar an dorchadas. An ceann a rugadh ar an cheo solais mar thoradh ar an oidhreacht na máistrí na lanna isteach ar an réimse an cath.

Nuair a ghlaonn an anam an bean sidhe a gabhadh amach, beidh na clocha ar an daingean ar an bhfianaise a bhriseadh agus titim ar a chéile. Beidh an bhiotáille an roghnaithe de Taelin uair níos mó a chur ar an réimse an cath i Cruinniú w i gcoinne an dorchadas.

Déanfaidh an tine an ghrian agus an ghealach dim agus céimnithe chun dorchadais. Ní mór don duine a rugadh ar an solas ag siúl amach as an scáth an tine an ghrian agus an ghealach agus an roghnaithe de Taelin mar thoradh.

Beidh an Dlí is Fiche ar an Tríú na lanna a shárú, i gcás roinnt de na roghnaithe de Taelin.

Mura ndéanfaidh an ceann a rugadh ar an bhfianaise thoradh an cúiseamh i gcoinne an arm na marbh, beidh an domhain titim isteach i dorchadas a bheidh gan deireadh. Ní féidir ach an cumhacht ag an Dlí Chéad na lanna threorú láimh an ceann a rugadh ar an solas.

Sa chath mar atá i ngach daoine eile a mbeidh an ceann a rugadh ar an solas troid, ní bheidh aon ráthaíochtaí. Ní ghlacfar ach le méid seo a leanas an eagna Taelin agus ag an ádh de Laeyra an ceann a rugadh ar an solas i réim.

The Age of Darkness

Ba chóir an ceann a rugadh ar an bhfianaise a bheith rathúil i gceannas ar an fórsaí an tsolais, beidh an domhan beo go buan coibhneasta ar feadh tamaill, ach ní bheidh ach ar feadh tréimhse chun a Dhia olc a thabhairt ar a thóir suas.

Más mian leis an duine a rugadh ar an bhfianaise a Cealaigh an damáiste de bharr an anam glaoch ar an bean sidhe a gabhadh, ní mór di teacht ar an Solas de Taelin agus a chuid draíochta a úsáid chun aon uair amháin níos mó a thógáil an daingean ar an solas.

Sna blianta tar éis dheireadh an chogaidh mór anamacha ba chóir, an ceann a rugadh ar an solas i casadh ar ais ar an dorchadas ar feadh tamaill, beidh sí a leathnú trí solas huaire. Ach leis an tríú, beidh sí a hionad i measc na spioraid na roghnaithe de Taelin.

Mar sin deireadh leis an bhfocal an tuar deiridh Bahala, an fiodóir de greams. Leis an gifting an tuar, cas mé an maintlín de chumhacht an fiodóir an aisling thar a fiodóir nua agus i bhfad níos óige an aisling. Creid na focail seo, beidh ar gach a bhfuil scríofa anseo teacht chun pas a fháil.

Is féidir na focail seo lá amháin a mbealach chun an ceann a rugadh ar an solas. Beidh an té a chosnaíonn a bheith in ann aistriú na focail seo a son, cé go mbeidh a fhios ag an bhrí nach taobh thiar de na focail nuair a fhaigheann siad iad.

Scríofa ag mo lámh,
Bahala Maranal, an fiodóir an aisling
Tríocha seacht mbliana anuas an bás mór de na máistrí na lanna.

The prophecy of the Great War of Souls
After three hundred years of peace in the world comes the Age of Darkness. The Dark God will return to begin his conquest of the world once more.

In the early days of the Age of Darkness, after the Blademasters have returned to the world of Calthea, the army of the dead shall arise in service to the Dark God. The dead shall rise and wage war across the face of Calthea.

When the twice dead city falls empty for a third time, the storm clouds will gather and the sabres will rattle in their scabbards. The blight of war shall be upon the land and only the one born of the light can lead the charge against the darkness.

The army of the light must uncork the magic of the bean sidhe to turn back the darkness. The one born of the light must lead the legacy of the Blademasters onto the field of battle.

When the soul of the captured bean sidhe wails, the stones of the stronghold of the light will shatter and crumble upon one another. The spirits of the chosen of Taelin will once more take the field of battle in the war against the darkness.

The fire of the sun and the moon will dim and fade to darkness. The one born of the light must walk out from the shadow of the fire of the sun and the moon and lead the chosen of Taelin.

The Twenty Third Law of the Blades will be violated for some of the chosen of Taelin.

If the one born of the light does not lead the charge against the army of the dead, the world will fall into a darkness that will be without end. Only the power of the First Law of the Blades can guide the hand of the one born of the light.

In this battle as in all others the one born of the light will fight, there will be no guarantees. Only by following the wisdom of Taelin and by the luck of Laeyra will the one born of the light prevail.

Should the one born of the light be successful in leading the forces of the light, the world will live in relative peace for a time, but only for a time for the Dark God shall never give up his quest.

If the one born of the light wishes to undo the damage caused by the wailing soul of the captured bean sidhe, she must find the Light of Taelin and use its magic to once more build the stronghold of the light.

In the years after the end of the great war of souls, should the one born of the light in turning back the darkness for a time, she will extend the light three times. But with the third, she will take her place among the spirits of the chosen of Taelin.

So ends the words of the final prophecy of Bahala, the Dream Weaver. With the gifting of this prophecy, I turn the mantle of power of the Dream Weaver over to a new and much younger Dream Weaver. Heed these words, for all that is written here shall come to pass.

May these words one day find their way to the one born of the light. The one who protects her will be able to translate these words for her, although neither will know the meaning behind the words when they find them.

Written by my hand,
Bahala Maranal, the Dream Weaver
Thirty seven years past the Great Purge.

The Elvish Language

(Author's Note: When I first decided that the Forestwalker Elves were going to have their own language and that it would be represented in the book, I thought I was going to make a language up. Then, I realized just how difficult that really is. I wasn't going to create a language for the Forestwalker Elves, but I still wanted to have a distinct language for them. Last year I hit on the perfect solution to my problem, and I put it into action.

The language for the Forestwalker Elves is the Irish language. I am currently learning the language. Those of you folks who speak Irish fluently (And I know there are, sadly, not that many of you) will most likely see that the translations are not very accurate. That's OK. They don't have to be. They just have to be good enough. And that's what I have.

Less than two million people worldwide speak the Irish language. I do not want the language to die as it is a truly beautiful language, which is why I'm learning it. My hope is that maybe some of my readers will see that this language is a beautiful language that needs to be saved. When I have children, I hope to pass the language down to them. But, for now, all I can do to save the Irish language is to use it. As the series goes on, I am sure this Elvish Language dictionary will grow. –Rick Bentsen)

An máistir na lanna – Blademaster

An té a chosnaíonn a – Protector

Bhuel le chéile – Well met

Cibé rud a tharlaíonn, deartháir, tá a fhios go bhfuil mé go raibh aon pháirt ann. – Whatever happens, brother, know that I have had no part in it.

Féadfaidh an ádh ar Laeyra agus an eagna Taelin leanann tú – May the luck of Laeyra and the wisdom of Taelin go with you.

feithidí – A type of insect that releases silk that is woven into clothing by the Forestwalker Elves.

Go dtí tú filleadh ar an gcathair sna crainn, mo dheartháir – Until you return to the city in the trees, my brother.

I ngach den saol, ní mór go mbeadh cothromaíocht. A chailleadh go bhfuil cothromaíocht a cuireadh chaos agus bás isteach Ní mór máistir na lanna a bheith i gcónaí ar comhardú i di féin agus ina cuid déileálacha le daoine eile. Sin é an fáth go bhfuil an dlí chéad cheann de na lanna chomh tábhachtach sin. Ní mór an grá roinneann sí lena fear céile bás caithfidh sí a chothromú déileáil ina seasamh – In all of life, there must be balance. To lose that balance is to invite chaos and death in. A Blademaster must always be in balance in herself and in her dealings with others. That is why the First Law of the Blades is so important. The love she shares with her husband must balance the death she must deal in her position.

Impigh mé de tú maithiúnas a thabhairt dom, mo dheartháir. Tá a fhios agat an grá agus meas agam duit féin agus do na mná grá agat. Ba mhaith liom rudaí a bhí difriúil ná ní mór cad a tharlóidh. Tá tú i gceannas ar feadh trialach nach raibh ach is féidir leat duine. Ní mór duit i réim. Gach ár saol ag brath air. Is é an meáchan ar an domhan ar do ghualainn. Tá eagla orm go bhféadfadh sé a bheith i bhfad ró-a iompróidh. Cuimhneamh nach bhfuil rudaí i gcónaí mar atá siad. – I beg you to forgive me, my brother. You know I love and respect you and the woman you love. I wish things were different than what must happen. You are headed for a trial that only you can face. You must prevail. All our lives depend on it. The weight of the world on your shoulders. I'm afraid it might be too much to bear. Remember that things are not always as they appear.

Is breá liom tú go mór – I love you very much

Is cuma cad a tharlaíonn sa lá atá inniu, tá a fhios go mbeidh tú féin agus an Alana Lady a bheith i gcónaí fáilte roimh chách sa chathair sna crainn, le haghaidh an banríon gheall an dílseacht na clan go siúlóidí i measc na foraoisí ar an máistir na lanna agus an ceann a chosnaíonn di. – No matter what happens today, know that you and the Lady Alana always be welcome in the city in the trees, for the queen has pledged the loyalty of the Forestwalker Clan to the Blademaster and her companions.

Is é sin é! Is é sin an réiteach! – I've got it! I figured it out!

Is maith a fheiceann tú arís, mo dheartháir. – It is good to see you again, my brother.

mo dheartháir – my brother

Mo dheartháir, le do thoil logh dom. Bhí mé ina páirtí do pian. Rinne mé rabhadh duit, ach tú a bheith gortaithe ar aon nós. Impigh mé de tú maithiúnas a thabhairt do mo mhuintir an pian go bhfuil muid ba chúis agat. Más rud é go mbeadh sé éasca do pian, a chur ar mo shaol mar íocaíocht as an méid atá déanta againn a thabhairt duit. – My brother, please forgive me for my part in the pain you have suffered. Although I did warn you, you have been hurt anyway. I beg you to forgive my family for the pain we have caused you. If it would ease your suffering, I offer my life as payment for what we have done to you.

Mo ghrá, Tá brón orm má ba chúis agam ort pian – My love, I'm sorry for the pain that I have caused you.

Múinteoir – A term of respect for a teacher of rangers in the Forestwalker Elves.

nathair an aeir a chosnaíonn – The dragon assigned to protect a Blademaster

Ní mór di a rachaidh isteach anseo chun aghaidh a thabhairt ar ndán di dul isteach le croí glan. Ní mór sí ag troid i gcomhréir leis an idéalacha Taelin agus Laeyra. Ní mór di cloí le Dlí na lanna má ghlacann sí ndán di. Teip ciallaíonn bás. – She who enters here to face her destiny must enter with a pure heart. She must fight according to the precepts of Taelin and Laeyra. She must abide by the Law of the Blades if she accepts her destiny. Failure brings death.

stát ndoimhneacht na tsíocháin inmheánach -- A technique used by elven rangers that allows them to be in a deep state of inner peace

Sí nach bhfuil grá nach bhfuil a fhios Taelin chun é Taelin ghrá. – She who does not love does not know Taelin for Taelin is love.

Turas go maith duit, an ceann a chosnaíonn sí an máistir na lanna. Go dtí go mbeidh níos mó ná uair ár cosáin trasna. – Good journey to you, Protector to the Blademaster. Until next our paths shall cross.

The Laws of the Blades

The First Law of the Blades:

You are commanded to love. Love your friends. Love your enemies. Love without reservation. Love without hesitation. Love without condition. Love without expectation of return. If you must fight, then fight with love in your heart. If you must kill, then kill with love in your heart. Never kill or fight with hate or anger in your heart. Hate leads to impotence, but love brings power. This is the law a Blademaster must live by more than any other or else she will be powerless to serve as she should. It is the First Law of the Blades because it is the most important. Live by it, or you will die.

The Second Law of the Blades:

True love breeds true forgiveness. Nothing is more powerful than the ability to forgive the one you love. And nothing brings you closer than the forgiveness of your own misdeeds.

The Third Law of the Blades:

Dark and light. Good and evil. Black and white. These are two sides of the same coin. Both sides must exist or neither will.

The Fourteenth Law of the Blades:

There are many things in life that are but mere illusions. Things are not always as they appear. A Blademaster must depend on the wisdom of Taelin to understand what is real and what is an illusion. Confusion brought on by false realities can lead to a gruesome death. Always remember to let Lord Taelin be your guide in everything you do. Remembering this will cause you to see through any illusion that is in your path.

The Fifteenth Law of the Blades:

In life as in battle, there are no guarantees. Victory and defeat teeter on the edge of a thin blade. It is belief in one's self that can make the difference between victory and defeat. A Blademaster must always believe in herself and be willing to seek the help of others in order to claim victory. This is the truth of life and battle. Live or die as you choose.

The Eighteenth Law of the Blades:

In all of life, there must be balance. To lose that balance is to invite chaos and death in. A Blademaster must always be in balance in herself and in her dealings with others. That is why the First Law of the Blades is so important. The love she shares with her husband must balance the death she must deal in her position.

The Nineteenth Law of the Blades:

We all make mistakes. The true test of a person is their reaction to making a mistake. Only by accepting the mistake and doing one's best to make amends can a person keep on the correct path.

The Twenty First Law of the Blades:

The Blademasters only owe fealty to the balance. They serve only the Southern Dales. Their only quest is for the truth. Only in this way can they fulfill their purpose.

The Twenty Third Law of the Blades:

The war never ends. Only the battles change.

The Twenty Fifth Law of the Blades:

All things must end. Nothing remains forever.

Blademasters and Protectors

Over the years of recorded history in Calthea, many women have held the title of Blademaster. Obviously, not all Blademasters have been mentioned in this series, but as Blademasters and their Protectors are mentioned, they will be listed here.

Blademasters of Old:

Raven Windrider and Richard Kale (The first Blademaster and her Protector)
Alyssa Nesbitt and Michael Westlund
Maria Davalos and Tarvan Draderis
Crystal Sapphire and Markus Sharde

Blademasters of Now

Alana Steeldrake and Colwyn Starseeker
Bella Starseeker and Cayden Antioch
Talby Swiftfoot and Tovar Greythistle

The Age of Darkness

The adventures of Alana Steeldrake and her companions
will continue in

Dragonsbane

Coming April, 2017

Since the first Blademaster, the dragons have always sent
one dragon to protect each Blademaster.

It is a sacred duty that the dragons have taken seriously
from the beginning. Now, with the Blademasters walking
the Southern Dales once more, the dragons have taken
their place by their side once more.

His name is hated amongst the dragons. He has made a
living out of hunting and killing them. And he does not
care what type of dragons he hunts.

And now, Malachi Dragonsbane is on the hunt once
more...and he is hunting for the Blademasters' dragons.

TURN THE PAGE
For a preview of **Dragonsbane**,
the fourth exciting book in
The Blademaster Chronicles

Prologue
Malachai Dragonsbane

he man sat in the corner of the tap room. From where he sat, he could clearly see everything going on in the room. It was his preferred location when he was in a tap room or tavern. It was the only way he could make sure that no one snuck up on him.

He was a man that needed to control everything that he possibly could.

The man sat sipping an ale. He did not, as a general rule, get drunk. That would be a giving up of control. In his line of work, giving up control like that would be fatal.

He leaned back in his chair, and he looked at where the bard was just getting ready to begin playing. He loved listening to a good bard play. Although he had no idea if the bard that was about to perform would be any good. He would happily listen, though, and make a determination from there.

Preview of Dragonsbane

The serving wench that had brought him his ale earlier came by with a bowl of stew. The stew was thick, with large chunks of meat, potatoes and vegetables. He had eaten in this tap room before, as it was where he tended to stay when he was home in Darcandale. He was not home near often enough though. He had been home for a long while this time, and he was itching to go out on a new adventure. Sitting at home did not appeal to him. The man was one that needed constant adventure in his life.

He was a hunter.

He did not currently have a prey, though, so there was nothing for him to hunt. He knew that the lack of prey would change, and that it would likely change soon.

It always happened that way.

The bard began to sing. It was a new song that the man had never heard before. He took a bite of his stew as he listened to the song, which was about the rescue of the citizens of Valendale. He listened carefully to the words of the song. He had heard about this new Blademaster. Like many people in the Southern Dales, the man had a deep respect for the Blademasters of old and all that they were said to have done for the Southern Dales throughout history.

As he listened to the song, though, he realized just how little he knew about the Blademasters.

As the bard sang, he weaved together the story of the great battle in Willowdale. The song brought the images of the battle to the man's mind as all good songs of heroic deeds should. He could see the great skeletal dragon wreaking havoc in the skies over the battle. He could see the great gold dragon give his life to protect the Blademaster and the people of Valendale. He could see the silver dragon attack out of nowhere and defeat the skeletal dragon.

He had not known that the Blademasters consorted with dragons.

The man opened his eyes and set his spoon down. He waved over the serving wench. It was time to settle up his bill.

Rick Bentsen

For Malachai Dragonsbane was about to go on the hunt once more.

Preview of Dragonsbane

About the Author

Rick Bentsen released his first novel in 2001. It was a simple science fiction story that was somewhat well received. Although it never sold very well, the people that read his first novel enjoyed it immensely. From that first moment, Rick was hooked.

Rick has long loved science fiction and fantasy books and movies and that love has turned into a writing passion. He has recently added a mystery/thriller series to his normal science fiction and fantasy series as projects to complete.

Rick lives in southeastern Massachusetts which he believes is the most beautiful place in the world. Fall in New England, he finds to be the most inspirational time of the year with all the colors.

Rick can be reached through his facebook page (www.facebook.com/RickBentsenAuthor).